Murder by Vegetable

A QUILTED MYSTERY

Murder by Vegetable

THE BABY QUILT

Barbara Graham

FIVE STAR

A part of Gale, Cengage Learning

GALE
CENGAGE Learning·

Detroit • New York • San Francisco • New Haven, Conn • Waterville, Maine • London

GALE
CENGAGE Learning·

LIBRARY OF CONGRESS CATALOGING-IN-PUBLICATION DATA

Graham, Barbara, 1948–
    Murder by vegetable : the baby quilt, a quilted mystery / Barbara Graham. — 1st ed.
        p. cm.
    ISBN 978-1-4328-2621-5 (hardcover) — ISBN 1-4328-2621-2 (hardcover)
    1. Sheriffs—Fiction. 2. Quilting—Fiction. 3. Tennessee—Fiction. [1. Music festivals—Fiction.] I. Title.
PS3607.R336M88 2012
813'.6—dc23   2012016868

Published in conjunction with Tekno Books and Ed Gorman.
Find us on Facebook– https://www.facebook.com/FiveStarCengage
Visit our website– http://www.gale.cengage.com/fivestar/
Contact Five Star™ Publishing at FiveStar@cengage.com

Printed in Mexico
3 4 5 6 7 16 15 14 13 12

For Huckleberry

ACKNOWLEDGMENTS

My thanks to all the "usual suspects"—my husband, friends, and family who accept my imaginary friends as well as me. Special thanks to Michelle Quick for testing the mystery quilt pattern and feigning interest when I am babbling about myself too much. As usual, grateful thanks to Alice Duncan, editor extraordinaire, whose pithy comments and suggestions greatly improve the story.

RUNNING IN CIRCLES
A MYSTERY QUILT DESIGNED BY
THEO ABERNATHY
FIRST BODY OF CLUES:

Finished size is a lap or crib quilt top, approximately 48" × 60". All fabric requirements are generous and based on standard widths of approximately 42 inches. The instructions assume familiarity with basic quilt construction and an accurate 1/4" seam throughout.

Fabric requirements:
Fabric (A). This is the main or theme fabric. Select a print—floral, novelty, or other non-directional print with at least five colors or shades of colors.

Fabric (B). A neutral, light or dark, should *not* be a busy print.

Fabrics (C), (D), (E) and (F) and (G). Select "interesting solids" (prints that appear to be a single color) of colors or small prints of colors found in the main fabric (A).

Yardage:
(A)—1 1/2 yards of print
(B)—1 3/8 yards of light or dark neutral
(C)—1/2 yard of print
(D)—1 1/3 yards of print
(E)—1/4 yard of print, a fat quarter will work
(F)—1/4 yard of print, a fat quarter will work
(G)—1/4 yard of print, a fat quarter will work

Cutting Instructions:

Be sure to label cut pieces with fabric letter and size cut.

(A)—from the 1 1/2 yards.

Cut 4 strips 4 1/2″ by LOF (length of fabric)

Cut 4 strips 2 1/2″ by LOF

From the remainder, cut 12 squares 4 1/2″

(B)—from the 1 3/8 yards of neutral

Cut 24 squares 5 1/2″

Cut 96 rectangles 4 1/2″ by 1 7/8″

(C)—from the 1/2 yard

Cut 12 squares 5 1/2″

Cut 4 squares 4 1/2″

Cut 4 squares 2 1/2″

(D) from the 1 1/3 yard

Cut 4 strips 2 1/2″ by LOF

Cut 3 squares 5 1/2″

Cut 12 rectangles 4 1/2″ by 1 7/8″

(E) and (F) and (G)

Cut 3 squares 5 1/2″

Cut 12 rectangles 4 1/2″ by 1 7/8″

CHAPTER ONE

Sheriff Tony Abernathy heard his twin baby daughters begin the snuffling sounds they made just before beginning to wail for their breakfast, and climbed out of bed. He felt unusually refreshed, and it was then he realized the girls had slept through the night. Glancing back at the bed, he saw Theo's tousled curls move as she rolled over onto her back. Her eyelashes fluttered and lifted. For a change, his wife's hazel eyes did not seem more bloodshot than green/gold.

"They slept all night? Both of them?" Theo whispered as she crawled from underneath the covers and pulled a robe on over her nightgown. Winter was finally over. The days had grown warmer, but nights and early morning were still quite chilly.

"Unless you were up with them and I slept through it." Tony rolled his shoulders, giving them a little stretch. "I didn't hear a peep." Before he could say more, the first baby's cry began, then her twin chimed in, the sound of their combined wails almost drowned out by the sound of a heavy boom from somewhere in the distance, echoing through the Smoky Mountains. Tony glanced at the clock. Six-thirty. "I guess I'd better have a chat with Quentin about his cannon. I think he needs to wait until at least nine before he starts shooting."

"Cannon?" Theo squeezed through the doorway before he did and vanished into the tiny room, little bigger than a closet, shared by their twin daughters and picked up one of the babies. Lizzie. "I know I've been distracted and sleep deprived, but

11

when and why did he get a cannon?"

"He built it. I know you've been unbelievably busy since our precious girls arrived." He made kissing sounds at the squalling babies. It had taken a bit of study before he and Theo could tell which baby was which and felt brave enough to remove their hospital identification bands. Little Kara had a dimple on her right cheek and Lizzie had none. More often, they depended on knowing Kara liked to shove three fingers in her mouth, disdaining a pacifier. Lizzie adored her pacifier and preferred to use her hands to grasp hair but not her own pale, feathery strands. In his dealings with Lizzie, Tony felt lucky to be bald. He winked at his wife. "I don't know how you could have missed hearing it before. Quentin and Roscoe have been working for months on their weapons."

"I know, I know. If I'd do something besides spend all day on the couch reading magazines, eating bonbons, and soaking up the peace and quiet around me, I might have some idea what's going on in the world."

Unable to suppress a smile at the far-fetched, and leisurely, picture she painted, Tony moved behind Theo and reached for the baby she hadn't picked up. Kara. Her tiny mouth opened wide, taking over her whole face, and she began screaming in earnest. It never failed to amaze him how such a tiny creature, barely bigger than a shoebox, could produce so much noise. He held her close to his chest and patted her back. Soon her screams quieted to giant shuddering hiccups. When he could be heard again, he returned to Theo's question. "Quentin has a vegetable cannon. It's not made from vegetables, it shoots them. He plans to participate in the demonstration at the Ramp Festival along with Roscoe and his medieval siege weapon."

"I've heard the sounds. I just didn't know where they came from or if I was dreaming them. Wait a minute; did you say a siege weapon? What is that?"

"I haven't actually seen it." He watched Theo change Lizzie's diaper quickly and move away from the changing table so he could do Kara's.

"Do they have to practice at this hour?"

"That's going to be my first question." He gave Theo and Lizzie quick kisses and carried Kara down the stairs. He'd give her a bottle well away from her mother and sister. Whenever possible, they switched the babies regularly at feeding time. Even at four months, Kara fit comfortably on his forearm. When her bottle was warm, he sat down with her and arranged her blanket. Wide blue eyes stared into his and her tiny hand grasped his smallest finger. Tony couldn't help thinking his girls were the prettiest babies ever.

His sons, Chris and Jamie, staggered into the kitchen, followed by Daisy, the family golden retriever. Chris let the dog outside and started rummaging for his favorite breakfast cereal.

"She sure can scream." Jamie patted Kara's fuzzy hair.

Distracted by watching her brothers, Kara hadn't quite finished her bottle when Theo and Lizzie appeared. Theo handed Tony his cell phone, which she had evidently answered, and supervised the boys eating breakfast while she packed their lunches.

Balancing Kara, her bottle, and the undersized telephone wasn't easy, but he'd been practicing. "Yes?"

"Sorry to call you at home, Sheriff." Tony recognized the voice. Rex Satterfield, his favorite of the dispatch officers. "I thought you should know there's been a big accident on the highway near Dead Man's Curve. The highway patrol notified me. It's a mess. I've sent about everyone out there but you, including the fire department and search and rescue. Didn't you hear all the sirens?"

"No. What happened?" Tony hated that stretch of road and its nickname. It was a vicious hazard. Because of the river, it

13

couldn't be straightened and because of the solid rock wall on the other side, it couldn't be widened. At least, not within the county's current budget.

Rex interrupted Tony's thoughts. "The preliminary report came in from Sheila. There's a heating oil truck on its side, blocking both lanes of the highway. Of course it's leaking all over the place. I guess the driver didn't want to observe the warning signs about the curve and the speed limit." His voice reeked of disapproval.

"I'm on my way." Tony disconnected the call and handed Kara off to Chris, who had already finished his cereal and stood close at hand. No longer starving, Kara gave her big brother a toothless grin which earned her a tickled chin. Shocked he'd been able to sleep through the sirens and apparent chaos on the highway, Tony took the stairs two at a time, understanding the seriousness of the situation. Not bothering to shower first, he dressed as quickly as he could.

Minutes later, Tony opened the front door just as the cannon boomed again in the distance. He carried a new jumbo jar of antacids, guessing he'd need all of them on a day beginning with a big accident. Not expecting to be able to see anything didn't keep him from glancing at the mountain. "What is Quentin shooting at up there?"

As Tony approached the blocked section of highway, his attention focused for a moment on a roadside cross constructed of two branches tied in the center with a leather bootlace and placed, like so many similar ones, at the site of a fatal collision. Tony remembered several deaths at this particular place, years earlier. Over time, many less serious accidents had occurred in the nearby area. What really caught his attention was realizing weeds growing around the cross had been mowed and daffodils were blooming, presumably planted in the fall. Someone's grief seemed unabated. A nearby pair of white wooden crosses had not received the same treatment.

The vision farther up the highway drove the memorials out of his thoughts. A small red heating oil tanker lay on its side. Because Park County was the smallest Tennessee county, the volunteer firemen were few in number but huge in willingness to pitch in. Their contribution to the community went far beyond extinguishing chimney fires. This morning Tony saw them hauling and stacking hay bales and doing what they could to limit the amount of oil going into the river. A heavy duty vehicle with a winch and a crane, presumably to set the tanker back on its wheels, eased past vehicles parked on the narrow shoulders. Tony recognized his deputy, Mike Ott, standing on the center line, directing traffic with flashlight and neon orange flag. There was a small crowd standing around watching, so Tony assumed his deputy was also receiving many unwelcome or unnecessary suggestions.

He parked his Blazer well out of the roadway and walked to the scene. Along with the firemen, the entire contingent of daytime deputies was hard at work—Mike Ott, Sheila Teffeteller, Darren Holt, and the one he normally worked with, Wade Claybough. Wade saluted with the shovel handle and went back to digging a narrow trench. Darren wielded a sledge hammer, pounding long wooden stakes into the hay to keep the bales in place on the slope. Sheila stood next to the driver, maybe for his protection, and was talking into her radio. The driver had a towel pressed to his face and bloodstains on his hands, but appeared to need no further medical attention.

Tony grabbed a shovel and started digging, working his way toward Wade.

Theo managed to load the children into her shiny yellow SUV in record time. Fifteen minutes. There was no such thing as doing it fast. Even with the boys carrying diaper bags and their school backpacks, it was an awkward series of events as she juggled her purse, two babies, and her keys.

She loved her new car. Its doors unlocked when she pressed the remote. It started every time she turned the key. The radio worked. The heater worked. She never got all the kids into it only to have to get out again and call the Thomas Brothers' Garage. The amazing yellow paint made it visible even on foggy mornings. Tony didn't love it because it had been a gift to her, and for some odd reason, she found his irritation entertaining as well.

She heard Quentin's cannon boom again. The sound echoed through the valley. This part of East Tennessee was filled with mountains, rocks, trees, and vegetation. Rather than requiring more water, in a normal year it required a Bush Hog to keep part of it mowed into submission. It also made determining the origin of sounds difficult. Now wide awake and knowing it was Quentin firing potatoes from a cannon, she recalled hearing that his friend Roscoe was involved with a trebuchet, a medieval siege weapon, and his plan was to have it hurling vegetables instead of stones. She had no idea what a trebuchet looked like but even the rumors involved "flinging" rather than "shooting." Theo couldn't wait to see their demonstration at the upcoming Ramp Festival. In the past, Roscoe's obsessions had ranged from his deep and abiding love of Dora-the-vending-machine to rescuing, illegally, an orphaned bear cub named Baby. Theo didn't know if the new siege weapon would replace Dora-the-vending-machine in his affections or if it had frightened away Baby-the-bear or if they were all one big, happy, bizarre family.

Theo liked Roscoe. He was honest, hardworking, and a free spirit. He pretty much lived on his own planet. A very interesting planet, but not one she dreamed of visiting.

Theo dropped the boys off at school and headed to her quilt shop. She hoped there would be minimal interruptions at the shop because she needed to work on the can-can skirts she had been volunteered to make. Clothing construction was not her strong suit, and creating dance skirts to fit six of the county's biggest men, including Tony, required miles of ruffles and acres of black taffeta. The six dancers, representatives of the sheriff's department and some volunteer firefighters, had been selected for their size, not their dancing ability, as part of a fund-raiser. They would be performing the can-can at the Ramp Festival.

Theo's contribution to the costumes began and ended with the skirts. She hoped. Some other wife was in charge of the wigs and bonnets. Instead of the standard dancer's bodice, the men would wear black sleeveless undershirts. She learned from Tony that footwear had been discussed endlessly. Only two men could find high heeled shoes that fit. Tony was not one of them. His footwear would be hiking boots. A couple of the firemen planned to wear their firefighting boots.

With such classy accessories, Theo didn't think the skirts needed to be special, just very full and round so they could be swished—black on the outside with rows of colorful ruffles on the inside. Miles of colorful ruffles for her to sew. She couldn't decide if she was looking forward to their costume fittings or not. She didn't want to laugh at the men, but couldn't imagine she would be able to keep a straight face under such difficult conditions. As small as she was, it might look like a mouse dressing a cat.

CHAPTER TWO

With the tanker situation more or less under control, Tony climbed into the Blazer and managed a three point turn on the narrow road. Cars, motorcycles, and small trucks were parked on the road, waiting for it to reopen. The occupants thereof were surprisingly calm. Many waved to him as he passed, so Tony assumed the more impatient drivers had turned and headed to town and would continue to their destinations the long way around.

The tanker truck was back on its wheels, and more volunteers had arrived to help clean up the, thankfully, fairly small spill. There was nothing he could add to the chaos on the highway. He thought he'd take a shower at the law enforcement center and put on a clean uniform. This one had started soiled and ended up covered with mud, oil, and non-specific grime. His hands weren't likely to be clean until he grew new skin.

It had been months since anything more serious than burglary, bar fights, and bad behavior had involved his department. Winter kept many people inside with the doors and windows closed. Even his desk was fairly orderly.

Just as he entered the building, his radio crackled, interrupting his musing. Dumb. He was just superstitious enough to feel as though he'd brought problems on himself. Rex's voice had dropped into an unnaturally calm tone. Tony felt the muscles in his back tighten in response. This could only mean the tanker disaster was growing for some unknown reason, or somewhere in the county something else bad was happening.

"Sheriff? There's a silent alarm going off at the bank, and everyone else is out at the tanker spill."

"Have you been able to contact anyone inside?"

"No, sir. I've dialed several numbers. The phones are ringing, but no one answers," Rex said.

Tony knew silence could mean the worst had happened, or it could merely mean the presumed robbers told the bank workers not to answer the phones. "I'll try the manager's personal cell phone. He coaches Jamie's baseball team." Tony punched some buttons.

"Yes?" Howard Halfpenny answered. His voice a bare whisper.

Tony spoke very softly so the sound wouldn't carry far from the earpiece. "This is Sheriff Abernathy."

Before he could say more, Halfpenny, the bank manager, interrupted, speaking in a slightly louder voice.

"Yes, you do have to be at can-can practice tonight." Halfpenny laughed, sounding almost normal, and said, "No excuses accepted. If I have to do it, you do too."

"How many?" Tony always wore a protective vest under his brown uniform shirt, but he reached for the heavier, bulkier one standing in the corner of his office. It looked like black nylon stretched over a bunch of bricks and wasn't much more comfortable.

"One."

"Is anyone hurt?" Tony slapped the vest straps in place and headed to his gun safe. "Are there hostages?"

"No sprains, no breaks. You show up at the south ball field and we'll work something out."

Tony grabbed a shotgun and shells on his way to the rarely used side exit from the law enforcement center. He gave Rex a running commentary on his radio. He could see the bank's south door a half a block away from him. He hoped there were not many customers at this hour. Nearing the door, he pressed his back against the wall, making himself as small as possible. A rattletrap sedan sat empty in a no-parking zone just outside the bank door. Tony knew the owner, and it still surprised him the man had passed a driving test. Tony waited.

He heard a car slowing to a creep behind him. Turning his head slightly, he recognized the driver, Mom Proffitt, and signaled for her to keep driving. She did.

Next to him the bank door began opening. Tony felt a surge of adrenaline hit him, and he inhaled a deep breath and blew it out. Slow Osborne, Jr., tiptoed toward his ancient car. The man was a little younger than Tony but much smaller. He was as mentally challenged as his father, Slow Osborne. Junior carried an antique Colt .45 Peacemaker in one hand, pointing it at the sky and clutched a plastic grocery bag, presumably holding cash, in the other. Slow Jr. stopped behind his car, where there should have been a rear bumper.

Tony thought the man was trying to figure out how to open the door with his hands full and made a judgment call. If he spoke, Slow might panic and try to fire the pistol, so Tony just took a long stride toward him, reached out with his left hand, grabbed the gun by the barrel and jerked hard like he was pulling a lever. Thrown off balance, the thief tripped over the sidewalk curb and landed in a heap in the gutter. "Owww."

"Hush." Tony said. Now holding two guns and having only two hands, he tapped the thief with his foot. "Stand up and put your hands on the car."

Slow Jr. sniveled and whined as he did as he was instructed. "Ya don't have to act so mean. The gun ain't loaded." He rested his hands on the mud encrusted trunk of his car.

Tony glanced at the revolver. It was dusty and ancient but there were at least two bullets in the cylinder. Better to be lucky than good, he thought, and placed it carefully on the roof of the car before reaching for the handcuffs on his duty belt. Slow Jr. didn't protest and stood still while Tony slipped them around his skinny wrists. Tony talked to Rex on the radio. "Ask Ruth Ann to bring a camera and come here. No one else is available."

Moments later, his secretary/assistant Ruth Ann appeared. She wore a big grin on her cocoa colored face and facial tissue stuck to the bright blue nail polish on her left hand. She carried a camera, a ruler, and a stack of yellow plastic numbered cards. "You point and I'll click."

It didn't take long. Starting with the paper bag containing 4,212 dollars in currency, they took pictures inside and outside and several shots of the Peacemaker, including one showing the bullets. The bank staff took turns popping out the door to chat. Tony shooed them inside. "I'll want to talk to each of you in a few minutes. Please don't talk among yourselves."

Leaving Ruth Ann with her photo project, Tony marched Slow Jr. to the law enforcement center and left him in the holding cell, locked up the revolver, and put away his shotgun. He went back to the bank to take statements. There weren't many employees and their statements were brief. All agreed that Slow Jr. had walked in carrying the revolver, put the bag on the counter, and demanded all the money in the bank.

Tony notified their county prosecutor, Archie Campbell, and the public defender, Carl Lee Cashdollar. And then he called Slow Jr.'s mother, Bernice.

The four of them needed to talk together before anyone interviewed Slow Jr. Tony didn't know where the line should be drawn between the ability to form intent and/or understand consequences. He wanted everyone to be on the same page. Bernice was the last to arrive, coming from work. Tony thought she looked even more tired and downtrodden than usual. Tears in her eyes were magnified by the thick lenses on her old-fashioned glasses. The woman's entire existence had to be work and worry. She and Slow had produced eight children. Most possessed average intelligence. Junior was the offspring most like his father.

"Where'd you get the gun?" Tony asked Slow Jr. He'd waited long enough to find out what inspired this morning's excitement.

"Found it in Grandpa's old trunk." Slow Jr. looked proud. "I'm going to be just like Billy the Kid."

"What do you know about Billy the Kid?" Tony asked.

"I saw a movie onest. Billy carried a gun and banks gave him money when he needed it." Slow smiled. "The banks have lots of money and won't miss none. They just churn it out when they need it."

"Do you mean making it, as in printing it?" said Carl Lee.

The man nodded.

Shaking her head, his mother wiped the tears from her cheeks.

Prosecutor Archie Campbell said, "I don't have a choice. Premeditation and use of a firearm."

Carl Lee cleared his throat. Everyone looked at the public defender. "I'm advising my client to remain silent."

Slow Jr. opened his mouth again, and his mother quickly placed her hand over it. "Hush, baby." For the first time, he seemed to recognize he'd made a serious mistake. Tears flooded his eyes.

Tony thought if Slow Jr. had once thought it would be fun to rob a bank, he knew differently now.

Carl Lee Cashdollar stopped in Tony's office doorway. He stood there making an odd humming sound.

"What's up, Carl Lee? Is Archie having second thoughts about sending Slow Jr. home until his trial?" Tony smiled and leaned back in his chair. Carl Lee wasn't wearing his lawyer face. He looked unsettled, so Tony waved the defense attorney into his office "You all right?"

Carl Lee shook his head as he sat down facing Tony. "I'm not sure."

Tony felt a jolt of curiosity mixed with concern.

Carl Lee said, "What do *you* do when you *know* someone has committed a crime and you don't have any proof?"

"I keep digging until the shovel breaks or until I have to work on something else. I don't mark the case closed." Tony leaned forward. "What's happened?"

"Don't laugh." Carl Lee's eyes flickered to the floor and up. "My wife's cat is missing, and I think Hairy Rags killed it and disposed of the body."

Tony did not feel like laughing. He believed the lawyer's story and similar ones he'd heard over the past few months. The game warden, Harrison Ragsdale, had long had an unsavory reputation, but recently there had been an exceptionally high number of missing pets in Park County. "Tell me." He reached for his notebook. In spite of more reports, they had not found more animal bodies than usual.

Carl Lee sighed heavily and reached into his pocket. He pulled out a photograph of a beautiful Siamese cat and handed it to Tony. "Two Bit."

"Two Bit?" Tony did smile then. "Looks like a fifty-dollar cat to me."

"When the previous owner gave it to my wife, he said the cat wasn't worth two bits. He was wrong." Carl Lee paused. "My wife adores the cat, and I'm almost as fond of it as she is. A few weeks ago, Two Bit followed me outside as usual, while I was putting the trash can out for Claude. Anyway, it was dark and there's a lot of trees and shrubs blocking the view, and I saw Two Bit lunge into a shrub and knew she was after a bird, but the bird flew away and at the same time I heard a car engine rev up and the cat was gone, and I'd swear the car making the turn belonged to Ragsdale."

"No cat body?"

"That's the only part I can't explain, but, we haven't seen her since."

Tony was still thinking about the cat and the bank robbery and the oil truck when Sheila tapped on his door frame. He waved her in, hoping she wasn't bearing bad news. "What's up?"

"You know I'm involved in an after school homework program for kids with problems?" Sheila settled on the chair and relaxed.

Tony nodded, relieved that Sheila didn't look upset. His only female deputy was smart, efficient, and a pleasure to work with. She could also shoot the antennae off a June bug from some ridiculous distance, one where he'd be lucky to even see the insect.

"Alvin Tibbles is my student. He's trying to be a good kid but Alvin's mom is a frequent flyer in the jail." Sheila paused. "Candy Tibbles is his mom."

Tony saw Candy's name on arrest reports frequently. She had a long record—mostly for drunk and disorderly. "Is there a problem with Candy?" Tony thought the homework program was a good one. It connected kids on the brink with positive role models. "Or do you think Alvin would do better with a male mentor?"

"I don't think so. Alvin and I actually get along pretty well. I'd like to see him have emancipated status." She leaned forward, clasping her hands together. "He's so old for his age he doesn't fit with any so-called normal family, but that's not why I'm here."

Tony felt his eyebrows lift.

Sheila continued. "What I came to ask you is for your permission to take Alvin on a tour of the jail, let him see what it's really like, where his mom sleeps when she's here and that she's not abused. He's *her* caretaker and he worries."

"Where does Alvin sleep when she overnights here?" Tony hoped it was some place safer than the backseat of an abandoned car.

"He's old enough to stay at home by himself, but I usually take him out to my folks' house." Sheila smiled. "My mom dotes on him, and he likes Dad."

"Bring him in any time. I'll escort both of you and he can ask me anything he wants." Tony thought in the long run it might save two lives, Alvin's, and his mother's.

CHAPTER THREE

Theo made it up the stairs to her office without dropping anything. Success. She was elated. Not only was she feeling stronger every day—her recovery from the twins' births was taking longer than she'd expected—but she was getting the hang of juggling. She knew her ability to carry both girls together wouldn't last long. The babies were growing like weeds, and she'd better rest while she could. Once they started scooting around on their own, she probably wouldn't get to sit down again until they went to school.

Gretchen, her only full-time employee at the shop, charged up the stairs behind them and stopped at the top, a pen and small notebook clutched in one fist and the mail in the other. "Jane's already called eighteen times." As if conjured by her announcement, the telephone on Theo's desk rang, and Gretchen trotted over to answer it. She claimed Theo had not arrived yet and would definitely give her the message. She disconnected. "Why is Jane calling the shop instead of your cell?"

Theo pulled her cell phone out of the diaper bag. "I turned this off." She did not turn it on. "Jane's afraid she'll wake the babies so she won't call the house phone. What does she need?"

Gretchen shook her head. "She won't tell me. She just wants you to call her."

Theo was torn. The twins were asleep, so she considered waiting until she'd gotten some work done on the can-can skirts and maybe even her new quilt pattern before returning Jane's call, but guilt won out. She dialed Jane's number. Her mother-in-law was a sweetheart, but disaster followed her and her sister Martha around like their shadows. Any guardian angel assigned to either of them was probably exhausted after one day. The two ladies were never without a plan for doing something bizarre. At least they had given up the idea of traveling around the state singing in bars, a scenario that had created many conversations and sleepless nights for Tony and his siblings.

"Oh, Theo dear, it's you." Jane didn't give Theo a chance to say a word. "I really hope you are planning to be a part of the quilting demonstration at the Ramp Festival on Saturday?" Theo shook her head at the voice. Jane, not seeing the gesture, of course, charged ahead. "I know you are busy these days, but really, it would be so sweet if you'd come and help for a little while and teach something simple. We'll find someone to cover for you at the ticket table."

Theo shook her head harder. She could feel her curls bounce and couldn't imagine her mother-in-law couldn't hear them. Four-month-old twins, plus two boys in elementary school, a shop to run, and a house and a husband sucked up every last second of each twenty-four-hour period. Wasn't working at the entrance table enough? Especially since she was sure her duty there would include dealing with people who didn't want to pay the fee. All that whining and complaining would wear down a saint. When would she have time to set up a demonstration? Where did Jane get these ideas?

"I really can't." Theo tried shoving the words out of her throat. They eventually came out, but sounded like "all right, if you need me" even to her own ears. She was sunk. Jane was ecstatic. How could she retract her words now?

Theo stared at the window, her thoughts immediately turned to what kind of quilting project she could demonstrate. She certainly didn't want to use any of her good fabric, especially since whatever she took would stink by the end of the day and need immediate washing or throwing away.

Ramps were intensely smelly wild members of the onion and garlic family. Whatever possessed Jane and her sister Martha to celebrate the coming of spring at their folk museum by having a Ramp Festival? They planned food booths involving the odoriferous vegetables. Soups, pies, snacks, everything would contain ramps. Everything would smell vile. Theo imagined even the food not containing ramps—the hamburgers, hot dogs and desserts—would end up with a vaguely garlicky onion aftertaste. Guilt by association.

Wasn't having the food enough? No. Not for those ladies. There was to be music all day, everything from bluegrass to rock and roll. Once they came up with the initial idea, they couldn't seem to stop. A quilt show, of course, and now a demonstration featuring Theo. Other demonstrations planned involved weaving, dyeing yarn with roadside plants, and making birdhouses out of gourds. Rumors Theo had heard suggested the ladies planned games, storytellers, a horseshoe toss, pony rides and, for something even more exciting, a display of vegetables as projectiles. Earlier in the morning she hadn't connected Quentin's practice blasting potatoes through a cannon with the full event schedule. Now she recalled others planned to celebrate with more ancient forms of weapons to attack the designated target with vegetables, even a catapult.

Jane and Martha's minimally paid assistant and newlywed, Celeste, looked like she'd aged twenty years the last time Theo had seen her. As Celeste had hurried past, she'd murmured, "You did warn me. Help."

The two women planned to import volunteer workers from all parts of their tiny county. The ladies fully intended to have as close to the total county population in attendance as they could. The senior citizens weren't immune to their recruiting plan either. Unable to outrun the sisters, seniors had been drafted as food server assistants; even the frail elderly like the Bainbridge sisters, Portia Osgood, and Caro, had been given jobs. Maybe they couldn't hoist a plate filled with a slab of pie, but they could hand out napkins and plastic cutlery. Poor blind Betty would probably be sitting in a corner telling stories to children or being the designated toothpick holder.

Theo moaned again. Trapped.

In the portable crib set up in the family corner of her office, Kara and Lizzie chortled and waved their hands and feet in the air. Pretty sad; it looked like even the infants thought their mother screwed up this time and were laughing about it.

It wasn't much past ten o'clock in the morning, and Tony felt ready to go home for the day. He hated the senselessness of traffic accidents. Slowing down by five miles an hour around Dead Man's Curve would not make a huge impact on anyone's timetable, certainly not near the delay being in an accident added.

He served his county's residents to the best of his ability. Today, he felt torn between the laws concerned with crimes involving guns and the sheer misfortune of Slow Jr. The man had committed a felony. He was competent to stand trial according to the rules. He knew right from wrong, the prosecution from the defense. He knew what the judge's role would be in a trial. Earlier, his office had been filled with a sense of impending doom. Nobody wanted to prosecute, yet they couldn't ignore the crime.

At least he'd finally managed to shower and change into a clean uniform. Maybe he could go to Ruby's Café and have a piece of Blossom's pie. Not only would it make him feel better because it would taste divine, but it would guarantee he put in his hour in the workout room in the basement of the law enforcement center. Sometimes he needed a little extra incentive to make sure he did his time on the treadmill and weights.

Just checking up, Tony drove the length of the county. The tanker was gone, towed away on its own wheels. The leakage had been less than feared but more than there should have been. Once all the measuring and discussion ended, it was clear the truck driver had been traveling too fast. He received a ticket and a lecture. Tony suspected he was going to get an earful from his boss as well. Wade told him how little the driver cared about the harm he'd done, and a string of curses and excuses had poured from the driver's belligerent face. Maybe his attitude stemmed from the shock of the accident itself, or maybe from the need to dramatize his life, but Tony didn't like him and would be pleased if he stayed out of Park County, Tennessee, for the rest of his life.

Tony drove carefully around the curve and headed for town. He noticed a small red pickup approaching, traveling slightly above the speed limit and swerving a bit. It was staying in the right lane. As it neared him, Tony realized the driver held a cell phone and was apparently sending a text message. Both hands flew over the device as the driver stared down at the screen.

A third hand, one belonging to a small passenger, gripped the steering wheel. Tony's daydream of continued peace and sane behavior shattered. He made a U-turn and fell in behind the pickup, flashing his lights and hitting the siren. The man behind the wheel—Tony wasn't sure he'd still qualify as the driver—leaned sideways like he'd dropped something and the pickup swerved hard, luckily not into oncoming traffic. The pickup finally stopped, half on the road, half in a ditch. The driver's side door opened and four hundred pounds of belligerent man shoved his way through the space. He clutched his cell phone in his left hand and dragged an ax handle from the open bed as he headed for Tony.

He didn't get far. Stopped by a scream coming from the pickup and the sight of Tony's semi-automatic aimed at his huge gut, he dropped the handle and raised his hands over his head.

Tony drove to Ruby's Café, went around to the back and sat outside. From his table he had a nice view of the ridge separating this area from downtown Silersville. The sight of spring foliage and the chirping of happy birds eased some of his frustration. He took a deep breath and slowly let it out, forcing himself to relax. Wrecks, robbery, texting, and attempted assault: what was next? He was sure it would be something stupid and spring fever would be blamed.

The incredibly beautiful café owner, Ruby herself, brought him a glass of water. "Good morning, Tony."

Ruby had married Tony's deputy, Mike Ott, in this very place only a few months earlier. Tony smiled at her and thought her voice held a happier than usual note. "You sound chipper."

"And why not? It's a beautiful day and one of my favorite customers has come by for pie? Cinnamon roll? Coffee?" Ruby didn't offer him a menu.

"Apple pie?" Tony loved his wife and children, but some days the pie ran a close second.

"Blossom just took one out of the oven. It should still be warm." Ruby's lips turned up at the corners.

Tony moaned, just a little, recognizing his lack of willpower. "Okay. Better make it a double."

When she returned with the pie, two warm slices on a dinner plate, she leaned close to his ear as she set down the plate, making sure the customers at nearby tables didn't hear. "Since you're one of my best customers, I'm giving you a news scoop— Mike and I are expecting a baby in the fall."

Before Tony could give her his congratulations, as well as

thanks for the news he beat Theo to, Wade arrived. He asked for the same size serving of pie. Ruby gave Tony a wink and headed for the kitchen.

Theo was surprised to see Tony arrive in her workroom. She thought he looked tired and elated at the same time. "What's up?"

"Can't a man come visit his three favorite females without getting the third degree?" He headed to the corner dedicated to the children. As well as a small table and chairs, a television and a refrigerator, the boys had video games and movies and books, and there was a microwave and coffee pot and a small pantry. Lately Theo had added even more equipment because of the twins. A changing table and crib, as well as a rocking chair and the usual trundle bed and floor chairs. "You're running out of space up here."

The twins napped side by side in their crib, so Tony just patted their tiny backs. One of his hands was still much bigger than each back, but the girls were growing every day.

"So true." Theo wasn't complaining. It was chaos, but it was happy chaos. "Maybe when Gus is finished adding on to Queen Doreen's shop and being your mom and aunt's museum slave, I'll have him add a floor above this one just for the kids. We'll be the tallest building in Silersville and maybe get an elevator and . . ." Laughing, she paused to take a deep breath.

"Ruby's pregnant." Tony whispered in the moment of silence.

Theo stopped chattering. "Really?"

"Yep." His bright blue eyes twinkled, and his whole face lit up with the smile. "I just got the good news directly from her, along with a double slice of apple pie. Very good, the apple pie, maybe the best one Blossom's ever made." Tony patted his stomach.

"I'm so happy for Ruby and Mike. Thanks for being the

bearer of such good news. It almost makes up for your mom trapping me into giving a demonstration on Saturday." Laughing, Theo gave him a big hug. "Do I need to keep this secret, or can I release the news here at gossip central?"

"Ruby says you can tell anyone you want." Tony looked at his watch. "It's eleven. Want to make a bet how long it takes before the news on the gossip express makes full circle and Ruby hears about it at the café?"

Shaking her head at his offer, Theo made one of her own. "For a kiss, I'll give you a five-minute head start. You better give the news to Ruth Ann before she hears it from the grapevine."

"So true. I'd hate to be decapitated for my bad behavior. I made her smudge her polish earlier today. A second transgression could have lasting consequences." Tony gave her a quick kiss, fluffed her curls, and charged for the stairs.

Theo actually gave him six minutes before she headed downstairs, baby monitor in hand, to start spreading the word.

Three elderly ladies were busy in the large, brightly illuminated classroom. It was the usual gathering place for many of the community women, and an occasional man. When there wasn't a class going on, anyone could come in and work on the charity quilt of the moment set up on a full-sized frame. In addition to the traditional hand quilters, Theo's shop now had a long-arm machine for those who wanted to rent time on it to quickly complete some of their projects.

Theo knew how to operate the long-arm machine, which resembled an oversize sewing machine with handlebars. The quilt sandwich remained stable, and the quilter moved the machine, making quilting by machine a completely new experience. Theo had taken classes on how to use the machine. She studied the video supplied by the company, and she practiced on some quilts donated to various charities. Theo just couldn't enjoy using it. Luckily for her and the shop, Gretchen had fallen in love with the machine and the process. So Gretchen not only gave lessons to their customers in using it, a requirement for anyone wanting to rent time, she also paid Theo a nominal fee and used it to do quilting for other people. The extra money she earned was going into Gretchen's children's college fund.

Today, so far, of the regular ladies, there were three. Oldest was legally blind Betty followed by her younger and better sighted friend Dottie. Compared to the physically gnome-like Betty, Dottie was a young, physically spry eighty-year-old. The ladies were drinking coffee and working on a jigsaw puzzle at a card table set up in the corner next to the coffee pot. Theo wondered how Betty could find the right place for the puzzle pieces without her sight until Theo studied them once and re-alized Dottie spent more time helping Betty find homes for her pieces than in working the puzzle herself.

This morning, the third woman, Ada Walker, served as their waitress. In one of the odd twists of fate guaranteed to make life unpredictable, Ada had moved to Silersville only two years earlier so she could live closer to her daughter. The situation seemed ideal. Ada's daughter and son-in-law owned a rental house on their property. It was tiny but cozy. Ada kept her own life and stuff separate from her daughter's. The house was also convenient to the senior center. Her daughter could keep tabs on her mother without either household feeling invasive or invaded.

Ada became one of the quilt shop regulars almost before she was unpacked. Life was good. Until the day it suddenly wasn't. In a freak accident, her daughter and son-in-law were killed. The property and its contents, except for Ada's personal belong-ings, suddenly belonged to strangers—the husband's brothers. They weren't unsympathetic to her plight, and wrote into the contract for the sale of the property her right to live in the cottage for life. And pay minimal rent.

Ada had clear desires for her after-death experience, and managed to work her plans for her afterlife into almost every conversation. She insisted on cremation, no funeral service, just a memorial luncheon and yard sale. Any proceeds over the costs incurred were to be donated to a designated charity. Her other recurring theme was a fluent, almost continuous, outpouring of profanity. Tony once said after chatting with Ada that, as a Navy man, he was surprised to learn that his vocabulary of certain nouns, verbs, and adverbs was shockingly sparse. Bright color highlighted his cheekbones, as Ada literally did make a sailor blush.

Theo's main issue with the woman was she didn't filter her language when children were present. She came to accept Ada's vocabulary with more grace after a whispered conference with her friends explained that Ada's tendency to use profanity started when she'd had a stroke or some similar neurological event.

The arrival of three more elderly ladies made the informal club gathering more festive.

Their group of older ladies came to the shop most mornings, sometimes to do puzzles, sometimes to quilt, and often to just sit and soak up the gossip and the fun environment of the shop. Theo's contribution was free coffee. At eleven-thirty, the ladies would make their way to the senior center, a block away, for lunch and whatever entertainment was available. They'd all be back in their own homes for the day by four-thirty.

"I have a bit of news for you," Theo said, and told them about Ruby's pregnancy. Then she suggested maybe their little quilting group might like to help make a baby quilt when Ruby's time came nearer.

They fell on the idea with great enthusiasm and began pulling quilting magazines out of a stack, looking for the perfect pattern. All of them knew their major job would be selecting the pattern and deciding on the fabrics. The younger members of the club, so to speak, would do the actual cutting and sewing and quilting. The older ladies, the day ladies, would get all the credit while the evening group would do the work.

Since Ruby had been initiated into the evening quilting group, known as the Thursday Night Bowling League, she would understand the rules of the game. In fact, she might end up working on her own baby's quilt for a while and be "surprised" when it was wrapped and given to her at a shower. Rules were rules, and as long as everyone understood and abided by them, there were no problems.

While Theo and the older ladies were chatting about the exciting new project, Portia Osgood tottered in, leaning heavily on a walker. While not Theo's favorite woman, she had fewer bad memories of having her for a teacher than Tony did. Theo had been an exceptionally sheltered and timid child who handed in all of her homework, and Mrs. Osgood had never needed to reprimand her. Tony, on the other hand, frequently clashed with the diminutive teacher. Self-confident and high-spirited, he rebelled against her rigid rules.

Theo greeted the elderly woman, pulled a chair over to the table for her, and asked if she'd like a cup of coffee or tea.

"Tea with cream." Portia glared, even as she struggled into her chair. "None of that non-dairy claptrap. There's nothing wrong with what cows produce. I've lived ninety years and had butter and cream almost every day of them."

Biting the insides of her cheeks to keep from laughing, Theo did as she had been ordered. As she walked toward the coffee pot, she heard the older ladies commiserating with each other about failing eyesight, poor health, and the loneliness coming from losing a pet or companion. "You never had children, did you, Portia?"

"Only the several hundred I taught over the years." Portia almost smiled when Theo delivered her beverage. "Some of them I liked more than others, but I did the best I could with what was given to me. I was occasionally surprised by the way they changed, but not usually."

"Like what?" Betty the gnome groped for her cup. "Or should I say who or whom?"

"Well, of course, there was Billy Ragsdale." Portia shook her head in disappointment or disgust.

"Is he the one . . . ?" Horror laced Dottie's words, but she didn't need to finish the question.

Portia answered, her voice brisk. "Yes, he moved to Chicago and later killed his girlfriend."

"What relation is he to Harrison Ragsdale?" Theo thought she knew but wasn't sure. Harrison worked as a game warden. He was not well liked.

"Billy was his older brother." Portia sipped her coffee. "They had a sister, and she was not exactly my idea of a fine human being either. I just don't know what possesses people to behave like that. Run around all hours of the day and night, drinking and carrying on like the devil's own."

Theo tiptoed out of the room when the ladies launched into a group discussion of how the world was going to hell in a hand basket. Their depressing chatter was destroying Theo's happy mood after Tony's wonderful news about Ruby. She decided to share the news with Gretchen instead and headed for the business end of her building.

Just as Theo arrived at the front of the store, Katti Marmot trotted in. Dressed in her favorite colors of pink and pink with more pink, she smiled broadly at Gretchen and Theo. "Is a good day."

Theo nodded. "It's always good to see you, Katti."

"Our Ruby is having baby." Katti stopped at the counter.

"What word is meaning more good?"

"Wonderful." Theo's delight was not only about Ruby's news, but she always enjoyed having the Russian mail-order bride around. Doc Nash had arranged for Katti to be her assistant during the last months of Theo's pregnancy with the twins, and Katti remained on the job for the first six weeks they were all home. It required more than one adult to deal with the newborns and Chris and Jamie. Tony was always on call. Katti might not work for Theo anymore, but she loved the girls.

Gretchen turned to glare at Theo. "You knew about Ruby?"

"I promise, I just found out and was on my way to tell you when Katti came in." Theo spread her hands in surrender. "Is it my fault she got her mouth open before I did?"

Gretchen's expression could have passed for acceptance. "So, Katti, how did you find out?"

Katti looked uncertain she should say anything. "I eat at café with my Claude, and Ruby tells me. I so excited I have my Claude bring me to shop so I tell you. Is wrong?"

"No. Not wrong." Theo gave her a hug. "It's wonderful news."

Katti looked over Theo's shoulder. "Oooh, new pink?" She released her friend and headed to a newly arrived fabric.

Behind Theo, Gretchen snickered. "Thrown over for some yard goods."

Her feelings not injured in the least, Theo might have offered a pithy rejoinder, but the baby monitor in her hand transmitted the sounds of soft baby chatter. "I'd better get up there."

After a late lunch, Tony drove, as he often did, the loop following the main roads of his county. It didn't take long and he liked to see what Mother Nature was up to as well as the residents. He'd swear the trees had been leafless the day before. Today, the buds on the trees and shrubs were fat and ready to burst open. The black walnut tree leaves were vivid green and he could see the catkins hanging like caterpillars in the branches. Flowering plants gleamed with white and pink. Spring had arrived overnight. No place he'd ever lived or visited could rival springtime in the Smokies. His window was down, and he could feel the softness of the air.

Although the possible combination of spring fever and the upcoming full moon might lead to escalating insanity in the locals was something he chose not to concentrate on, he found himself growing wary. He hoped the morning activities would be the extent of foolish behavior.

Daydreaming of a world where he'd be able to banish people he didn't like from his county, Tony gradually became aware of the sound of a rifle being fired, probably a .22 caliber. He pulled off the road and cut the engine. Stepping out of the vehicle, he listened intently, hoping to be able to determine the origin of the shots. It wasn't unusual to hear occasional gunshots, but a road sign sniper was costing the county a fair amount of money and time. Drilling road signs had been going on unchecked for almost half a year. Who was so determined and so elusive?

His cell phone rang at the same time he heard Rex's voice on the radio. Not knowing where to go for his sign sniper, Tony climbed into the Blazer.

"Sheriff?" Rex was backing up his radio call with the telephone. "Are you coming by your office any time soon?"

Tony thought Rex sounded irritated. Strong emotion from him indeed. "I'm on my way now. What's the problem?"

"Blossom Flowers has a pie for you, and she says she's not sure you'll get it if she leaves it unattended in the lunch room." Rex's voice reflected the insult he'd been given.

"I had pie at Ruby's this morning."

"She's here now." Rex's words snapped through the earpiece.

Tony sighed. He supposed he ought to put a stop to the pie deliveries. In his head, it always sounded like a good idea to tell

Blossom not to bake for him. Unfortunately, the scent of one of her pies drove Tony's common sense out the door. He congratulated himself on being better at sharing than he used to be. The first pie she made for him, he ate with his office door locked. "I'll be there in a few minutes."

He was almost back to town when he saw the game warden's vehicle, lights flashing, parked behind a small van with a giant plastic insect on the top. Tony slowed. Although he thoroughly detested Officer Harrison Ragsdale and was one of many who shortened the name to Hairy Rags, it was Tony's sworn duty to lend assistance to anyone if needed. More so, because, whether he liked it or not, Ragsdale was another sworn officer. Luckily, Ragsdale glanced up from his study of something in the bed of the pickup and waved Tony on. Ragsdale's face bore its normal expression of anger and disapproval. The two men standing with him appeared unhappy but noncombative.

As Tony expected when he reached the law enforcement center, Blossom sat in his office, and a fresh pie rested on his desk on the top of a stack of files. She sniffled. "I don't like Rex none. He always looks at me like I'm carrying plates of poisoned apples in here."

Irritated, Tony shook his head. "Rex is just doing his job. You answer his questions, and he'll leave you alone." He studied his guest. Since Blossom's social life had developed into the county's favorite spectator sport, she hadn't been baking for him as much as she used to. Kenny Baines and DuWayne Cozzens were both hotly pursuing the plain but incredibly sweet woman with thinning orange hair, bulbous blue eyes, and more-than-slight weight problem. The men often had to settle for a group date. Blossom's increased social life had caused her a bit of weight loss for a while, but she had come to terms with dating, and although she was a good forty pounds lighter than she'd been a year ago, there was still enough of her to please both men. "Maybe you could offer *Rex* a dessert."

In response to his reprimand, Blossom's face turned pink and she pouted, her lower lip protruding like a three-year-old's. "I don't trust him with your pie."

"Blossom, as much as I enjoy your pies, I'll have you barred from my office if you don't stop sulking." He gave her a stern look. "Rex lets you into this wing of the building because I've told him to. I can change that right now."

Tears rose in her great protruding eyes and rolled down her face. She brushed them away with her forearm. "Sorry."

"So, what's really bothering you?" Tony wasn't sure why he knew pie was not what Blossom wanted to discuss, but he did.

"I've been gettin' notes." Blossom twisted a strand of her thin hair around a chubby finger and stared toward the quilt hanging on the wall behind him. "Lots of nasty notes about my likin' two men." She blinked. "You said it was only bad if I was to marry both of them." Her frown held a hint of accusation, as if he'd misled her intentionally.

Now he understood the problem. There weren't a lot of single men in Park County, and Blossom was probably dating two of the best ones. Tony skipped over the legality question, hoping to satisfy his curiosity. "Do you like one more than the other?"

Blossom touched the center of the dip just below her lower lip with a finger and made a "hum" sound. She glanced down. She glanced up. Finally, she shook her head. "Well, DuWayne's a better dancer, and Kenny's got great kids. I know I ought to choose, but they've both been good to me."

As she went on to detail the pros and cons of her beaux, Tony had to leave his office for a moment so he wouldn't burst out laughing. She was taking this issue very seriously, not just giving in to emotion. Who would have ever guessed Blossom would be the center of a love triangle or a gossip firestorm like this one?

Ruth Ann stared at him and slipped the brush back into the bottle of fingernail polish. "Is there a problem?" Her dark eyes sparkled brighter than the glitter in her tangerine polish.

Tony thought for a millisecond. "What she really needs is a woman's advice. I'll send Blossom out to talk to you." He turned and vanished into his office before Ruth Ann could voice a protest.

Convincing Blossom to talk to Ruth Ann was harder. Finally though, she grudgingly waddled out to share her problem with Ruth Ann, sniffling the whole way, and Tony slipped past her and out of the building. He'd be lucky if Ruth Ann didn't add a little something extra to the pie on his desk. Something like drain cleaner.

On her way home for the day, Theo descended upon Nina. Her best friend was such a sweetheart. She hated mystery quilts. She didn't like not knowing what the finished project should look like, mostly, Theo believed, because Nina loved to make changes to patterns. When she tested for Theo, it was critical for her to hold firm to the instructions. She was perfect. Even though Nina had plenty to occupy herself, what with teaching high school French and raising her own children, she accepted the task.

Visiting Nina was also an excuse to take a beautiful drive. Nina's home was built on the farthest lot in the subdivision created by her father on the family farm. Poor for farming but rich in beauty. It had the best view in the county. The road formed an oval, and the homes were on the outside of it. The center was an undeveloped park, filled with animals and ancient trees. The view across the valley was of the taller mountains of the Smokies. Like most of the new homes, Nina's was built to take advantage of the view. Her nearest neighbor was five hundred yards away and hidden by the trees. Expensive lots. Nina's dad was no dummy.

As Theo carried the twins and her bag containing the pattern and a variety of fabrics into Nina's house, she couldn't help but notice a huge heart-shaped box of chocolates, still wrapped in cellophane, sitting on the entry table. Valentine's day was long past. The box was covered with dust. "If you're not going to eat the chocolates or throw them away, you ought to at least dust them."

Nina only laughed.

"Seriously." Theo knew they were a gift from Nina's ex-husband. "What's going on? Does he want you back? Do you want him back?"

"The kids want him back." Nina led the way into her spacious great room. The panorama of the Smoky Mountains made a majestic backdrop to her comfortable furniture. "I am willing to let them spend more time with him but dread the moment when he disappoints them again. I know him too well to believe otherwise." Her expression was pensive. "I hate to see them get hurt again."

Theo, being Nina's friend, understood. She had never been one of her ex's fans. "But why keep the chocolate out there?"

"As long as I don't open it, the kids can see I'm giving it proper consideration, and the answer is still no." Nina did smile then. "I imagine the dust will be a foot deep when they figure it out." She took Lizzie from Theo and gave the baby a big kiss on her neck.

"I've brought you something else to play with besides the girls." Theo handed Nina a few sheets of paper and a paper bag containing a variety of fabrics. "Have fun."

"Anything special you want me to watch for?" Nina stared at the first page. When Theo didn't say anything, she glared. "You know I hate to do mystery quilts."

"Yes, and thank you anyway. It makes you the perfect pattern tester." Theo made herself comfortable on an old rocking chair. "Speaking of knowing things, have you heard about Ruby being pregnant?"

"Yes, it's so exciting! She'll be the most gorgeous pregnant woman ever. Her ankles probably won't even swell." Nina peeked into the bag. "I don't suppose you packed baby fabrics for me to play with?"

Theo had, the moment she'd heard Ruby's news.

CHAPTER FOUR

Remembering his promise to Theo, Tony thought he'd put his escape from the office to good use and deal with the noise of Quentin's cannon. The last time Tony had an employment update on Quentin, he was still working for Gus. Tony's oldest brother had been working on the folk museum project for their mother and aunt for over half a year. Tony decided to drive out and talk to Quentin and see what was happening on the site of a former dreadful—what was it called? Not a motel. It finally came to him: an old fashioned tourist court. That was the name for it. Until Gus tore the remains of it down, a series of individual cabins dotted the acreage. Rotting and falling down, nothing could look worse than they had. Gus's crew, including Quentin, had leveled them and cleared out not only the buildings but truckloads of kudzu and dead trees.

Of the original buildings, only the cinder block one used as the former office remained. It had been gutted inside and painted and now served as the private museum office. On the rest of the grounds, Gus's crew had moved and rebuilt, on site, an antique barn, built a new museum building with climate control to protect the more delicate items on display, like the antique quilts and clothes, and separated the parking area from the recently planted grass with new split-rail fences. A few sheep and a goat inhabited a large undeveloped pasture filled with wild grasses, shrubs and weeds. Besides adding a bucolic touch, the animals helped keep the rampaging vegetation in check.

The old barn and the new museum building looked splendid in the morning sun. A cabin recently moved onto the property now filled a space near the far end of the barn. Across the parking area from the complex of buildings, he spotted his brother and two helpers busy setting up a stage facing a neatly mown field. Tony climbed from the Blazer and headed in that direction.

"Hail, Caesar!" Although Tony was the youngest of the Abernathy siblings, he thought he most resembled Gus, named Caesar Augustus Abernathy at birth. Like Tony, he was tall, muscular, and short on hair.

"Oh, yoo-hoo, Marc Antony," Gus called as he ambled toward Tony, tossing a small sledge hammer from hand to hand. "I baked you some cookies." He batted his eyelashes.

Tony thought Gus's imitation of Blossom was spot on. "It's better to have a fan than be a slave. What's our mom got you doing now?"

Gus waved toward the construction area. "After we get the stage set up, we're supposed to start work on the outdoor dining area for this weekend's fun." His forehead developed deep grooves and his voice dropped. "Mom and Aunt Martha seem to expect hordes of hungry diners. Do you think many people will come out here to eat ramps? Have you ever smelled one?"

Tony shook his head. He'd heard of the pungent vegetable but had never, at least not knowingly, eaten one.

Gus stared into the distance. "Think onions with garlic sauce."

Tony's stomach flinched. "I think there will be a crowd, but I don't know how many folks will plan to be eating much. There's already been some whining by the cheapskates in town about having to pay admission to hear the music and see the crafts show. The ramp dishes are free, but the rest of the food won't be."

"A full day's entertainment costing less than a movie ticket?" Gus looked stunned. "Do they think it should all be free?"

Nodding, Tony looked past his brother at the parking spaces. "If there's a crowd, where are they supposed to park? There's not more than thirty spaces here."

"Mom's worked out a deal with Sam Brown, the owner of the property across the road. He's letting her use a cow pasture as an overflow parking lot." Gus frowned. "She won't say what he asked for in exchange, but you can bet there's something on his mind."

Tony studied the house on the small dairy farm. Not new, not ancient. The house was in reasonable repair, the yard non-descript, the nearer pasture held a herd of milk cows and the farther one showed signs of having been mowed recently. Tony actually felt relieved he knew so little about Mr. Brown. Either Brown stayed on the right side of the law or was extremely clever. His first son had died in an accident at the age of thirteen. Tony and Brown's remaining son had been friends in school, mostly because they played the same sports. The son had been a decent guard in basketball, not exceptionally bright or dull, and Tony guessed he'd moved away after school to get out of milking. "It's been six months since Brown's wife passed away. Maybe he's looking for a replacement."

"Do you think our mom would put up with mud and manure being tracked into her house?" Gus squinted toward the farm house. "I think Brown's nice enough, but I can still remember the time I saw him walk into the house wearing his barn boots. I was selling Christmas wreaths with the scouts, and he went in to get the money."

Tony whistled. "Mom would have gone ballistic, for sure, but maybe there was a mud room for that kind of thing. I never saw mud on the floor when I visited his son." Thinking of complaints reminded him why he'd made the trip out here. "I need to talk to Quentin for a minute."

"Let me guess," Gus said. "The potato cannon?"

"Oh, yeah." Tony grinned. "I'm sure you've heard it. Everyone's heard it and called to complain. Have you seen it?"

"Yes. Quentin and Roscoe invited me to drive up the mountain after work the other day. The cannon was quite impressive, but when it comes to the vegetable weapons I prefer Roscoe's trebuchet." Gus shifted his ball cap and lowered his voice. "I think it actually belongs to Roscoe's lady friend."

"A trebuchet? I heard the rumors." Pausing in mid-step, Tony glanced over his shoulder. "And there's a real live lady friend? A woman? Not a bear or a vending machine?"

"You haven't met her?" Gus grinned like he'd won the lottery. "Wow! What are the odds of my meeting her before you?"

Too insanely curious to waste time in a verbal sparring session, Tony raised his hands in mock surrender. "Tell me."

"She's a professor at the university. Something to do with European history, and she is wildly enthusiastic about medieval weaponry and armor and our Roscoe." Gus leaned close. "Do you suppose he's told her about holding the county record for spending the most years in our middle school?"

The concept of their educational differences rendered Tony speechless. He couldn't wait to meet the woman. Even more thrilling was being able to scoop Theo with yet another bit of information she hadn't gleaned down at gossip central. When he could talk again, he said, "Mom tells me Berry and Callie are both coming." It was the closest thing he had to a news bulletin.

"Tiberius is leaving his patients unattended?" Gus glanced at the sky as if expecting it to fall. "Who is saving the world from cavities and overbites?"

Tony considered Gus's surprise understandable. Their brother the dentist often used his work as an excuse to let his

48

brothers deal with their mother. Their sister, Calpurnia, on the other hand, was frequently victimized. Callie didn't have enough sense or, more likely, wasn't mean enough to refuse to participate in one of Jane's plans. One woman's dream trip was the other's nightmare. Tony thought he, Gus, and Berry should scrape together enough money to send Callie to a spa, far from any body of water, all expenses paid. After the nightmare cruise several months earlier during which she'd suffered seven days of being seasick, Callie deserved a treat. The only thing they lacked was the money to do it.

Stepping away from Gus, Tony walked over to Quentin. Tall, twitchy, and skeletally thin, Quentin listened to Tony's concerns about the early morning cannon practice, his head bobbing in agreement.

Tony said, "I haven't seen it, but look forward to it and I am impressed by the sound it makes. Unfortunately, the loud booms have been disturbing a fair number of people."

"I didn't know it were a bother as I live so far out." Quentin was contrite. "I'll not shoot it before I come down to work."

"Thank you, Quentin. Even though you live far from town, I'm sure the mountains make the sound travel oddly, creating the problem. It might be a good idea not to shoot it after eight at night either." Tony had no authority to request it, but hoped Quentin would agree.

Quentin nodded vigorously and turned, motioning for Roscoe to join them. Roscoe's homely face paled and he dragged his feet as he came toward Quentin, his friend and the owner of the land where he lived in a battered camper trailer. When Roscoe got near, Tony heard Quentin say, "Don't worry. It ain't about Baby."

"Sheriff?" Roscoe's voice was a mere whisper. "Do you know where Baby is?"

"No." Tony hadn't heard anything about the bear in months.

"Is she still hibernating?"

"She's gone away from her sleep spot." Roscoe's eyes began to water and he wiped his dripping nose with the back of hand. "I ain't seen her since last week. She's never been gone like this. Maybe a day, but not more. I filled her bowl with fresh water and put an apple next to it. Baby ain't touched it, 'n' she loves apples." He cleaned his hand on the seat of his jeans. "I thought maybe you heard somethin'."

Tony had no information. "Since you can't legally keep the bear and she's not your property, I'm not sure I can send out a search party for her." Tony couldn't help but sympathize with the man. After game warden Harrison Ragsdale had expressed plans to euthanize the cub, Roscoe had saved it from certain death and raised it mostly in the wild. Having weighed the issues, including the fact keeping the bear was illegal, Tony decided to turn a blind eye. Baby lived outside and came and went at will. She was not caged or tethered. Tony understood Roscoe's concern about the young bear. There were more dangerous things in the woods than bears and wild hogs. People.

Theo glanced up to see two of her favorite younger quilters, Melissa and Susan, coming through the front door. They were both married to executives at the fertilizer plant and had taken her beginning quilting class soon after moving to town. They were now true quilting and fabric addicts. Good people and good for her business.

Melissa, a pleasant looking brunette and the older of the two friends, had a couple of boys in middle school. They kept her busy with sports events, class projects and, she claimed, industrial level grocery shopping and cooking. She often laughed about how much food boys that age could eat and encouraged Theo to start making regular deposits into a special account, saving for the day Chris and Jamie turned into eating machines.

Theo always joined in the merriment, even though she knew it was not a joke.

The other one, Susan, was not quite thirty. Exceptionally tall for a woman, she stood over six feet. The California native had gone to college in Virginia on a basketball scholarship and never returned to her home state except for occasional visits. Her features were slightly sharp and marred somewhat by the unevenness of her nose, which had obviously been broken in several places. Her hair was a drab light brown and usually held back from her face with a big clip. Susan was a lot of fun and had a wicked sense of humor, which probably kept her sane because she had three children. The youngest, a little girl, was just over a year old and a very determined child. She wanted to walk wherever her brothers did. The younger of the brothers was four and a half. It was the oldest child who had the most interesting history.

Theo remembered the night at the Bowling League meeting when Susan told the quilters that her husband had a son before they married he hadn't told her about. To be fair to the man, he was unaware the boy named Zach existed until one day when the boy was about three years old. Susan was pregnant at the time and stunned when her husband brought home Zach, whom he had received, delivered like a package, at his old office. An envelope and a note from his birth mother were pinned to his jacket. Essentially it handed all rights and responsibility to Susan's husband, John. No exchanges, no returns.

The family had struggled for a while to incorporate Zach into their lives about the same time they dealt with the birth of Nicholas. They succeeded. Now Susan was Zach's "mom" and Zach was a handsome, sweet boy who was in Jamie's class at school and played on his baseball team.

At the end of the day, and on his way to do his workout, Tony stopped by the jail. This half of the law enforcement center was comprised of several types of cells. Men and women were separate, of course, but there were also accommodations for youthful offenders and exceptionally violent or suicidal prisoners. A large portion of the population was addicted to illegal drugs or medication, which added another dimension to the job.

If he had to house Slow Jr. in his jail, Tony wondered where the man would fit. He was not a juvenile. He wasn't a hard case. Tony wasn't a doctor, but he guessed insanity wasn't the issue. As the man's name indicated, he was just slow.

Running on the treadmill, Tony tried to push away his depressing thoughts. He heard the door open and smiled when he saw Wade trudge inside. If anything, his deputy looked worse than he felt himself, which, given Wade's good looks, took some effort. "What happened to you?"

Wade shook his head, remaining silent. He stepped onto the other treadmill and started his warm up. Tony left him alone. Sometimes he'd felt the same way after dealing with the things people did to themselves and others.

After about fifteen minutes, Wade broke his silence. "I thought about shooting someone today."

Tony nodded. He'd guessed it was something like this. Similar temptations had come to him over the years. "Anyone I know?"

Instead of answering the question, Wade said, "You mean you've actually thought about handing out punishment without going through the legal system? I always think of you as being better than me." Wade's troubled expression darkened his blue eyes to black. The skin over his cheekbones stretched tighter than normal, emphasizing their contours.

"I'm not better than anyone." Tony remembered wanting to dispose of Possum Calhoun and a few others, specifically people who abused the innocent. Right now the Farquhar clan was on top of the list of residents he'd like to be rid of. "There have been several times both here and back in Chicago when I've been tempted to show someone what it's like to be on the receiving end of abuse. Don't act on it. That would only lower you to their level."

Wade nodded. "I wanted him to throw a punch at me." As if unaware of his actions, his hands flexed wide before balling into tight fists. "So help me, Sheriff, if he so much as touched me with his little finger I'd have decked him first and then cuffed him."

"For assaulting a police officer?" Tony sympathized. Every time he thought he'd seen or heard the worst people could find to do to their "loved ones," someone managed to surprise him. Where did such depravity come from? he wondered. "I'm guessing someone is tormenting a child or a spouse." Wade didn't disagree, and Tony felt the all-too-familiar frustration and anger surge through him. "You have the authority to place children in protective custody."

Wade finally spoke. "Thankfully, it was not a child. I never wanted to learn about the darker side of some of our, so-called, fine, upstanding citizens. Until today, seeing it for myself, I wouldn't have believed someone else if they told me whose secret life is so vicious." He increased the speed on the treadmill. And ran. His silence broken only by his feet pounding on the belt and his labored breathing.

Tony finished his workout. As he turned to leave he said, "Go home. Kiss your wife. Don't watch the news. It will only depress you more." He hoped he could follow his own advice. He was in no hurry to find out who'd done what. He'd read Wade's report in the morning. "I'd hate to have to arrest one of my deputies."

After dinner, Theo dug through the overflowing basket of

recently washed laundry sitting on the kitchen table. "All these tiny socks and none of them match." She stacked about ten mateless socks in a pile. "Is the washing machine flushing them into the sewer?"

Not being particularly helpful, Tony inserted his thumb into a sock. It fit perfectly. "I suppose it could. I know it's chugged out chunks of mud bigger than this." He put a sock on each finger and waggled them in Theo's face. He grinned. "Puppets."

Theo rolled her eyes but couldn't suppress a smile. She pointed to the mass of clean infant clothes. "Fold."

Fingers still covered, he did. Little socks decorated with elephants, daisies, even camouflage, danced as he folded shirts and onesies and stacked them in neat piles. "Blossom's love life is getting noticed. She's receiving anonymous letters of disapproval."

"Poor Blossom." Theo smoothed wrinkles from a yellow towel decorated with pink bunnies. "She's not hurting anyone. I wish people would let her have some time to work out her personal life."

"If it were up to you, would you prefer Kenny or DuWayne?"

"Neither." Theo winked at him. "And she can't have you."

CHAPTER FIVE

Tony studied the reports on his desk. Burglary wasn't an unusual crime in Park County. Money was tight and a fair number of the older generation had never gotten into the habit of locking their doors. If they didn't lock them at night, they sure weren't going to do it when they ran to the store. His department received calls about stolen televisions, stolen computers, radios, some jewelry whose owner wasn't sure if it was stolen or just lost, and, not too long ago, a stolen sheep. The sheep was the easiest case to solve. The bright mind behind the theft put a collar on it and staked it out in his own yard, never thinking the owner could identify it. "They all look the same to me," was not a defense, at least not an effective one.

Claude Marmot filed a complaint about someone littering at the dump. A sticky note attached to the front of the report was written in Sheila's clearly legible handwriting. "Can you litter at a dump?"

This list of recent burglaries was disturbing. Several newer homes, ones with good locks and garage doors with coded entries had been victimized. A couple of them had alarm systems that had gone off and alerted his office. Unfortunately, even with the best of intentions, it took them long enough to reach the residences that the burglar or burglars had a chance to take a few expensive items and vanish. So far, Tony and his deputies had discovered nothing but a few small clues about these puzzling crimes.

Tony wasn't even certain if the stolen items were being sold, pawned out of town, or if they simply became part of the thieves' property. A stolen chain saw would take down a tree branch as easily as one that had been purchased. Jewelry, unless it was an extraordinary piece, could be worn in front of the former owner and might go unrecognized. No one could probably use six televisions but maybe the thief wanted to be able to watch six channels at the same time, or several thieves each got two.

He suspected either the Farquhar "darlin' boys" or one of the Lundys. Both families produced litters of dishonest children, male and female. They filled jail cells in most of the counties on the eastern end of the state and several had graduated to the state penitentiary in Nashville. Suspicion wasn't the same as proof. Still, his staff was doing the best they could to solve the problem.

Wade's report told an ugly story of an abusive husband who took great care to not strike his wife in the face. The photographs attached to the report showed massive bruises and contusions on every other part of her body. A footnote on the report listed her address as in care of the women's shelter. Tony suspected she had been moved out of the county by the volunteers led by Mike and Ruby Ott. There was not much hope of hiding someone anywhere in the county. He could only hope she'd participate in the group discussions and learn her husband did not have the right to use her for his punching bag. It usually took more than one rescue before a woman fought through the brainwashing and learned to live free.

Tony made a note reminding him to have everyone pay extra attention to the husband's whereabouts and activities.

On his way to the dump, Tony drove past Blossom Flowers' new house. On the surface, the woman looked like an unlikely object of as much male adoration as she had. Large, she claimed openly to be fat. Blossom was sweet but not a beauty. He noticed Blossom sitting on her front stoop with Kenny's little girls while the two men vying for her hand worked together.

Kenny and DuWayne were putting up a brand new white picket fence around her yard, enclosing the house. The men were using one of the newer vinyl products that came in sections and didn't need painting. They already had the posts set and the men seemed quite well suited to working together. Maybe the months of both of them dancing with Blossom at the same time had taught them a valuable lesson in teamwork.

Tony stopped, as always curious to see what people were up to and to visit a bit. Over the time he'd been the sheriff, Tony had probably learned more about the criminal activity around the county from casual conversations than in actual interviews with apprehended crooks.

"Hey, Blossom," he called to the source of his pie supply. "Kenny. DuWayne." The men nodded a greeting but kept working.

Blossom waved from the stoop but didn't get up. One of Kenny's little girls had fallen asleep with her face pressed against Blossom's leg, and the other girl ran toward him carrying a picnic basket. "Want to see the pubby?"

"Sure. I love puppies." Tony dodged the men and their fence panel. "I gather the puppy is the reason for the new fence."

The little girl nodded, a serious expression on her cherubic face, and she gently set the basket on the ground. She reached inside under a towel and with both hands picked up a very young yellow Labrador retriever puppy. Almost snow white, with chocolate-brown eyes, it displayed the heart-stealing puppy expression used to sell everything from toilet paper to cars. "Her name is Miss Cotton."

"Nice name. Did you pick it?"

"Me and my sister, an' we helped Daddy pick her out too."
She extended the pup toward him. "She's a present for our
Miss Blossom."

He was thankful neither of his boys was along, because his
family needed another dog to go with the hundred-pound dog
they already owned and the four children they had like he
needed hemorrhoids. Still, he couldn't resist holding the soft,
chubby pup with its tiny paws, and admired its teensy toenails.
He'd bet in two weeks the paws would grow to be the size of
shovels, and those toenails would become big claws capable of
digging huge holes in mere seconds.

Tony glanced at the men. Since the little girl belonged to
Kenny, it had to be he who was the gambler. The puppy could
sway the affections of the fair Blossom in his favor. Or, if Miss
Cotton ate something Blossom treasured, DuWayne might win
the day.

Blossom placed a hand vertically against her face at the
corner of her mouth like she thought it would shield the little
girls from what she said. "The fence is 'cause we don't want the
game warden running over our Miss Cotton a-purpose. He has
a house just down the street and we don't want to take chances."

"Do you really believe he would?" Tony had heard many
unpleasant rumors about the man, but so far, he had not been
able to substantiate any of the vile accusations. He saw Blossom's normally cheerful expression turn dark and she nodded.
Tony said, "Why do you think so?"

"I'm mostly in the kitchen at Ruby's, but word gets around.
You know, good and bad. It ain't been long since that old
woman's cat and Nem's dog was both done away with by him.
He coulda swerved, but he didn't try to miss them."

Tony decided he would see what he could learn about the
game warden, maybe later.

★ ★ ★ ★ ★

Tony drove out to the dump. He barely had time to climb out of the SUV when he saw Claude Marmot's head pop up over a rounded piece of scrap metal, the doorless body of a small, rounded compact car. Claude waved his arms over his head like he was signaling someone much farther away than the ten feet separating them.

"Sheriff, you've got to put a stop to it." Claude's face flushed almost purple. "See the sign—some idiots have been stacking their trash right next to it."

Tony studied the hand lettered sign. No Littering. He had to agree it was clearly stated. A glance at the mess near the pole holding it made him sympathetic to Claude's outrage. Piles of unbagged garbage, a mixture of recyclable items and some nasty smelling stuff. A few long bones attracted flies.

"It's on my yard!" Tiny droplets sprayed from Claude's lips.

With a sigh, Tony pulled out his notebook. He wished Wade was with him. His deputy was really much better with paper-work. He took several photographs.

Claude dived behind his car-part project but continued to provide commentary on everything Tony saw, smelled, and made notes about.

Feeling like he'd done what he could, Tony sauntered over to watch Claude work. Claude was a wizard at repurposing castoffs. He'd once turned a Crown Vic into a pickup. "What's this going to be?"

"Making a cover for my motorcycle. I'll have shelter from the rain."

After lunch, Tony headed to the museum. The stage construction looked to be well underway, and he wondered if his brother ever got to go to his own home in nearby Townsend.

He knew there was a plan to the upcoming festival. His mom

always had a plan. Some were not bad, others were hideous. He told himself she always meant well. Over the course of the afternoon, this plan included multiple musicians and a few dancers scheduled to perform. Jane had confessed to inviting everyone she could think of who might want to be on a stage and was shocked when everyone accepted. Now she stood in front of a newly erected outdoor table and appeared to be struggling to produce a workable schedule.

Tony offered to help her weed out the rotten performing apples and turned the list on the table so he could read it. He only had time to read a couple of the names and recognized a few moderately pleasant entertainers. He opened his mouth to protest when his mother pulled the list away from him and planted her elbow on it to keep it in place.

"You don't need to be involved," Jane said. "I appreciate your willingness to help, but I asked them and they all said yes. No matter what you think, if they're on the list they get to perform. I'll just have to limit the amount of time each group is allotted."

"Well, if they ask you if they can perform, you can allot a mere thirty seconds to the brother and sister singing group called the Elves, and it will still seem like eternity." Tony gave a shudder and tapped her list. "I hope they're not on this. If you recall, they had a captive audience at the community Christmas program."

Jane twitched slightly at the hideous memory and pressed her lips tightly together.

Tony stared at her. "I had people offering me money if I would shoot the Elves, and if not the singers, the members of the audience just to put them out of their misery. I claimed I was saving all the bullets for myself, greedy soul that I am."

"That's not funny, Marc Antony." Jane tried a reproving glare, but it failed. "They were pretty awful, but I'm sure they've improved."

"Is that like saying it would take more than one bucket of rocks to fill the Grand Canyon?" Tony suddenly realized what she had told him. "Are you saying what I think you're saying? Did you invite the Elves?"

Jane sidled away from him, her eyes focused on the dirt near her feet. It must have been some incredibly interesting dirt because she wouldn't look up.

"Mom?" Tony leaned closer and bent so his lips were near her right ear. "Tell me you didn't invite them."

Her expression told the whole story. Finally, with a sigh of surrender, she nodded. "But, I also have Pops Ogle and his little group, and there's a husband and wife bluegrass duo and a couple of small groups to play music for dancing." Jane ticked groups off on her fingers. "I don't remember all of them, but I promise we have lots more entertainment planned. There's even going to be a juggler."

Hating the expression of total despair on his mom's face, Tony decided to ease up. "It will be fine," he lied. "Just set time limits." He didn't mention that fifteen seconds of caterwauling Elves was much too long for mortals to bear.

Jane folded her entertainers list and shoved it into her purse. "Enough of that, dear."

Out of sight, out of mind? He hoped not.

Jane gave him a sunny smile. "Tiberius and Calpurnia are coming and bringing the kids. All my grandchildren in once place for the whole weekend. It's going to be splendid. Isn't it?"

"Yes, Mom." Tony watched Jane as she trotted toward the office building. He hoped she wasn't going to be crushed if the festival wasn't well attended. He wandered over to the stage area where Gus, Quentin, and Kenny Baines were pounding nails as fast as they could. Between his fencing project and work, Tony wondered if Kenny had time to eat.

They hadn't gotten around to building stairs, but had a

makeshift cover of a blue tarp nailed to poles casting shade on the back of the stage.

Gus waved a nail gun in his direction. "What do you think?"

Tony gave him two thumbs up. "What's the tarp for?"

"If we have some rain showers, I want my tools, especially the electric variety, to stay dry." Gus flexed his biceps. "I'm much too puny to drive a nail with a plain old hammer." He proceeded to laugh at his own joke. Both of them knew Gus could drive a nail into a board with a soup can. Tony had seen him do it, but the story made Jane cranky. Evidently their mom still remembered the living room sprayed with tomato soup concentrate when one of Gus's mighty blows sank the nail point down into the board and drove the nail head up into the can at the same time. Then he proceeded to wave the can around, showing off and at the same time releasing a fairly steady spray of soup. Gus had been thirteen at the time and since then had added a hundred pounds of solid muscle.

"Are you in charge of the sound system too?"

Gus shook his head. "I can wire a house or set up a computer, but I do *not* do sound systems. Is there supposed to be one?"

"I hope not." Tony mumbled. "One of the singing acts is the Elves."

The normally healthy color leached from Gus's face. "Tell me it's not so."

"I have an idea." Tony moved closer and lowered his voice. "If I can find out when they're due to appear I'll let you know, or vice versa. At minimum, we can put in some ear plugs. We'll be the town heroes if there's a power failure."

Gus extended a hand.

They shook.

"Has Mom ever heard them perform?" Gus looked as panicky as Tony felt. "Those voices can peel the bark off trees."

Gus's cell phone rang. He checked the screen and shook his

head. "No good deed goes unpunished." He answered it and moved away from the hubbub around the stage. "I explained all this before." Seconds later he was holding the phone away from his ear. The sound of a woman's voice poured from the phone. A very angry woman's voice.

"I've a good mind to fire you," were the only words Tony could understand. The sound of the phone disconnecting was pretty obvious as well. Tony couldn't help himself. "Who?"

"Queen Doreen. I told her when I began her expansion project at the gift shop that I'd be taking some time off in order to do work for the festival. She was fine with it until today." He rubbed his ear. "She's called five times already just to threaten to fire me. Damn, why not go ahead and get it over with?"

"Sound likes you're between a rock and a hard place."

"Nope." Gus grinned. "With Mom and Queen Doreen, it's between dynamite and C-4."

Tony heard the dispatch radio call for all available members of their volunteer search and rescue group. He presumed Mike and his bloodhound, Dammit, were going to be unavailable to the sheriff's department for the rest of the day. His small force was shrinking.

He dropped by the search and rescue hall to learn more. A hiker had not returned to his car, which remained parked in a turnoff near the boundary of the national park. A note on the dashboard gave his name and his plan to hike for two days. The note was dated three days earlier.

The men and women who were involved with search and rescue, like the Silersville fire department, consisted of volunteers. They trained hard and were willing to risk their own safety and long hours away from jobs and family to help find lost souls. Nothing gave them greater joy than the safe return of a missing man, woman, or especially a child to an anxious family. Sometimes the problem was nothing more than miscommunication and easily solved. Other times, injury made locating and retrieval extremely tricky and dangerous for all involved.

"Who called?" Tony asked Halfpenny, the lead volunteer and fellow can-can dancer.

"His brother. He knew where the car was parked. When his brother didn't call in, he drove out to see if the car was still there. It was. He waited a few hours and no one came, so he left. He considers this our problem now."

"That's a pretty precise schedule. No other contact information? Cell phone? Satellite phone? Hiking partner?"

"Nope. The brother says he likes to go it alone." Halfpenny sighed, a look of disgust on his face. "At best, the brother is unconcerned. At worst, he's happy his brother has vanished."

Tony felt the muscles in his shoulders tighten and thought for the millionth time about taking his family and running away from it all. He knew there was nowhere to go. Life was like a caravan in the desert—following a camel was better than dying on a sand dune. He forced himself to focus.

"Did the brother bring a photograph?"

"No." Halfpenny's expression grew grim.

"I'll get you a copy of his driver's license photo." Tony shook his head. "The things people do for fun." Halfpenny nodded and strode away.

Tony stared out the window at the mountains in the distance. He knew the Smoky Mountains didn't possess anywhere near the height and grandeur of the Rocky Mountains or the Himalayas, but they could be dangerous. The canopy of vegetation provided dense cover, inhibiting aerial searches. Trees, rocks, and vines, along with the rushing waters of spring runoff, added to the danger to a solitary hiker. Within the national park, there were a multitude of trails, some for more advanced hikers than others. Outside the park boundary, which is not an obvious line, are areas as untouched as they were two hundred years ago.

The spotter plane was already in the air.

On his way out to search on the ground, Deputy Mike Ott stopped to talk to Tony. His companion, the magnificently homely bloodhound named Dammit, sat and began a leisurely exploration of one his oversize ears with a back paw. Mike said, "He could be anywhere. We'll start at the car and see where we go."

Tony had heard frequent complaints from the S & R group about lack of visible clothing on the people they rescued. It was a miracle any of them were found. "I don't suppose he's wearing something easy to spot, like a bright blue and yellow shirt or jacket?"

Mike's burst of laughter did not sound particularly amused. "Camouflage. According to his brother, everything he wears, from his pants to his pack, is designed to blend with his surroundings. If he's fallen and broken his leg, he'll blend right in with the bushes and grass." Mike bent over and carefully massaged Dammit's legs, preparing him for long, strenuous hours of searching.

Rocks, water, and rumors of feral hogs were just a few of the possible hazards the hiker and his want-to-be rescuers might face. Tony could remember a time they'd searched for days and finally spotted their missing person—decidedly not hoping for rescue—but he was trespassing, and his arrest had been one of the more entertaining searches since he'd taken office. The man was dumb as a brick and turned out to be a felon missing from a work release program. He'd chosen to focus on the "release" portion of the agreement.

But nothing Tony had learned about today's missing hiker indicated anything more suspicious than a bad attitude, or his brother's, mixed with poor judgment.

Tony had to admit he was dying of curiosity as he stared at the small group of vegetable weapons sitting in horse trailers, now parked in the far end of the museum parking lot, near the hill. According to Gus, the intriguing cannon Quentin built was just big enough to launch a potato. In comparison to the other weapons, it was a modern marvel. Its long barrel looked like nothing more than a length of pipe with about a five-inch diameter. The two medieval weapons going on display were a trebuchet and a catapult. They were almost fascinating enough to get him to join their medieval weaponry club. Almost. The weapons were built to scale but well smaller than the devices designed to lay siege to a castle.

Roscoe, the owner of the trebuchet, had borrowed a Bush Hog and cut down all the vegetation in the area designated for the war machines before vanishing from sight.

With Tony watching, a small caravan of enthusiasts soon arrived, parked near the trailers, and went to work. Quentin trotted past Tony and joined the group, leaving Gus and Kenny still working on the stage. With great good cheer, the group did hard physical labor, carrying bits and pieces Tony guessed weighed well more than a hundred pounds each. It took four men to carry the long arm of the trebuchet up the hill to the place chosen for its setup. Tony suspected the location had something to do with the broad, reasonably flat surface of packed-down red clay. The catapult had wheels, but they were wooden and looked handmade. They lacked something in roundness, so to haul it up the hill, the workers got help in the form of a twenty-first century tractor.

Fearing they might try to enlist him into what appeared to be grueling manual labor, Tony backed away, but anticipated the demonstration with interest.

He didn't back away fast enough. "Sheriff." The word was softly spoken about at the level of his left shoulder blade. "I'd like you to meet someone." As shocked as he was to have Roscoe slip up behind him, it was his companion whom Tony found interesting.

Skinny little Roscoe who possessed bad teeth and a loving attitude didn't release the arm of the woman at his side, a slender woman with exceptionally long dark chestnut hair. Tony could see some strands of silver glisten in the single braid hanging down her back, stopping at her knees. Large, dark eyes glowed with humor and intelligence. They were her best physical feature, but what Tony liked best was her laugh. He'd heard her laugh while the equipment was being unloaded.

"Professor Veronica Weathersby." Roscoe's grin was delighted and exposed every bad tooth in his head. "Sheriff Tony Abernathy."

The professor held Roscoe's hand with her left and offered her right to Tony. They shook hands briefly before she withdrew hers and placed it gently on their clasped hands. When she spoke, her voice was soft and had a faint, almost British, accent. "I'm always pleased to make the acquaintance of one of Roscoe's friends."

Tony felt like making a courtly bow. If he'd had any idea how to do one, he might have. "I am pleased to meet you too." He wondered how many questions he could ask without being considered unbearably nosy. He started with a straightforward one. One he knew the answer to already. He hated to admit he'd heard gossip. "Professor of what?"

"My specialty is medieval life and culture."

Tony did wonder how she and Roscoe had met. Roscoe's major social functions were sports events, particularly baseball. While Tony sorted through various ideas about how to probe into their relationship without being considered boorish, Veronica voluntarily explained.

She waved in the direction of the weapon. "We met at the organizational meeting of a new group. Our group tries to recreate as faithfully as possible some of the culture of the past—weapons, clothes, food. We hope to do demonstrations, and maybe someday there will be enough of us to have a full-day celebration of our own and invite the public."

Tony decided she might have more degrees than the average university, but she was cheerful and pleasant and had no air of superiority about her. She liked Roscoe. Tony thought inevitably someone would stick Veronica with the nickname Ronnie—and the couple would become known as Ronnie and Roscoe.

"Do you get along with the bear?" Tony still wondered if Baby had run away or was lost or something more sinister.

"Yes, she's very sweet."

"Any sign of her?" said Tony.

"Baby's still missing." Roscoe's voice sounded froggy, like he'd been calling the bear too much or was percolating a head cold.

Veronica patted his shoulder and pressed her forehead to his. "I'm sure if something bad had happened to her, we'd have found out by now." She lifted tear-moist eyes to Tony. "With the unusual white spot on her chest, she's very identifiable."

"I'll ask Harrison Ragsdale," Tony promised. "He's the game warden and not much for cooperation, but I think you're right. Bad news does travel pretty fast."

Roscoe snuffled into a handkerchief.

Veronica smiled gently and led her beau toward their machine. "Would you like to see our beauty, the trebuchet?"

Tony didn't have to be invited a second time, and walked up the hill with the unlikely couple. The moment Tony finished talking with them and examining their trebuchet, he planned to call Theo to tell her all about the professor, and to gloat. This was the second piece of really exciting news he'd heard before Theo. If he kept a journal, it would be written in big letters right after "Ruby is pregnant." Tony patted the siege machine. "It's fascinating. I can't wait to see it operate. Who did the actual construction of this?"

"I built it and Quentin helped." Roscoe cast an adoring look at the professor. "We couldn't have done it without Veronica's instructions. She knows all about these things."

Veronica actually blushed. "It is a scaled-down model, but one quite capable of launching stones and melons and pumpkins with remarkable force and accuracy."

Quentin charged past them, evidently having finished his task with the weapons, at least for the moment, and waving to the threesome. He jumped up on the stage and went back to his task of shoving the boards tightly against each other while Gus and Kenny nailed them down.

The festival site was taking shape, but Tony's enthusiasm for the event dropped another notch as he watched the stage floor taking shape. The idea of doing the can-can in a ruffled skirt didn't hold any appeal. He might have dreamed of a career playing baseball, but never once had treading the boards of theater appealed to him.

He glanced at his watch. Speaking of the can-can, he needed to get to rehearsal. Their choreographer, Miss Cindy, had volunteered to work with them after her creative movement classes for four-year-olds ended. She was almost seventy and could still kick higher than any of his group. The dance studio was simply a large room with a smooth wooden floor at the back of the carpet-remnant business owned by her husband.

Before he turned on the ignition, he couldn't resist calling Theo and gloating about meeting the professor.

Theo was miffed. Tony got to meet Roscoe's girlfriend before she did. The injustice of it all had her pacing the floor in her workroom. Over in the corner, out of her range, the twins slept in their small crib. Chris and Jamie wouldn't be out of school for another hour. Carrying the baby monitor with her, she went downstairs to the shop.

Gretchen was cutting fabrics for a customer. They were deeply involved in determining just how much of each were needed for a project.

In the workroom, a few ladies were gathered around their latest group charity quilt. This one was to be raffled at the Ramp Festival to raise money for the food bank. People could donate either canned goods or cash in exchange for a ticket. The quilt top was one Theo had built while testing the pattern for one of her mystery quilts. The overall illusion was of a series of eight pointed stars within larger stars. The fabrics were all deep blues, maroons and browns. Even though it was quite elegant, it had served its purpose and Theo had donated it, hoping they would sell lots of tickets.

The quilters chatted quietly as they worked. When they saw Theo, they waved her over. "Grab a chair and needle, sugar, you might as well put in a few stitches with us."

Theo obliged, pulling a chair closer to the frame and picking up a needle where someone left off quilting. "Do you think it will be ready by Saturday? I know we can work on it at the festival, but usually more talking than quilting happens in public, and we can sell more tickets on a finished quilt."

"That's for sure." The oldest woman laughed. "I do enjoy a good gossip and a barbeque sandwich."

"What about the ramps?" Theo didn't care for them herself, but would nibble a bite of ramp pie just because it was the reason for the gathering. "They are pretty pungent."

"I remember going out with my grandmother to gather them in the spring. She always said they'd keep us healthy. But really,

I think it was all about money. We had nothing, and eating ramps and dandelion leaves was one way for us to get vegetables. It wasn't like now when we can buy greens any time of the year at the grocery store."

"How do you prefer your ramps? In a pie, soup, sprinkled on a sandwich?"

"Soup, I think. When I have them in pie I like to sprinkle a lot of pepper on it. It kind of balances them out and you kind of don't notice the strength of the ramps."

"Interesting." Theo wondered how to pass on the information about Veronica and decided just to spit it out. "Have you all heard about Roscoe's girlfriend?"

"The vending machine or the bear?" The speaker got the giggles and could barely finish her question.

"Neither," said Theo. Suddenly her needle was the only one still moving in and out of the quilt. The other quilters were frozen in place. Taking pity on them, Theo elaborated. "A real live woman. She's a professor at the university."

"Well, cut off my legs and call me shorty." The elderly woman leaned forward. "Tell us more. Have you met her?"

"Not yet, but Tony has, and she's going to be helping the medieval warriors show their machines. He says she's very nice."

"Speaking of Roscoe, did that pet bear of his ever show up again? I'd sure hate for Hairy Rags to catch it, because that awful man likes nothing better than causing some animal misery."

"So why is he a game warden?" Theo threaded another needle. "If he dislikes animals."

Three heads shook in confusion.

"All I know is he swerves his truck in the direction of any animal, a pet or a wild thing, crossing the road." Tears welled in one woman's eyes. "I know he's responsible for my kitty going missing."

"How do you know?" Theo thought if there was evidence,

they could get him fired, fined, and run out of town. Ragsdale's absence would make Silersville a nicer place to live. Before anyone could come up with an explanation, a faint cry came through the baby monitor. "Oops, my fan club is waking up." Theo headed upstairs.

Lined up in the dance studio, facing a wall of mirrors, Tony wanted to run away. Five of the six dancers, himself included, listened to Miss Cindy's careful instructions. The sixth, Halfpenny, was still out searching for the missing hiker. The energetic older woman talked nonstop, and put them through a series of warm-up exercises apparently designed to make him feel larger and more awkward than before.

"How is Theo doing with the skirts?" Miss Cindy asked Tony.

"I know she's been working on them. I'll call." Tony grasped any excuse to delay the inevitable. It turned out to be a brief delay; he hadn't even gotten the phone out of his pocket when he spotted Theo struggling to open the glass fronted door while buried by the frothy black, orange, red, and yellow of the skirts.

He hurried to help her. "Get me out of here," he whispered.

Theo ignored his plea. Instead of helping, she actually winked at him and headed for Miss Cindy.

"It's so much easier to practice with the skirts and whatever you plan to wear on your feet." Miss Cindy squealed and clapped with delight. "I love the skirts, Theo. Thank you!" Cindy turned to face the men. "By the way, I've ordered some black fishnet stockings that should fit y'all just fine. Isn't it amazing what you can shop for on the Internet?"

Before any of the men could raise an objection, two of the smallest women in town started handing out the skirts. The men grumbled but stepped into them and tied them over their day clothes. Tony decided Napoleon's dictatorial nature probably had more to do with his diminutive height than his ambition to rule as emperor.

Tony looked into the mirror again. The image of the shiny black skirt tied over his chocolate brown uniform shirt, complete with badge, froze him in place. At least his khaki pants hadn't been transformed into black fishnet stockings. "I can't do this."

Miss Cindy, whom he decided to nickname Miss Napoleon, reached up and patted his back. "You'll be fine, Tony. Once you have your bonnet and wig on and aren't wearing your uniform, you can pretend to have fun."

Bonnet and wig? He thought he shook his head, refusing to cooperate, but Miss Napoleon didn't seem to notice.

Miss Napoleon demonstrated how to grasp the skirts so the dancers could swish and flip them. Checking the mirror, Tony decided there was safety in numbers. They all looked equally bizarre. Even the normally handsome Wade appeared less so than usual. Claude Marmot, whose body hair was thick and dark, was going to look like a dancing bear. Their former sheriff, Harvey Winston, didn't seem as tall as he once had, maybe because of the ever increasing size of his belly. Tony relaxed a bit and experimented with flipping his skirt. This might turn out to be fun.

"I'm Veronica. Are you Theo?"

Theo bobbed her head even as she said, "Yes. I'm glad to meet you." Theo *had* wanted to meet Veronica. The extent of the understatement made her laugh. In fact, she was obsessed with curiosity about a woman who was both a university professor and Roscoe's girlfriend. A real live girl. And now Veronica was here, standing in her quilt shop. If Theo wasn't seeing her in person, she might doubt the woman's existence.

Veronica spoke softly so Theo stepped closer and thought Veronica smelled like roses. "I wanted to ask you a question, Theo."

"Would you like to go upstairs to my office, or would you rather have coffee in the workroom?" Theo made her offer in front of witnesses. If Veronica preferred the privacy of her office, Theo couldn't be blamed. Theo was sure every ear was tuned in, waiting for Veronica's answer.

"Let's have coffee down here. I'd love to see what your group is working on." Veronica headed for the workroom and stopped just inside. It was a busy day in the workroom and women of all ages and description were busy working on the raffle quilt.

Standing near her, Theo was struck by the woman's ordinariness. She was a bit taller than Theo herself and thin, but the curtain of hair was real. Thick and glossy, it practically begged to be touched. Her features were closer to plain than pretty, but a little makeup might be all she'd need to swing to the gorgeous end of the scale. "Your hair is beautiful. Has it always been long?"

"Thank you. And no." Veronica pulled the mass of it over her shoulder and sat on one of the folding chairs. "Some days I get so tired of it I'm tempted to grab a pair of scissors and just whack off a couple feet of it."

"You could donate that much to Locks of Love and not miss it much," said Caro. "Some cancer patient would love a wig made from it."

Veronica smiled at the older woman. "What a splendid idea. Let's cut it now."

And so they all agreed. Seconds after meeting Theo's group of friends and customers, Veronica was standing on a box and one of the shakiest hands in the room held the scissors. Theo opened her mouth to protest, but a booming voice behind her silenced them all. "Don't."

Prudence Sligar Holt, hair stylist, arm wrestler, and mother of a herd of children, was not the kind of woman who could be intimidated by others. Rising from her seat at the quilt frame, she lifted the scissors out of Caro's trembling hands. "If we're going to do this, let's do it right. I've cut hair for Locks of Love before." She bent over and glared into Caro's sweet face, but her voice was gentle. "Let me do it, Caro, honey?"

"I'm so relieved you're here." Caro wobbled toward her chair. "I'd have nightmares for the rest of my life if I mangled it."

In seconds there was a party at Theo's shop. The grapevine was operating at full power. Quilters and non-quilters alike joined the party, met Veronica, admired her hair, both the donated and the stuff still on her head, cooed at Theo's infants, and generally indulged in laughter and socializing.

While Theo's brain worked on a civil approach to being nosy, others stepped in.

"How did you and Roscoe meet?"

"What do you think about the bear?"

"What do you think about the vending machine?"

"Who are your people?"

"Is marriage a possibility?"

Theo admired Veronica's poise, but she supposed anyone who was smart enough to earn a Ph.D. and teach at a large university was no stranger to rude questions. "You don't have to answer," Theo whispered, then held her breath, hoping Veronica would tell them all about herself.

Theo watched as Veronica held up a hand, signaling for silence. Her gesture worked. The quilters, usually an unruly, but not rude, bunch, settled onto their folding chairs and sat, leaning forward, mouths closed. The only sound was the puffing of one quilter's portable oxygen tank.

"I'm Veronica Weathersby." She stood straight, hands held low in front of her. She was gripping her thumbs. "I certainly understand your curiosity about me. I'm a bit curious about all of you too." She flashed them a smile. "I'll admit that Roscoe is not like most of the men I meet in the world of academia, and that's good. He's honest, hardworking, and has built me the most amazing trebuchet. I cannot imagine a more romantic gesture."

"A whatzit?" The question came from the back row.

"Oh, you'll see it at the festival. It's a small version of a siege weapon. It has a swinging arm and a net. Back in the Middle Ages, it was used to throw rocks or whatever at castle walls during an attempt to break in." Veronica's smile was radiant. "Roscoe and I met at a picnic for people interested in learning about life, tools, and weapons from a much earlier era."

"Well, I can certainly believe Roscoe would love to throw rocks at things." Prudence's voice rang through the room.

"Oh, not as much as I do." Veronica spread her hands. "I love siege machines the way your group loves sewing machines."

As a way of shutting down the conversation, her comment failed. The noise level in the room skyrocketed. The general consensus was a question. "How could anyone not love quilting?"

"I do love Baby." Veronica regained their attention with a whisper. "She's the sweetest animal."

"Is she talking about that bear?" An elderly woman bellowed. "Ought to be shot before it eats one of us."

Veronica stopped smiling. "Baby is a good bear. She eats bugs and grubs and berries."

Theo stepped forward. "Thank you, Veronica. You've been more than gracious about dealing with us." She glared at the bear-hater. "I'm sure we can all enjoy the differences as well as the similarities between us."

Gretchen slipped through the back door carrying a takeout box from Ruby's and set it on the counter next to the coffee pot. "I bought cookies."

The audience dissolved, heading for treats in a more or less civilized manner.

"What a great idea." Theo looked toward the front door. "I didn't even see you leave."

With a laugh, Gretchen handed Theo a cookie she'd removed from the box on the walk back. "I thought with Veronica as our impromptu guest, a few treats might produce a banner day of sales."

Watching the cookie eaters begin to prowl around the workroom, Theo could tell they'd soon be out in the fabric area, shopping. "You deserve a raise."

"So true, Boss, but that's life." Gretchen trotted toward her cutting table, preparing for the expected onslaught.

Theo was surprised when Veronica pulled her aside. "Roscoe thinks you're the perfect woman." If Theo had a moment to decide what would be the least likely statement she could imagine, she wouldn't have come close to that one. She just stared at Veronica.

"Really." Veronica nodded for emphasis. "It's because you make beautiful things and because you don't make him feel worthless." She whispered. "Plus, you like watching baseball."

At that Theo laughed. "I don't suppose *you* like baseball?"

"I love it. But"—Veronica's voice dropped even lower, and she spoke the words as if she were confessing to a terrible crime—"my favorite team is his team's arch rival."

Theo gave her statement some thought. "Do you get along with Baby and Dora?"

"I love Baby." Veronica looked discouraged. "I just can't warm up to the vending machine. Maybe it would be easier if she was filled with chocolate."

"You'll do fine." Theo gave the professor a quick hug and went to help Gretchen.

Tony received frequent updates from the frustrated search and rescue ground crew as they moved from the parked car into the ancient forest. Not surprisingly, given their missing person's predilection for dressing in camouflage, the search plane failed to spot any movement the size and shape of a hiker. The dogs, including Dammit, were their next best option.

Late in the afternoon of the second search day, they found him, almost by accident. He lay on the ground, dressed in camouflage, half under a rhododendron. Its heavy, glossy leaves formed a natural shelter for him, and his clothing blended him into the leaf and shadow pattern.

Mike relayed their position and the condition of the hiker. Through the radio, Tony heard angry words from the hiker.

"What took you so long? I saw your plane fly over at least three times yesterday."

Mike said, "You've made yourself invisible."

"I'll sue."

Mike muttered into his radio. "Can we leave him out here?"

"I'm afraid not." Although Tony sympathized.

By the time the rescuers shepherded their ungrateful charge back to civilization, there had apparently been a series of threats on both sides. The rescued man suffered from diarrhea and dehydration. His disagreeable attitude didn't endear him to anyone. As soon as the doctor finished his examination and assistance, the man stomped away with no offer of thanks to anyone.

In a county the size of his, Tony didn't have enough deputies to lose one to a fool's errand. He thought he'd enjoy sending the hiker a bill for wasted time, and certainly understood now why his own brother had not been concerned about his disappearance. He might have been hoping never to have to deal with his sibling again.

RUNNING IN CIRCLES
A MYSTERY QUILT
SECOND BODY OF CLUES

Sew a 4 1/2″ by 1 7/8″ rectangle of fabric (B) on two opposing sides of 4 1/2″ by 1 7/8″ rectangle of fabric (D). Make 12. Label (B+D)

Repeat, sewing fabric (B) with fabrics (E), (F), and (G).

Press to darker fabrics.

Trim to 4 1/2″ square

Label (B+E), (B+F) (B+G) and set aside.

Layout:

Place the 4 1/2″ square of fabric (A) next to the 12 blocks labeled (B+D) with rectangles of fabric (B) along one side of (A). Sew.

Repeat on opposite side of (A) with blocks (B+E).

Press to (A). You will have twelve strips—D+B+A+B+E.

CHAPTER SIX

Saturday morning dawned bright and beautiful. Spring was putting on a show of fresh green leaves, colorful flowers, birds, and vistas to inspire poetry. The bright blue sky highlighted the distinctive haze on the mountains, tinting the hills rather than masking them like the heavy summer air. People poured onto the museum grounds.

Tony thought the turnout for the Ramp Festival had to exceed even his mom's optimistic plans. At least no one could say his mom and aunt gave a party and no one came. What was she thinking now? Too many people? Not enough people? He watched her trotting around the craft booths on the far side of the lawn. Separated from the rest of the festival booths and events, the lines at the food booths snaked around the eating area, allowing people waiting to get food to chat with those eating. There wasn't an empty chair or bench in sight. A small flock of enterprising and fearless ducks wandered through the diners, pecking at any fallen treat.

The mixture of aromas coming from the food booths made his stomach rumble, suggesting he explore the foods offered. There were a couple of booths run by restaurants and professional caterers. Ruby's Café booth offered mostly desserts. He'd seen Blossom and her coterie of suitors carrying pies and cakes to it. He wondered if he should start with apple pie. Next to Ruby's booth was a small tent shelter providing shade to the two men cooking popcorn in a giant black kettle. The barbeque

80

sandwiches at the Baptist church's booth came on paper plates and were accompanied with a handful of flimsy napkins. Not to be outdone, the Methodists were cooking hamburgers and hot dogs on a pair grills made from salvaged steel barrels.

Slightly removed from the other food offerings, the actual ramp dishes had their own little area. Those products were being given away as part of the contest and celebration. Empty commercial-size condiment jars with slots cut in the lids had been decorated and labeled by competitor. The voting was monetary. Whichever jar collected the most money determined the winner and would win the grand prize, a trophy—a ramp created by a clay artist. It was actually quite attractive. All the money donated was to go toward the senior citizens' programs and facility.

Wearing matching bright blue T-shirts printed with "Relic Squad" in fluorescent yellow, the six oldest participants—Nem, Portia, Ada, the Bainbridge sisters, and Caro—handed out napkins and forks, sprinkled pepper, red or black, added salt, offered ketchup. Gnarled, shaking hands perhaps took longer to do the work, or failed to spread the seasoning across the food's whole surface, but no one complained. It was part and parcel of the event. Their tip jar was kept busy.

Members of several youth organizations, including the scouts and Chris and Jamie's baseball teams, had been hired to clear tables and pick up trash. The boys and girls were earning their pay. Tony didn't know when he'd ever seen so many paper napkins. Some of the diners were actually leaving tips on the tables for the cleanup kids. Maybe his team would be able to buy a couple of new bats for the coming season.

On the stage, the Elves were performing. The dreaded group sounded a bit less hideous than Tony remembered. It might have had something to do with crowd noises and the unexpected problem with the speakers. No sound could be heard coming

81

from them. Tony hoped the issue would be resolved, only after
the Elves finished. The schedule allowed them ten minutes. If
they tried to go over the limit, Tony might grab a pitchfork and
lead the charge, like villagers chasing Frankenstein's movie
monster.

The Elves stopped singing, which inspired a wave of
enthusiastic applause. Everyone smiled, clearly relieved to have
it over and done, performers as much as the audience. The
Elves took a bow. As they headed from the stage, they received
another big ovation. Luckily there was no time allowed for
encores.

The Elves looked excited by their warm reception. Tony
wondered if the audience ought to have provided so much
encouragement. The way he saw it, either the Elves would plan
on performing at every public event, or they would head for
Nashville, expecting to make it big. He hated for the kids to be
crushed. On the other hand, he'd heard worse sounds on the
radio, so maybe they would end up being rich and famous and
having groupies follow them around. The idea made him laugh
out loud. A few heads turned his way, but no one asked him
what he thought was so funny.

Miracles do happen. The sound system recovered from its
technical difficulties just in time for Mayor Cashdollar to announce the next part of the entertainment. The vegetable
weapons were going to fire their first rounds, and he directed
the audience's attention toward the field.

At the far end of the museum property, a colorful series of
pennants separated the food, crafts, and music portion of the
festival from the vegetable warfare, as Tony thought of it. Quentin prepared to blast a potato from his cannon. Roscoe and his
lady friend stood next to their small trebuchet, and a visiting
scholar from the medieval club waited near his catapult. The
group had arranged everything so the festival goers would be

able to see both the machines do their work and the result of their collection of vegetables striking the targets.

Tony heard the cannon boom and saw a potato fly through the air and slam into a temporary wall of straw bales, totally missing the target, a stock tank filled with water and little yellow rubber ducks.

Even without hitting the intended target, Quentin and his cannon received wild applause. Turning to face the audience, Quentin crossed an arm over his waist and made quite a courtly bow.

The medieval scholar with the catapult fired next. The roly-poly visitor was obviously having a great time. Whenever Tony saw him, the man wore a wide grin. Dressed in a period costume of black tights and what looked like a long crimson shirt, the little man looked like a bright red apple with toothpicks for arms and legs and a red "Robin Hood" hat with long pheasant feathers hanging off the back of his head. His catapult was a fairly straightforward weapon—it worked like an oversized spoon in a food fight. The catapult threw a small pumpkin, probably past its prime. The orange projectile slammed into the front of the stock tank and shattered, sending a plume of rotting vegetable marrow into the air. The audience cheered and clapped. The owner tipped his plumed hat.

Even from this distance, Tony saw the little man's belly bounce as he laughed.

Roscoe and Veronica's trebuchet was the oddest of the three weapons. What looked like a net holding a melon dangled from the weapon's arm. The couple cocked the thing with a lever, then fired. Tony wasn't quite sure what happened. A counterweight pushed back, the arm flung the net up and released the melon. It flew through the air, crashing into the stock tank and sending rubber ducks splashing onto the grass. The cheer was tremendous.

Veronica gave Roscoe a big kiss. If possible, the onlookers' enthusiasm for the kiss was even greater than for the duck splash. Veronica made a curtsey and threw the audience a kiss as well.

The performance was scheduled to occur again in half an hour. Tony was having a great time. He couldn't imagine watching anything more fun than flying vegetables at a festival celebrating spring and a noxious vegetable.

He still had an hour before it was time to change into his can-can ensemble. He already wore the sleeveless black T-shirt under his regular shirt and shorts and his hiking boots. At least he was not in uniform. When it was closer to performance time, he'd remove his outer shirt, add the skirt, wig, and bonnet. The comedian in charge of wigs had supplied him with long curls exactly matching the improbable red of Blossom's hair.

"So, who's the handsome newcomer dancing with Blossom?" Theo whispered into her mother-in-law's ear. "I'm sure I'd remember seeing him before."

Jane's answering sigh didn't mean she took her eyes off the couple dancing. "He's the new dentist in Tiberius's office group. He's not from the area and thought it would be fun to see our festival and meet the rest of the Abernathy family."

"Why weren't we introduced?" Theo frowned at her brother-in-law. Berry stood on the far side of Jane.

"I met him." Jane turned. "We were all together this morning. At breakfast." She waited a moment, then added. "At Ruby's. Honestly Theo, don't you remember?"

Theo remembered she hadn't gone to Ruby's Café for breakfast because she had been too busy packing everything she could possibly need for the day's outing with two infants and two rambunctious boys and a quilting demonstration featuring herself. The boys had gone with Tony, and she and the baby girls had taken a little nap. Survival strategy. No one bothered to mention the handsome new dental partner. "I wasn't there."

"Really?" For a moment it looked like Jane was going to argue the point. "Oh, that's right. It was just Tony and the boys. There was a mob at the table, and I was sitting next to Dr. Looks-so-good. I wasn't paying attention to much else."

Theo's laugh burst free, drawing several glances. "Is that his name?"

Jane actually blushed. "No. I was too busy staring at him to hear what Tiberius said his name actually is, so I made one up."

"It certainly fits."

"Yes it does, dear. Just because I'm older than you doesn't make me blind."

"Dr. Looks-so-good?" Nina laughed. "Our Jane gave him the name? Well, I must agree. The name does have a certain resonance." She tilted her head slightly watching the dentist, now dancing with Martha. "I may have to develop some dental issues."

"I'll bet his entire practice is women's dentistry."

A couple of the quilters overheard the conversation. One suggested they plan a field trip day to Knoxville; they could visit all the fabric stores, have lunch, and drop by the dentist's office just to have a look.

"Do you think he knows DuWayne and Kenny are probably looking into hiring a hit man?" Nina glanced over to where Blossom was now dancing with her regular pair of suitors. "Two's company and three's a crowd."

"At least the men are smiling again. For a moment I was afraid there was going to be violence."

Theo saw Katti and Claude Marmot arrive in her pink convertible. Katti jumped out in a swirl of black and pink polka dots and trotted over to Theo, or, more accurately, to Theo's twins. She cooed and patted their chubby cheeks and whispered things in Russian to them. They grinned back.

"You have smart babies." Katti hugged Theo. "Already they know Katti's language."

Theo agreed. Since Katti became her personal assistant, she had thrown Russian words into their conversations for months. And since Theo was a proud mom, she certainly wouldn't discourage Katti from praising her children.

Katti patted her polka dot–covered belly. "I have baby too. I wait to tell all as Missus Ruby deserved days of celebration first."

"How wonderful!" Theo hugged Katti. "When are you due?"

"When is?" Katti asked Claude. Before he had a chance to open his mouth, Katti chattered on. "Is holiday."

"Halloween." Claude kissed his wife's cheek. "A fun day, my sweet, but not a holiday."

Theo was mesmerized by the difference in Claude since his mail-order bride arrived. It was hard to call him Marmot-the-Varmint anymore. His wife had civilized and transformed Claude, at least the exterior. "Theo." He tipped an imaginary hat to her. "Excuse us but I'm going to dance with my wife before I have to dance with your husband. I'll leave it to you to decide how to combine pink with pumpkins and spooks."

Jolted by Claude's vision of a baby quilt, pronounced just as she tried to swallow her cold drink, Theo started laughing, choked, and blew lemon-lime soda through her nose. Valentine's Day meets Halloween? Impossible. She glanced furtively around as she mopped her face with a baby wipe. "What if it's a boy?"

Theo needed a break. Her cheeks hurt from all the smiling she'd been doing. She'd chatted and stamped hands as proof of payment, and now was working hard to keep a happy expression on her face when she was actually ready to drop. The girls were getting cranky, and so was she. She wouldn't say it was all bad. She'd had a good time for a while, chatting with folks she rarely saw and hearing compliments on the twins. Now she wanted some peace. The twins wanted lunch.

"Can you believe the crowd?" Nina shimmied into the folding chair next to her. "And hand over the money box and stamp."

"You're my replacement?" Theo turned.

"Yep." Nina scooted closer. "I thought I'd give you time for a break before you have to do your quilting demonstration. What quilting technique are you planning to show a mixed group like this one?"

"Before or after I strangle my mother-in-law?" Theo massaged her back with one hand. "To answer your question, I decided English paper piecing is simple enough for beginners and requires no sewing machine and not much skill. I really need to grow a spine."

"Too late, dearie. Everyone already knows you're a pushover." Nina offered her a cookie. "You've got to try one of these. It's sinful. I'm not sure what's in it besides oats and chocolate and pecans. Blossom says Tony loves them, and they're her new favorite to bake."

At that point, Theo might have chewed on a rock if it was painted to look like chocolate. She nibbled on a corner of the cookie and moaned. "That is *so* good. No wonder Blossom has so many men chasing her." She chewed quietly, letting Nina handle the incoming tide of festival attendees.

Jocko, Geordie, and Shawn, the three Farquhar "darlin' boys" tried to slip past without paying while Nina was taking money, making change, and stamping the hands of a family of four. Theo stepped in front of them to make them stop. She had known them all their lives and didn't like any of them. She couldn't tell them apart. One of them had a patch of whiskers on his neck—Theo didn't know which "boy"—from the front it looked like a tiny goatee but from the side it turned into an unshaved group of hairs. There was no chin. None of them was under thirty or gainfully employed in honest work. They were universally shifty, dishonest, and spewed profanity and tobacco juice like crazy. They ran in a pack, and Theo wasn't sure any of them could function alone. Of course, being the nephews of Angus didn't give them much of a chance to learn better. No, that wasn't a fair excuse. Theo remembered their late aunt had tried to civilize them, but not even one was interested in her lessons.

Theo wrested seven dollars from each of them, which she assumed was stolen, before she left Nina to deal with the table and pushed the stroller toward the museum office. She planned to rest for a few minutes and feed the girls before her demonstration.

Tony's vantage point allowed him to keep an eye on the entrance. He watched Nina join Theo, and saw the women dealing with festival attendees and the Farquhars. Seeing no reason to interfere, he returned to his supervision of the scouts and their cleanup program. He did make sure all of his deputies knew the location of the darlin' boys. Prevention was the motto. Keep the day safe and enjoyable for everyone.

A squabble on the far side of the grounds was turning ugly, but it looked like Wade had it under control. Tony wasn't stupid. He knew some people would smuggle alcohol onto the premises in flasks or the more inventive gelatin concoctions, and as long as they were adults and not overdoing it, he didn't care. His men would keep an extra sharp eye on them as they left.

He saw Theo and the infants vanish into the office and made his way there. Feeding time with only one person was horrendous. He considered Theo's relieved smile more than generous thanks. "Are you having any fun at all?"

Theo, busy gulping water from her insulated bottle, nodded. Water splashed onto her neck and made her squeal. "That's what I deserve for being piggy. It is tiring but fun." She offered a cookie to him. "Nina and I tried some of Blossom's new cookie recipe. Have you tasted one?"

"Are you kidding? You know my whole office is filled with her official taste testers." Tony patted his stomach. "I do think her new cookie is splendid."

Theo shook her head in mock despair. "You know, my friends are concerned you'll run off with Blossom, lured away from a loving family with brown sugar and nuts. Does she cook anything not filled with those ingredients?"

"Nothing I'd want to eat." Tony headed for the door, a baby draped over his arm, a baby bottle in one hand. "We'll be outside."

"I didn't mean to kill her."

Theo heard a man's low-pitched voice somewhere behind her. His words fell into one of the odd silences that sometimes occur in a generally noisy gathering, almost like everyone paused to take a breath and listen to what he had to say. Theo didn't recognize the voice. She tried to move her head just a bit to pick up more of the conversation. Her quilting demonstration blissfully brief, Theo had returned to her post, sitting at the ticket table. Nina left; going to check on her children as well as Theo's.

"What good does it do to talk about it now? Dead is dead." A woman's voice, also unfamiliar, held no discernable emotion. "What did you do with her body?"

Theo teetered backwards on her chair, wanting to hear more, hoping to see who was talking. The mancuver got her maybe an inch closer.

"I buried her in the—" The rest of his words vanished in the boom of Quentin's cannon and the wild applause from the crowd.

"No." Theo almost shrieked in frustration. Eavesdropping was impossible now with all the cheering and commotion. She considered standing on her little table so she could see better and maybe try to memorize every unfamiliar face. Better yet, she wanted to back up time and move close to the conversation, maybe take a picture of whoever was talking with her cell phone. Behind her she saw a short, middle-aged man wearing a plaid shirt and khaki pants held up by wide suspenders. His companion was certainly exotic for Silersville. Thin, and very tall, he wore a long black leather coat with a hood. The hood was up but didn't disguise the skeletally narrow, almost transparently colorless face and shaved head. The angel of death. She looked for Tony, thinking he might know who they were.

Because of Tony's height, augmented by the ladder he stood on, Theo could see him at the far end of the museum grounds. It looked like he was picking something out of a tree branch. A cheer for him went up when he pulled an errant balloon from its spot and handed it down to the toddler in a man's arms. Good for Tony; he'd probably be reelected sheriff in a landslide if Winifred Thornby put a photograph of his action in the newspaper.

Failing in all attempts to identify the man and woman whose conversation so intrigued her, Theo grabbed her purse and rummaged around in it. At last, she found an old shopping list and a pen. She wrote a note about the conversation she'd heard—the words and what the voices were like. What really struck her was the lack of emotion from both the teller and the listener. Were they cold and callous monsters? Not knowing the whole story, was she jumping to inaccurate conclusions? Was this dead thing a person? A goldfish? A possum on a dark road?

She used the camera built into her cell phone to take a few random photos. Maybe if she showed them to Tony later, he'd be able to answer her questions.

Theo wondered if she could deny a county resident entrance to the festival. Angus Farquhar offered her seven dollars in limp singles. Without touching them, she could tell they would be damp with the man's sweat or maybe something worse. Angus leaned forward, his little piggy eyes were red rimmed. He belched directly in her face. The whiskey fumes almost knocked her off the folding chair.

"I don't think . . ." She began, hoping inspiration would come to her, but her mind remained blank. Angus slammed his big hands on her table, making her ink pad, rubber stamp, and change box bounce.

"I'll bet you don't think, little missy." His lip curled back from his yellow teeth. "My money's good."

Theo saw strands of meat hanging from his teeth and smelled something rotting. She leaned back, trying to evade the sight and smell. "Alcohol is not allowed on the premises."

"Don't have any on me." He leaned closer, lowering his voice to a whisper. "I'll let you pat me down. You can take your time."

"I'll have to object." Tony's voice came from just behind her. "If there's any patting down, I'll do it."

Theo wasn't sure when she'd been happier to have her husband appear.

Angus straightened. "We was just chatting. Your little wife don't think my money's any good. I got as much right as anyone to be here."

Theo opened her mouth to protest, but Tony's hand on her shoulder cut her off.

Tony's voice was calm. "I'm going to take your money, Angus, and I'll stamp your hand to let you into the festival. If you so much as breathe too close to anyone, I'm going to haul you out of here in chains." Tony took the cash, coughing a bit when Angus's overall aroma hit him. "A few ramps might improve your breath."

As Angus stomped past them, Theo turned to watch his progress. While she and Tony were dealing with Angus, a fair-sized crowd had gathered behind them. "Ticket sales as a performance art." She laughed. "Thanks for stopping by. I don't like that man."

"Sheila hates him. I don't want to have to arrest either one of you for putting something extra in his pie." Tony ruffled Theo's curls and kissed the babies. "Call me if you see him do anything that I can use as an excuse to get rid of him."

"He smells like a distillery," Theo whispered. "I think he's drunk."

Tony hadn't appeared to be listening but he nodded. "Too bad we couldn't have caught him driving down here. I doubt we can charge him with eating under the influence."

"Even as crowded as it is, I bet he'll have a table to himself." Theo fanned her hand under her nose.

"In the meantime, I'm collecting you for the taking of the family photo." Tony leaned over her shoulder. "I forgot to tell you earlier. Mom insists we have a picture taken of the whole family. She's rounding up everyone."

"Who's the photographer?" Theo checked the girls. They were perfect. Without looking, Theo knew Chris and Jamie and their cousins would look normal in a photograph, not like the unnatural poses of overly clean children at Easter. On the other hand, she would like to change her shirt. This one had barbeque sauce on it.

Interrupting her thoughts about clothes, Tony said, "Nina volunteered. She thinks the light will be great in front of the old barn."

Theo understood why Jane would want a photograph of all her children and grandchildren together. She would like one too. The last family portrait didn't include Kara and Lizzie, of course, but then it had been taken years earlier when Jamie was an infant.

"What about the ticket table?"

Tony nodded toward the barn. "Here comes Celeste. Since she actually works at the museum, she offered to hang out here as long as necessary."

The delightful young woman who worked for Jane and Martha hadn't been married for long. She and her school teacher husband strolled to the ticket table. "Patrick volunteered to keep me company."

As she and Tony walked toward the office, Theo studied the Abernathy family. Oldest and biggest was Caesar Augustus. Solid, dependable, and the one most likely to set up an elaborate prank. She still laughed whenever she thought of his buying an old metal canning device to can all the Christmas gifts, and then hid all the openers. Christmas morning had the children in a panic. And the women, too, for the cooking as much as the presents. Next to Gus stood his wife Catherine, elegant, beautiful, and sweet. They had no children, but they loved to baby-sit. Could anything be better? Probably only if they ever produced a child or two of their own.

Next to Gus stood Tiberius. Although slighter than Gus and Tony, Berry was not small. His skin was bronzed. If he wasn't at work, he was usually out on his bass boat. He lived to fish. His wife was pleasant, but she tended to avoid being too involved in the Abernathy gatherings. Their twin boys were fifteen and it looked like they planned to grow as big as Gus. Standing to the side, Calpurnia was wiping something off her daughter's face. Her husband was talking to Jane, who, in her late sixties, was still trim and energetic and dyed her hair a soft blond.

Posing sixteen adults would be tricky. This was a logistical nightmare. Theo watched Nina frown as she attempted to organize the nine adults and seven children. Trying different arrangements of small groups and straight lines, Nina took lots of shots. Theo's diminutive size usually put her in the front row with the younger kids. Berry's twins towered over her and they loved it, patting her on the head as if she was a puppy. Most of her baby weight was gone but some still lingered, in all the wrong places. Theo felt like a mushroom standing in a forest.

Tony made his way to the museum office as soon as the photograph session ended. A storage room had been set aside for the can-can dancers' dressing room. In a few minutes he would have to step onto the stage for his debut. He wasn't sure how the community might react to the entertainment supplied by the combination of firefighters and law enforcement, but he hoped the dance would be popular enough to fill the hats passed afterwards. Being able to buy some new rescue equipment would make the humiliation worthwhile.

Retired sheriff Harvey Winston was tying his ruffled skirt on over a full set of bright red long underwear, opting to tie the skirt below the widest part of his belly. With the red long johns and his luxurious white mustache, Harvey looked like Santa Claus in drag. Tony relaxed, guessing no one would be able to focus on him. All eyes would have to be trained on Harvey's ensemble or Halfpenny's hitherto secret assortment of tattoos. The two of them made the remaining four dancers appear rather bland.

Once onstage, the dancers in high heels spent most of their time trying not to have their toes crushed under hiking boots or firemen's boots. Miss Cindy's choreography was quickly abandoned. It became a case of every man for himself. The gaudy hats were tied under their chins and served the secondary purpose of holding the garish wigs in place, but a couple slid to one side, causing intense merriment among the dancers. The audience laughed, showing they thought the dance was funny too.

Bow-legged Halfpenny, the bank manager, one of the dancers who had donned high heels, bent forward and flipped his skirt over his head, displaying the full cascade of gaudy ruffles and the unmistakable sight of blue denim shorts. The audience howled and clapped and whistled. Some people threw cash onto the stage. More money went into the hats and helmets being passed. The dancers descended into the throng, posing for pictures, for a fee.

In spite of newspaperwoman Winifred Thornby's unpleasant editorial the previous week, she even put a few dollars in a hat and promised to praise the men, in print, for their enthusiasm. Tony had seen her deposit the money. He'd believe the rest of it when he saw it.

CHAPTER SEVEN

Garbled sound came from the loud speakers. Mayor Calvin Cashdollar was taking this moment to make a speech to welcome all the visitors to the First Annual Silersville Ramp Festival. Considering the party had been going on for hours already, most people laughed or ignored him. Calvin made it sound like he'd slaved for months working on setting up the event. Tony wanted to yell at the man, and announce to all present that the mayor had absolutely no part in the organization or actual work of putting the festival together. He took a step forward, only to have his mom grab him by the arm.

Jane's eyes sparkled with merriment. "Don't you dare."

"Dare what, Mom? I'm not causing any trouble." Tony squeezed her hand. He doubted he could fool her any better now than he could when he was eight. He'd removed his hat and wig but still wore the can-can skirt in case more cash for photos was offered.

"I invited the mayor to introduce the acts." Jane fluffed her curls. "It gives him something to do. Even a part-time mayor needs to earn his keep."

Appeased, Tony glanced back at the food booths. "Are you going to have enough food?" The glimmer of panic in her expression told the story. "What can I do?"

Jane rubbed the little line forming between her eyes. "I don't know. Those people are eating everything but the plates. And the bags of trash, mostly plates, are indecent. I had to send

Tiberius into town for more garbage bags."

Once her words began, Jane babbled, mostly nonsense. When she ran out of steam, Tony heard an agonized plea, "Can you get them interested in something else, like the music or those vegetable weapons?" Jane's expression was a cross between horror and delight at the idea of another potato flying through the air, distracting the mighty diners.

Tony nodded and turned, nearly tripping over two little boys in team shirts gathering trash and shoving it into a black plastic bag large enough to hold a man's body. It took both of them to haul the bag from table to table.

Up on the stage, the mayor stepped away after introducing the next performers, a husband and wife team, Eddie and Ginger. Eddie plucked at the strings of a guitar while his wife arranged her skirt and settled on a stool, a zither on her lap. They played well, sticking to the old mountain songs, plaintive and at times cruel.

Satisfied the musicians would help slow the diners, Tony headed for the ticket booth, thinking he could juggle the babies for a bit and let Theo have a break. Hairy Rags plowed into him, not bothering to glance up or apologize, and then veered away, walking toward the woods. As rude as ever, he had one hand pressed against the back of his neck, covering the space between ear and spine, and one over his chest. Mostly what Tony noticed was the odd sound he made: kind of a wheeze.

Dodging people carrying plates of aromatic foods, Tony weaved his way through the "relics" until he found Theo. She looked pathetically happy to see him.

"If I don't get to the bathroom, there's going to be a puddle right here." Theo shoved one baby at him and then the other, climbed off her chair, and trotted toward the main office building.

"Should I watch the girls?" Tony kept an eye on her back.

When it went stiff, he knew she'd heard him and would talk about it later. He couldn't understand why he enjoyed ruffling her feathers, but he did.

"Say, Sheriff." The words came from the far side of the makeshift ticket booth. "Don't suppose you'd let an old man in without a payment? I kin promise not to eat much, but I purely desire some ramp pie."

Orvan Lundy. Tony couldn't believe his luck. He'd been at the ticket table for maybe ten seconds and was already in a quandary. Tony was sure the old sinner couldn't afford the seven-dollar entry fee and equally sure he shouldn't let the old guy in for free. Orvan sidled closer, rubbing his gnarled and weathered hands on the bib of his overalls. "Maybe there's chores I could do, you know, as a trade?"

Tony thought it sounded like a good plan. "Why don't you go help the kids who are doing the trash collecting? Just tie the tops of the garbage bags closed, good and tight, then carry them out and put them in the back of Gus's pickup. Some of those boys are a little short for the duty." Tony congratulated himself for not mentioning Orvan's own lack of vertical stature.

Orvan stood at attention, clicked his heels, and saluted. Less than a minute later, Tony saw Orvan carrying a trash bag with one hand and a slab of ramp pie in the other. The old guy could probably qualify as a "relic" too, but would never admit to his age or do anything civic-minded. There certainly was nothing wrong with either his arm strength or his appetite.

"I leave you in charge for two minutes and you've got Orvan working?" Theo's voice teased him. "And I heard what you said about holding the girls."

Before he could respond, the musicians stopped and an appreciative audience began to clap. Above the applause a boom announced Quentin's potato cannon had launched another spud. Tony turned to watch. The potato fell short of the stock tank again. The crowd cheered in spite of the miss.

A scream cut through the noise.

"I killed him." From his vantage point, Tony saw Quentin bolt down the hill, his long arms flapping like featherless wings. "I killed him. Where'd he come from? I killed him." His words fell into a shocked silence.

Tony handed Theo the infants and took off running toward Quentin. It wasn't easy to dodge the crowd, a task made doubly difficult when people began shifting around trying to see what had happened. Mike Ott arrived first. When Tony made it through to the scene, he saw Mike bending over the prone figure of Hairy Rags. Wade was charging toward them from another direction. Like Tony, he still wore his can-can costume.

Tony noticed Doc Nash hustling as fast as he could, weaving through the surging festival goers. Right on his heels was Wade's wife, Dr. Grace Claybough. A few people headed in the opposite direction, jamming up the doctors even more. At least the crowd wasn't screaming with panic.

Theo hated being left behind. She was too short to see over anyone taller than a small child, and holding two babies didn't make climbing onto the chair feasible. The decision about what to do was taken from her. The curious crowd hurried toward the clearing. She was carried along by a tidal wave of newcomers, forcing her to leave the ticket table unguarded. Luckily she was able to stash the cash box in the stroller, but then had to abandon the stroller.

A glance into the concession area showed Jane and Martha and Callie standing on chairs, trying to see. To her right, the musicians on the stage waved their arms and sang louder to attract the attention of the audience but no one seemed interested in watching them. Giving up the fight, they stopped their music and turned to face the action. The "relics" clumped together,

Nem taking an obviously protective stance near the cluster of frail old ladies.

Hoping to find someone to hold the now-squalling babies while she returned for the cash box, Theo headed toward Nem and the relics.

The Bainbridge sisters were huddled together, looking like they expected something awful to happen and they wanted to die together. Tiny Portia Osgood planted herself and her new walker firmly behind Nem and next to Caro. Ada walked in a circle around them all, swearing steadily under her breath. Nem waved Theo closer, "Miz Theo, you're welcome to join us."

"Thank you." Theo walked over to the group, shifting the babies higher in her arms. "I don't suppose you have any idea what happened?"

Ada's description was certainly colorful, but lacked details. Ada ignored Caro's attempts to stem her tide of profanity.

"I saw it all." Nem cleared his throat. "That wretch Ragsdale got himself shot with a spud. Walked right into it. Served him right, but I hate to see Quentin suffer for it."

"They ought to give him a reward," Caro whispered to Theo. "I just never could like that man. Not after all the things he's done." She reached out and smoothed Kara's hair. It stood away from the baby's scalp as if she'd touched a static electricity machine.

Lizzie began squalling and if there were any other comments her wails drowned them out. Theo did manage to see Tony, Doc Nash with Grace, and Mike approach the prone figure of Harrison Ragsdale. She tried, but failed, to feel sorry for Ragsdale. Mostly she was concerned because the man appeared to have collapsed during Jane and Martha's big festival. She spied Chris and Jamie, all pretense of cleaning tables gone, trying to creep around the outside perimeter to get closer to the motionless body, and called them back. "You boys do something useful instead of nosing around where you don't belong. Chris, will you please go get the stroller for me. And Jamie, I'm sure we could all use some water."

Ada's steady stream of profanity attracted the boys' attention. Hesitating only briefly, they went off to do as they were bidden. "It's not like there's any blood," Chris muttered. "Just a guy lyin' on the ground."

"Chris!" Theo waved him back. "The money box is in the stroller. Don't let it fall out."

The boy looked at the entrance and back to her. "Mom, there's people coming in without paying."

"I know. I know, and people are leaving just as fast." Theo took a deep breath, forcing herself to use reason rather than frustration. "I'll go back as soon as you bring me the stroller. Your sisters are getting heavy."

Caro held out her arms. "I'd love to hold a baby for you."

With a grateful sigh, Theo passed Kara to her elderly friend and focused on calming the now hysterical Lizzie. "Poor baby."

Only moments later, Chris ran toward her pushing the stroller much faster than he would if it was occupied. The cash box bounced out and Jamie scooped it up, hanging on to it like a football. The boys skidded to a stop, garnering great applause from the elderly onlookers. The boys wrapped their arms across their waists and made dramatic bows.

Theo had to laugh. Sometimes it took very little to be in the entertainment business.

Doc Nash squatted next to the body of Harrison Ragsdale, stretched out facedown in the grass, and confirmed the man was dead. No reason to hurry now. He waved for Grace to join him. "If you're going to doctor in these parts, you'll be checking the dead as well as the living." He squinted in Tony's direction and winked at Grace. "Especially as long as Tony's the law. But doesn't he have nice legs?"

Tony didn't respond to the gibe. He watched as the doctor hooked a finger into Hairy Rags's collar and pulled it back so Wade could take pictures. Several scratches ran in parallel lines across the skin between the shirt collar and his thick, snow white hair. Tony asked, "What do those marks look like to you?"

His deputy had made his way through the crowd just seconds behind everyone else, took one look and disappeared into the woods for a moment. Wiping his face with his handkerchief, he retrieved his camera bag from the car and now was all business, placing markers and rulers and making notes about the photographs he was taking.

The doctor leaned closer and tilted his head back so he could focus through the magnifying part of his bifocals. "They look like claw marks. Maybe one of his charges took a swipe at him. I'd guess a game warden might interact with some of his furry charges but I've seen some similar marks left by angry humans. I'll take a good close look during the autopsy."

Tony nodded and looked up the hill to where Quentin had his potato cannon set up next to the trebuchet and the catapult. "How accurate do you think that cannon is?"

"It's not a big cannon. I know some of the mega cannons can blow a potato through a wall." Doc Nash chuckled. "As far as accuracy, a small cannon, in a professional's hands, and at closer range, it might be pretty good, in Quentin's shaky world, not so much."

Tony looked at Quentin, who had started running down the hill the moment Harrison fell. Now standing next to Mike, he was panting and wringing his hands, threatening to twist one off. Tony walked over. "You all right?"

"I didn't see him." Quentin's head bobbed twice and he wailed, "Wh-hat was he doing out here?"

Tony glanced around, trying to ignore the horde of curious

onlookers. "You and your friends clearly marked this area as a potentially dangerous place to be. I don't think you can be held responsible for someone ignoring the warning signs and walking into your potato."

"Bless you." Quentin's shaking subsided a bit. "Bless you." He turned and hustled back up the hill to where his friends waited.

"Tony." Doc Nash stood and brushed grass off his hands. "There's something iffy about this body."

"Iffy?" Acid poured into Tony's stomach. He reached into his pocket for his emergency antacid supply. "Iffy how?"

Doc Nash watched Wade working with his camera. "I'm not sure. It doesn't look like the potato hit him hard enough to form a bruise, much less kill him. There are ways to determine force, but in my experience I'd say the spud is definitely innocent of any wrongdoing. I have no idea what he died of, though I'm pretty sure it was not natural causes."

"Pretty sure?" Tony wrote himself a note. "Those words don't exactly warm my heart."

Grace pointed at Harrison's mouth with a blade of grass. "It looks like some skin irritation here. Maybe he ate something he shouldn't have or something stung him. Does he have any allergies?"

"Not that I'm aware of, but he's not a patient of mine." Doc Nash searched the man's wrists and neck. "He's not wearing any kind of medical alert information." He dug through Harrison's pockets. "No medications so far." He pulled out Harrison's badge and placed it into a paper bag before reaching into another pocket. He extracted a revolver. "I'm giving this to you, Sheriff."

Tony checked it. It was fully loaded. He unloaded it and placed the gun and cartridges into an evidence bag.

Doc's inventory continued. "I'll keep the knife, cell phone, comb, and handkerchief." Doc made his own notes. "You take the keys." Doc pulled out the wallet, flipped through the contents. "Nothing here about allergies." He placed the wallet into the bag of personal items and stared at the body for a moment, then said just loud enough for Tony to hear, "Maybe poison?"

Hearing the "P" word, Tony reluctantly turned to face the milling crowd standing just beyond the makeshift fence. Would he see hordes of people falling to the ground, poisoned at his family's party? Thankfully, there were just the normal gawking faces, some serious, some gleeful. "Go back to the food and crafts and the music. There's nothing to see here." He began walking forward, shooing the leaders, like he was moving cows. Jumping into the spirit of the situation, Berry and Gus worked their way around the outside of the crowd and added their assistance.

Without warning, Martha grabbed one of the musicians, who, startled, fought her briefly and inadvertently scratched her arm with his fingernails. After a mumbled apology, he climbed the steps to the stage, pulling his partner with him. They launched into an upbeat favorite, and soon the audience was just that again, a group of people clapping and singing and eating and enjoying the beautiful spring afternoon. It wasn't like they'd lost someone they all cared for and there didn't seem to be anything much to see at the death site.

Tony lined up the vegetable weapon crew, spacing them too far apart to allow for any conversation. He considered Quentin's potato striking the man nothing more than a fluke, but he thought the foursome demonstrating vegetable warfare might be able to help him. They would have had a great vantage point for seeing something out of the ordinary. "The four of you were looking down at our little event. So, one at a time I'd like to ask you some questions, and I don't want you talking to one another."

"Ladies first." Wade beckoned to Veronica.

Tony had no idea what had caused Ragsdale's death, so he decided to go with the generic, "Did you see anything that struck you as unusual?"

Veronica gazed down the hill. "We were all having a great time. The weapons performed better than expected." She paused, reining in her enthusiasm. "I didn't see the man on the field until the potato was in the air. Looking back, it seems like he might have staggered an instant before he was hit, but the ground is uneven and I've come close to turning my ankle several times."

"Staggered?" Tony considered the implications of the word.

"You know, like he'd had too much to drink, or maybe as if he stepped in a hole and was losing his balance."

"Anything else?" Tony stared down the hill at the ambulance arriving to cart off the corpse.

"No." Veronica shrugged. "Sorry. It was a tremendously fun day until then. I hope we get to do it again."

Tony sent her to change places with Roscoe. Their conversation didn't last long. If anything, Roscoe had seen less than Veronica because he was "gazing at my lady love" instead of looking down the hill.

The professor strode toward them. With each step, his great belly swung right, and then the other way. Up close, his red velvet tunic was well sewn and highly decorated with embroidery and jewels. Tony thought Theo would be proud of his ability to judge the quality of needlework. It had taken her years to train his eye—a long transition from Neanderthal to an appreciative viewer. "Who made your outfit?"

The professor's wide smile broadened. "My wife." He waved to someone in the crowd below. "That's her, the gray-haired woman buying a ticket, or more likely twenty of them, for the quilt being given away. She's more interested in the crafts than our weapons."

Tony thought he detected bewilderment about his wife's lack of interest in the weapons. Although he couldn't see the woman, he believed she was in the crowd. "How, or why, did you decide to participate today?"

"Are you kidding? I live for this." The professor's belly bounced, making the jewels flash in the sunlight. "Food, music, and the chance to blow rubber duckies out of a trough with a vegetable. Can life get better?" He lowered his voice and reined in some of his exuberance. "Except for this incident and that one hideous musical act." He shuddered at the memory.

Tony had to admire the man's enthusiasm. He wasn't too sure what it would take to get him out in public in a miniskirt, but to each his own. Tony managed to convince himself the can-can skirt was much more masculine, at least while the black satin hung straight down covering the inner ruffles. "I understand you're from Knoxville. Have you ever met Harrison Ragsdale?"

The jovial expression vanished. "I have." The professor averted his eyes and his lips pressed tightly together.

"Under what circumstances?" Tony always found it curious how disparate lives so often intersected with each other.

"You might find this hard to believe, but we were roommates our freshman year at the university." The professor shook his head. "To be precise, we were roommates for the first month of freshman year. After that, I was able to make other living arrangements. To be frank, I'd have rather slept under one of the bridges than share with him any longer."

"Wow." Totally gobsmacked, Tony stared. "Why?"

The professor looked as if he might not answer. Then, exhaling loudly, he began talking. "It was not awful the first week. We were young, away from home for the first time. He was from this end of the state, but I grew up in Pulaski, so I was farther from my home. The first few days, he was the only person I knew on campus." The professor's hands shook as he pulled a handkerchief from a hidden pocket in his tunic and blew his nose. "I'll not get into more detail unless necessary, but I quickly learned he delighted in cruel behavior toward people and animals."

"Were you aware he lived and worked in this county?" Tony paused. "As a game warden?"

"Hell, no." The feathers on his hat whipped from side to side. "I might not have come if I'd known there was a chance Ragsdale would be here."

Tony felt his eyebrows climb. "When was the last time you saw him before today?"

"The day I moved out of the dorm. The university is large and our majors led us to different parts of the campus. I found joy and love in the history department and he I don't know what he found." The professor slipped his handkerchief into a secret pocket. "I don't think he wanted to be happy. You ever meet someone who seems to revel in unhappiness, whether theirs or someone else's?"

"Unfortunately, yes." Tony had met several people in the category and couldn't understand their penchant for misery.

"That was Harrison." The professor jiggled impatiently. "Can we go back to our machines?"

"Yes. I have your contact information." Tony beckoned Quentin forward. "But I can't have you firing down at a possible crime scene."

"Crime scene?" Quentin leaned forward as if he'd be able to see something special from up on the hill. "We've been up here all afternoon. Honest, Sheriff, when I fired the cannon, no one was anywhere down there."

"I'm sure that's true." Tony absolutely believed him.

Quentin started twitching more than usual. "What crime then?"

Tony had no answer and thought Quentin nailed the crux of the problem. If there was a crime, Tony didn't think it actually happened here in the field but more likely it occurred in the crowded public zone. Tony glanced at the hordes of restless party goers. "Never mind. Have fun. Shoot all the spuds you want after we clear the area." Tony could only hope he was making the right decision.

"I've been replaced on the ticket table by Ruth Ann and Walter. Isn't it nice to see her husband out and about again?" Parking the stroller with the angelic—now that they were sleeping—babies, Theo sat down next to Callie and grinned at her sister-in-law. "Has your mom always been a magnet for mayhem?"

Callie, who had been on the verge of answering, froze. Looking past Theo she said, "Hi, Mom."

"Can you believe it?" Jane plopped onto an empty chair, nearly causing the folding chair to do just what it was named for. Both Theo and Callie grabbed to support it. Jane thanked them sweetly before taking a long drink of her iced tea. "Honestly, I don't know why these things happen around me."

Callie turned to Theo. "Does that answer your question?" She reached for Jane's hand. "I don't think you have anything to do with it, Mom. If you stayed home alone, you'd miss too much fun."

Theo mumbled something about not wanting the roof to cave in around her mother-in-law so it was safer for her to be out and about, and made everyone laugh. "Now that we're all feeling better, why don't we see what's for sale in the crafts booths. I heard the senior citizens' craft group has worked for months making hot pads, doll clothes, and place mats."

Nina came close enough to hear them and chimed in. "My French Club kids hope to sell enough cookies and brownies and cakes to fund a collection of music and movies in French. Their goal, since no one can afford to travel to France, is to have enough entertainment to last through an all-night party."

"I'm sure I need some cookies and hot pads." Callie rose and led her mother in the direction of the crafts area. "Now that most people have eaten, let's go see what all is for sale over there. I was afraid of being trampled earlier."

Theo handed Nina ten dollars. "Buy me something chocolaty. I need to get back to the ticket table and see if Ruth Ann and Walter have had enough fun yet."

CHAPTER EIGHT

"Sheriff?" Doc Nash called Tony over to the ambulance. "I've changed my mind. I'm not going to do this autopsy."

Tony looked into the doctor's serious brown eyes. "Why not?" He really didn't need to ask. Over the time they had worked together, Tony had come to understand the doctor was willing to admit when a situation was beyond his training and available equipment. What the statement really meant was Doc Nash believed the body was evidence in a murder case, and he wasn't going to risk destroying evidence that might point to the killer, and he didn't want the killer to get away with it.

Doc Nash pointed to Ragsdale's face. "Now that he's on his back I can tell you this is not normal. See the way there's a bit of swelling around the lips. He probably ate something he was allergic to or some insect bit him, or I don't know what I'm talking about. He's not one of my patients, but people with strong food allergies are normally very careful about what they eat and routinely carry medication to counteract a reaction until they can reach medical help." The doctor's bright brown eyes met his. "Plus . . ."

"Plus?" Tony actually felt his stomach fall. An expression he now understood. "What is plus? Plus doesn't sound good."

"Look at this." Doc Nash peeled back the jacket, exposing the end of a wooden stake about as thick as a wooden spoon handle. It was definitely not a twig, and it was jammed into the deceased's chest. "What does that make you think of?"

"Old vampire movies." Tony leaned closer and Wade jumped forward with the camera, photographing the thing from several angles. There was a small amount of blood on the point.

"Yeah, my thought exactly. But in the middle of the afternoon? Shouldn't it be midnight in a cemetery?" Doc Nash sighed. "I don't know if it penetrated the heart or not, but it punctured something. I'll leave it to an expert to find out."

Tony studied the surrounding area. On this side of the rope marked with brightly colored pennants, there was a wide space, clear of trees all the way up to the mostly level space where the cannon, trebuchet, and catapult sat. The medieval enthusiasts' Bush Hog mowed all the vegetation in the area to a height of about eight inches. In his viewpoint, the idea of someone being able to hide before, during, and after stabbing Ragsdale with a wooden stake was ludicrous.

On the festival side of the rope, hundreds of people milled about, some watching the show on the stage, some roaming around the food and craft booths, some just standing around talking, and some staring at him and the ambulance. With such a crowd, there was little room to move around. Tony couldn't help but wonder how someone could be stabbed with no one, apparently, noticing. Or maybe someone had. A groan worked its way up from his stomach. They needed to talk to everyone at the festival.

He saw Rex Satterfield dancing with his wife in the space in front of the stage. Although Flavio Weems had made progress as far as becoming a good dispatch officer, he would not be as efficient and professional as Rex for another twenty years. Tony didn't have his radio with him, so he used his cell phone to call Flavio. "I know where Wade and Mike are—I need you to contact Sheila and Darren and tell them to come to the museum. Now. And tell them to bring plenty of paper."

Tony thought they could set up tables in the barn/exhibit hall and run everyone through to get statements. He didn't want their life stories, just their names, addresses, where they were standing and anything they might have seen that struck them as unusual. His stomach growled. He was probably the only person here who hadn't eaten. He decided some lunch would improve his attitude, if not his heartburn, and he headed for the food booths.

Avoiding the ramp dishes, he settled on a barbeque sandwich. It came with a huge pickle and a bag of potato chips. Carrying his plate with both hands because the weight of the pickle alone would cause it to collapse, he made his way to Theo's table at the entrance.

Her smile was welcoming but strained. He placed his lunch on the table and settled onto an empty chair. "You can have the pickle."

Theo's smile brightened a bit as she reached for it. "People are getting cranky about not being allowed to leave. Others are still arriving, or returning."

"And other than remembering them, how do you know they've paid?" He took a big bite of the excellent barbeque and started opening the potato chips as he chewed.

Theo looked at him like he'd arrived from Mars. "I stamp their hand when they pay." She waved a small rubber stamp under his nose. "Like they do at just about every event we attend."

Tony had to admit he'd forgotten he'd stamped hands earlier and had overlooked the most obvious solution to his dilemma. "Do you happen to have another stamp or another color ink we could use?"

"Yes, both, but the pickle isn't enough of a bribe. You have to tell me what's going on."

Theo, following Tony's instructions, found a rubber stamp with a second design and gave it to him. Each person would need to be checked for a second stamp, a red heart, before they'd be allowed to leave.

Thankfully, Berry stepped in to help her at the gate. While not built anything like Tony and Gus physically, Berry was nonetheless an Abernathy man and, like the other two, he wasn't intimidated by a few cranky people wanting to leave without checking in with the sheriff's office representatives. No red heart on their hand, no departure. His authority was undisputed.

Theo stayed at the table and continued to take money and let Berry deal with those leaving. It didn't take her friends and quilt shop customers long to find her and attempt to extract information from her. It was easy to stay quiet about Tony's investigation, because he hadn't told her anything.

Nina brought the plate of brownies Theo had ordered and stayed to help with the twins. Even she attempted to extract information from her. Nina's eyes sparkled with mischief. "Really, Theo, I'm sure you know something."

Theo didn't have to feign ignorance. "No. I don't." She lowered her voice. "If you learn anything, please come tell me. I hate being the only person left out of the loop."

"Deal." Nina patted Lizzie's tiny back and cooed, "Aren't you the sweetest baby?" She winked at Theo. "I say the same thing to Kara. Does that make me a big fat liar or what?"

"I'll forgive you for them. I'm afraid I do the same thing. They'll be warped for life, each one claiming to be my favorite."

Nina glanced past Theo. "Berry doesn't look at all like Tony and Gus, does he?"

Theo studied the dark-haired brother and shook her head. "He and Callie take after Jane's side of the family while Tony and Gus are built like their dad." She glanced over to the table where Berry towered over Orvan Lundy, preventing the little old man from leaving without being cleared. Orvan's whine wasn't getting him anywhere. "Berry's not exactly small, you know, he's just a lot smaller than his brothers."

Nina agreed. "Plus, he has a lot more hair. I know hordes of women who would give their back teeth to have a mane of black hair like his."

"No kidding. It looks like something in a shampoo commercial." As they talked, Theo realized she hadn't seen their elderly friend for a while. "Have you seen Caro?"

"She was over with the rest of the 'relics.' " Nina half-stood, looking toward the concession stand. "I don't see her now. Why?"

"I'm a bit concerned about her. She hasn't been at Thursday Night Bowling League lately, not even in the daytime, but then, neither have you."

"I expect to be there this week. Last time was parent teacher conferences, and I don't remember why I couldn't come before. How's Caro doing?"

"She feels so guilty when she can't go see her husband more often, but when she does visit, he has no idea who she is. Alzheimer's has taken him far beyond her reach." Theo sighed. "It's amazing his body can keep going for so long without his mind."

"It's too sad to contemplate." Nina looked beyond Theo's shoulder. "What *is* fun to think about is Blossom and her coterie of gentlemen. How many beaux does she have now?"

As a change of subject, Theo thought it was inspired. "Well, let's see. The last I knew, Kenny and DuWayne were sort of co-stars. Why?"

"Because she's dancing with Doctor-looks-so-good again." Nina stared at the dancers. "He's very easy on the eyes."

Unable to resist, Theo turned to look. Flamed-haired and quite light on her feet for a plus-size woman, Blossom was dancing the two-step with a tall man with broad shoulders and narrow hips. Neither Kenny nor DuWayne had any height to speak of, so it wasn't one of them. Theo said, "That new dentist is gorgeous, isn't he?"

"Only if you think tall, dark, and handsome is gorgeous. I'm jealous of Blossom. Where does she find them?" Nina sighed. "All the men I seem to meet these days are married, losers, or married losers."

Theo saw the expressions of concern on Blossom's beaux' faces. "Maybe you could cut in. I'll bet her boyfriends Kenny and DuWayne wouldn't mind." There was nothing more Theo could suggest. With not a lot of men in Park County, few were single and even fewer were stellar. As Theo watched, the musicians stopped playing and the dancers applauded. A girl, maybe thirteen, carrying a guitar, took the stage. She sang poorly, but the audience stayed to listen and applauded generously when she finished. All in all, hers was a much superior performance to that of the Elves.

Theo's younger quilting friend Susan dropped by the admission table and told Theo that the quilters guarding the display in the barn reported a lot of sightseers but not much in the way of sales. Normal. For them this festival was a chance to show what they liked to do and perhaps interest onlookers in joining their fabric-filled world. Self-appointed quilt guardians were fiercely protective and handled the quilts with white gloves. No one else was allowed to touch them. The combination of fabric and weeks, months or years of work did not welcome hands smudged with barbeque sauce and ramps. Just thinking about greasy red-orange smudges on an heirloom made a couple of women withdraw their quilts from the exhibition.

The senior citizens had set up their booth to make money, and they were cleaning up, monetarily, selling their small homemade items to all and sundry. The biggest sellers were the hot pads, microwavable fabric potato pockets, followed by the place mats and, running last, crocheted toilet paper roll covers disguised as girls in flamboyant colored full skirts.

Theo knew how much work those covers were to make and hoped not too many of them would soon be disposed of, to be collected by their trash hauler Claude Marmot and taken to the dump. Mostly because she was sure Claude would rescue them, and poor Katti would have fifteen hoop-skirted toilet paper–holding girls in their small house. Not all of them were pink, so they could create a major decorating issue for Katti.

Between Claude's penchant for finding new uses for much of the trash he collected, and Katti's love of pink, visiting the Marmot home was always an adventure. Theo admired the mind that converted a sedan into a pickup. Now Tony had described a hard shell motorcycle cover. What would Claude use to build a baby stroller?

When the new little Marmot arrived, space was such an issue, it would probably have to sleep in the sink. Theo hoped Claude would find enough scrap lumber to build on another room or two.

Tony wondered if any of his deputies had learned anything more interesting than he had. So far, the most important thing he learned was to hand each person a breath mint before asking them any questions. Ramps were almost a tie with garlic if there was a contest for a vegetable producing the most pungent breath. The mints didn't fix the problem, but did serve as a distraction and also gave the interviews a more social feeling.

Most of the citizens of Park County were either okay with Harrison Ragsdale being deceased, or pleased by the situation. No one shed a tear. No one admitted to being his friend or even to having had a conversation with the man at the festival. This was hardly surprising. For as long as Tony had known the man, he seemed to have been in a bad mood. He openly professed to disliking animals, which made his job choice fascinating. Tony had asked him once why he'd decided to be a game warden. In a weak, or surprised, moment, Harrison had admitted he enjoyed knowing people who liked to kill animals. Tony didn't want to know anything more.

Tony wasted little time with each person. He asked his questions, jotted down the answers, and sent them back to the party. He wasn't prepared for everything. When an old man settled into the chair, sighed, and laced his fingers together, Tony tried his usual approach even though he doubted it would work. "Name?"

"You know me. I'm Sid Lundy."

Tony did know. "Did you see Harrison Ragsdale?"

"Say, Sheriff, look here." Sid opened his mouth wide, releasing a gust of ramp infused air, and pointed to his false teeth. "Kin you tell if they fit? They seem a bit wiggly. Make's me disbelieve these is mine."

Coughing from the noxious fumes, Tony decided to stamp Sid's hand and send him away. "They look fine to me." His eyes were watering, but he was able to point out his brother. "Get Berry to look."

Queen Doreen was next in line. Tony wasn't sure he'd ever been so delighted to see her. He waved the mayor's wife to the chair facing him, offered her a mint, and asked her the same questions he'd been asking everyone else—did she know Ragsdale, did she notice anyone approach the man or see anything notable or suspicious? It was like dropping dynamite into a well.

"That wretched man!" Doreen slapped her hand against the blue leather purse in her lap. "I know people in this community think I'm cold, but I'm not. It's just that my interests are different from theirs. Harrison Ragsdale was the coldest excuse for a human being I ever saw."

Tony watched her squeeze the purse strap like she was trying to strangle it. He waited.

"On more than one occasion I saw him swerve to intentionally hit some poor animal—it didn't matter what—squirrel, cat, dog, or possum. If animals had money I'd say one of them had hired a hit man. If someone killed him, I don't think you need to spend much time looking for the guilty party."

"Did you have personal experience with him?" Tony couldn't recall ever seeing Doreen or Calvin with a pet.

"You mean did he kill one of my animals? No. I don't have pets. But Pansy Flowers Millsaps has come to work crying a couple of times because she's seen him do it. And Carl Lee's wife swears he ran over her cat on purpose, just like he did Portia's." Doreen pressed a trembling hand against the side of her face, catching a tear. "I did see him hit a possum with his car once. He stopped, got out, and kicked it into a ditch. Rotten bastard."

Surprised by the depth of her emotion, Tony sent her on her way. Doreen wasn't leaving town, and he didn't believe she was guilty of anything worse than speaking ill of the dead. But her words made him think about Roscoe and his missing bear. Where was Baby? Had Harrison taken the bear? Destroyed her? Was he responsible in any way for her absence? If so, Tony could imagine Quentin deliberately shooting the man with a potato in hopes of exacting revenge for his best friend. Was Quentin goofy enough to think he could murder a man in front of witnesses and get away with it? He was about to go after Quentin when he remembered the facts didn't match, even if the motive did. No one could have predicted Harrison would walk into potato range, and what they needed was someone who could, and would, stab the man with a wooden stake.

Tony felt a prickling at the base of his neck. Who else possible was left then? Carl Lee, Mr. Espinoza. Where was Angus now? Tony radioed, asking Flavio to relay his question. The answers came back—no one knew where he was or when he'd left. Given her post in the front, Theo might know, but she was not on radio. He dialed her cell phone.

Theo picked up on the second ring. "What is going on, Tony? People are leaving in droves and another group seems to be arriving. It's like a tidal wave. Is there bus service I don't know about?"

"Damn. I should have sent someone to help you and Berry right away. I don't want anyone else to leave, I'll send you Darren." Tony waved to his deputy, calling him closer, even as he spoke to Theo. "I know you're in a jam down there, but please try to remember who left and make a list."

"But, Tony." Her voice sounded strained. "How can I make a list? I don't even know a lot of them."

It was late in the afternoon by the time Tony and his deputies had talked to everyone and made notes on what, if anything, they'd seen. He stood and stretched and walked back toward the food concessions. Clustered in a warm place, sitting on folding chairs upwind of the rancid ramps, the six "relics" appeared to be sound asleep. Wondering why they were still on duty, Tony glanced at his aunt.

Martha shrugged. "I tried several times to get them to let me call for their ride. They don't want to miss anything, and they want to do their jobs. Until they wore out, it looked like they were all having lots of fun."

"I'm guessing this is the most excitement any of them has had for a while. Lots of activity and people to talk to and music—no wonder they want to stay." Tony hoped they weren't overdoing it. "I haven't seen your friend, Mr. Espinoza, for a while."

"He left early. Before you began the interviews and hand-

119

stamping business." Martha's eyebrows pulled low. "You don't think he had anything to do with Harrison's death?"

"I don't know what I think yet." Tony didn't like missing Mr. Espinoza. "Why did he leave so early?"

Martha's shrug told him nothing.

"What excuse did he give you?"

"He said he had an appointment he couldn't be late for." Martha's eyes met his. "Really, Tony, he's a very nice gentleman."

"When did he tell you about the appointment—before or after Harrison died?" He scribbled two words in his notebook. "Find Espinoza." He showed it to his aunt.

"It was right after everyone ran toward the field." Martha paused, clearly trying to remember the sequence of events. "I tried to see what was causing the commotion, but didn't want to abandon the cash. Orlando passed by me. I think he couldn't see me for the crowd, and he did tell Jane to let me know he had left."

"Did you expect him to stay the whole afternoon?"

"Yes. He told me he would spend the day here and help us shut everything down." Martha kicked the ground with her toes and shrugged. "He must have gotten an important phone call."

"Does he get them often?" Tony didn't approve of the way Orlando was treating his aunt. He considered her silence an answer. She deserved better.

Almost all Tony knew about Orlando Espinoza was that he was an exotic-looking man for East Tennessee. He was short, stout, and combed his oiled, thinning hair straight back from his forehead. Dark brown, almost black eyes vied with a lustrous mustache for his most noticeable feature. He tended to dress formally, even for informal occasions, so he was the only man at the festival wearing a suit. And not just a suit, but a three-piece suit complete with a vest, tie, and jacket pocket handkerchief.

Most of the time he carried another handkerchief in his hand, using it frequently to dab perspiration from his neck and forehead. Tony thought he was a pompous bore.

He claimed he was a visiting professor at the university and enjoyed meeting the locals, but in truth he rarely mingled. It wasn't because of a language barrier. His English was totally fluent and idiomatic. A wide line of snobbery ran through him and, although he found the locals interesting and very nice, as a rule he shared no common interests with any of them. As far as Tony could see, he enjoyed Martha's company because he found the English teacher not only amusing but extremely well read in the classics, his preferred reading material. The two of them often attended lectures and book events together. And they enjoyed ballroom dancing.

"What do you really know about him?" Tony rubbed the side of his nose. "You're the only one who has gotten more than two words out of the man."

Martha looked uneasy. "I never doubted anything he said. Do you think he's not what he appears, a very pleasant gentleman from South America?"

Tony sighed. "I don't *think* anything. I'm just curious, more so because of the timing of his exit." Martha's late husband had been a secret womanizer, gambler, and loan shark, and finding out about him hadn't made her cynical. On the contrary, she now operated on the assumption that having already having dealt with a cheating liar, everyone else must be telling the truth. Tony knew it was not necessarily accurate. "I am going to dig a bit deeper into Mr. Espinoza's background."

"And if you find something unpleasant?"

Tony thought "unpleasant" was the least of their worries. "I'll be sure to let you know."

Tony felt trapped. He was sandwiched between two men, angry

men, who came looking for him. They must have partaken of liberal amounts of ramp pie and had the breath to prove it. "What's the problem?"

"I parked in the overflow lot across the road and just went over to lock my popcorn and cookies in the car. It looks like someone crashed into it hard. The whole thing looks like an accordion, crumpled in front and back."

The man on the other side piped up. "I was going to leave, but this guy's rear bumper is jammed into my car's front end. There's no way my car's drivable."

A glance around the festival grounds showed all of his deputies were occupied. "Show me."

The two men kept up a steady stream of complaints about the parking situation, at least when they weren't threatening to sue the museum or asking if the museum's insurance company would pay. Tony thought their own automobile insurance would have to pay. Unless the culprit left a note taking responsibility and an offer of cash. They walked only halfway across the road when Tony saw the cars. Neither man had exaggerated the problem.

This was not a simple parking lot bump—the cars looked like the losing entries in a demolition derby. Tony checked the two cars and noticed some deep dents in several nearby vehicles. Staring at the mess, he massaged the back of his neck while mentally running through his list of profanity. He considered using several new swear words he'd picked up from Ada but managed to contain them. "I'll get a camera and call for a tow truck. If your insurance agents are over at the festival, you might want to show them this mess."

Sheila had just finished talking to a gentleman when Tony went to get the camera. "I'll do it, sir, I could use the fresh air, and I know every insurance agent in a five-county radius."

Tony couldn't even work up a token protest. "I'll go chat

with Farmer Brown and see what he can tell us about the damage." Tony checked Farmer Brown's house, including both porches, the milking barn, the pastures. No one. Circling around, Tony returned to the house, where Mr. Brown sat on a ladder-back rocking chair on his front porch. Tony knew he hadn't missed seeing the man there earlier.

Tony thought Sam Brown resembled his name. Sturdy, simple, and utilitarian, dressed in a festival of browns. Thanks to Theo, Tony had been exposed to nuances of color, tone, and shade. As he did now, Sam often dressed in brown work clothes of heavy canvas—waterproof, warm, and long wearing. Chocolate with overtones of red clay. His hair, deep mahogany with strands of silver, was shaggy but clean. There was less silver in it than most men in their late sixties had. Gleaming under heavy brows, his eyes were almost black except for flecks of amber. His face and hands were the color and texture of old saddle leather.

Sam's wife had passed away about six months earlier. The two living children, a boy and a girl, had long since moved away.

"How are Anita and Junior?" Tony leaned against the roof's support post.

"Junior's moved again," Sam said. "Wish he'd move home, but now he's in Virginia coaching girls basketball. College. At least he's closer than he was."

"And Anita?"

"She was always too busy to settle down." The amber in his eyes faded. "Now she's in LA. She still wants to be in the movies, but meantime she works at an amusement park sewing people's names on hats."

Pleasantries over, Tony said, "What happened over in the parking area?"

"Nothing."

"Those dented-up cars would indicate otherwise." Tony said. "There are several cars with pretty severe damage."

"Then they came like that. I was here." Sam shook his head. "I'd know." After his pronouncement, he stopped talking.

Tony wondered what he was hiding, and why. Tony had a fair amount of experience with lies and automobile accidents—this incident was a whopper on both counts.

"You heard Harrison Ragsdale died?"

"Good news travels pretty fast." Brown's face showed satisfaction. "I do hate him—did hate him, you hear. I know he killed my boy and claimed it was an accident. I hope he suffered a lot." He pulled out a faded blue bandana handkerchief and wiped his eyes. "I don't suppose you'll tell me what happened?"

Tony shook his head. But the old man's question made him curious.

Tony still remembered the accident that had occurred when he was young and new to Silersville. The Brown boy had been riding his bicycle after dark out on the highway when he was struck by a car. Tony's own mom had been so upset by the incident she'd locked all the family bicycles in a shed and made all four kids walk everywhere for a month.

As a parent, Tony fully understood how the unthinkable event would never fade in the old man's memory. What Tony wanted now was to know if Mr. Brown came to the festival and if so, had he been carrying a sharp stick? Had Ragsdale even been the one driving the deadly car? How many years had passed? More than twenty for sure, maybe closer to thirty.

CHAPTER NINE

Early the next morning, after a semi-sleepless night disturbed even more by heartburn and nightmares of zombies driving cars and catapults tossing vegetables, Tony retrieved the Sunday edition of the Knoxville newspaper. A real newspaper. Their local *Silersville Gazette* provided gossip, school lunch menus, and event listings twice a week. For news and, more particularly, sports news, it held nothing national. Baseball season was his favorite time to read the paper. This morning's headline stopped him.

"Killer Spud in Silersville." The byline, his nemesis, newspaperwoman Winifred Thornby. The accompanying photograph showed people charging toward a prone figure on the ground. A second photograph was of him, can-can skirt and all, standing near the body. The article began, "Sheriff Tony Abernathy is investigating the suspicious death of long-time Silersville resident, game warden Harrison Ragsdale. To this reporter's questions, he merely claimed to have no comment. Only time will tell if the sheriff's department will be able to clarify the events to the satisfaction of this reporter and the citizens of Park County."

Tony wondered who would write the follow-up article, "Sheriff Strangles Reporter." He envisioned a photograph of Winifred's body, wrapped in a blue tarp, lashed to the roof of his vehicle. He started to slam the door behind him, but remembered his family sleeping upstairs. To release some of his tension, he threw the newspaper at the wall. Predictably, it just became disordered. Not satisfying at all. He picked it up, shuffled it into some semblance of order, and went upstairs to shower and change. This Sunday was going to be just another work day. He'd read the paper when he got home.

Tony wanted to talk to the mayor's nephew. Carl Lee Cashdollar was as honest a man as Tony knew, but everyone had a breaking point. Maybe his wife had encouraged him to give the game warden a taste of his own medicine. Tony had seen the younger Cashdollars dancing before the cannon episode, but not after. A series of radio calls established the couple had to have left during the confusing moments immediately after the body fell. They had not given a statement at the museum.

Wade joined Tony at the Cashdollar house.

Carl Lee opened his front door when Tony knocked. He smiled a greeting. "Come in, Tony. Wade."

Tony handed the attorney the Knoxville paper they'd picked up from the sidewalk. Tony and Wade went inside and stood just inside the door. "This isn't a social call. Is your wife here?"

"Yes." Carl Lee's expression was suddenly wary. "Is there a problem?"

"I hope not." Tony didn't move. "Can you ask her to join us?"

Carl Lee loped toward the kitchen and returned with his wife. Jill was wiping her hands on a kitchen towel. While not a beauty, she had a sweet face and had always given the impression of being quite shy. "Sheriff?"

"You two were at the Ramp Festival." Tony began. It wasn't a question.

"Yes, we left early," said Carl Lee.

"Any particular reason why?"

"It was the smell." Jill waved a hand in front of her nose. "At first it was just awful, and then it got even worse. I couldn't eat my hamburger because the air around us smelled so bad. We had to leave."

"My wife's a diabetic and has to monitor her meals and eat on a schedule." Carl Lee wrapped an arm around her slender waist.

She nodded. "It's not usually such an issue, but yesterday I needed to leave. A little breeze would have helped a lot."

"What's this about?" Carl Lee's attorney radar must have signaled him again.

"Harrison Ragsdale."

"That man!" Jill's eyes flashed with anger. "I'm sure he killed my cat. Carl Lee thinks he ran over her like he was trying to do it." When her husband squeezed her gently, she went quiet but shook her head, her fury still evident.

"Ragsdale's dead." Tony watched for a reaction. He wasn't disappointed.

Jill smiled.

Wade looked up from his notebook. "What time was it when he ran into you?"

"Close to one-fifteen. We were on the way out."

While Wade wrote the information in his notebook, Tony said, "I don't suppose you're his lawyer or know if he has a will?"

Carl Lee laughed. "The man was never a client of mine. I'd be surprised if he buys anything local. What happened?" Carl Lee looked directly into Tony's eyes. "He was alive when we left. He bumped into us as we were trying to make our way to the parking area. Almost knocked me over and spilled Jill's diet drink all over her shirt."

Tony saw the cola stain on her T-shirt. "Are those the clothes you wore yesterday?"

"Just the shirt. I decided that as long as it was dirty I'd wear it while I do some work in the flowerbeds before church. It's much too pretty a day to stay inside."

"Thank you." Tony believed the couple and was relieved to finish their interview and cross them off one list. "I just have to verify who was where."

Tony and Wade drove to the university and tracked down Orlando Espinoza. The dapper little man sat at a library table, a newspaper spread before him. When Tony approached, Espinoza tipped his chin down and looked over the top of his reading glasses. "Sheriff?"

The man's snotty attitude raised Tony's hackles. What did his aunt see in him? "You left the festival rather abruptly yesterday."

"Yes."

If possible, the man managed to convey even less personal warmth than before.

"Would you care to tell me why?"

"No." Espinoza tightened his lips making his mustache quiver.

"If you prefer I can take you back to Silersville with me. You can call an attorney, and then the two of you can decide what your next move might be." Tony was just irritated enough to do it, and it must have shown.

"There was someone there with whom I did not wish to speak."

Tony gripped his pen a little tighter, pretending it was Espinoza's throat. "Whom?"

"Mr. Ragsdale."

"Ah," Tony drawled the word, giving it several extra syllables. "And why not just avoid the man? Why leave?"

"Because, he's a nasty worm, and Martha was busy, so I left." Some of the fight went out of him. "It's all because of Martha. You know, some women were born to be the cause of duels. Can I be faulted for finding her worth dying for?"

"And Ragsdale?"

"The pig! He said he'd kill me if he ever found me within ten feet of your aunt. He not agree to my offer of duel." Mr. Espinoza pressed both hands to his heart, his fingernails looked sharp but not clawlike. "That man carries a gun and a cane he swings like club. I no match for him if not in fair duel. Martha busy. I leave."

Tony wasn't sure if Espinoza knew of Ragsdale's demise. In his agitation though, his flawless English clearly had certainly developed a few cracks. "What time did you leave?"

"Why these questions?" Espinoza's face flushed and a fine bead of sweat formed at his hairline. "I dislike you."

A glance around the area showed no one close enough to overhear the conversation. "I dislike you too. I wasn't fond of Mr. Ragsdale, but I will find out why he died even if I have to haul your sorry butt out of here in handcuffs and shackles."

"Died?" Espinoza withered, deflating like a leaky balloon. "I left at half past two."

Wade drove them back to Silersville. "Did you have any idea Harrison was duel level interested in your aunt?"

"No." Tony felt a bit dazed. "I wonder if she knew."

"I think your aunt is a wonderful woman," Wade's voice trickled off.

"I do too, but fighting a duel over her? In this day and time, that's a bit unusual." Tony coughed. "Assuming what he says is the truth."

"Are you going to tell her?"

Wade's eyes were covered by very dark sunglasses, but Tony would swear he saw them sparkle with merriment. "I think what you're saying is that *you* want to be there when I tell her."

"Yes, sir." Wade bobbed his head. "I would enjoy seeing her reaction. A lot."

Minutes later they were ushered into her kitchen. In Tony's opinion, Martha's kitchen was one of the great places to visit. It was warm and full of light. It wasn't homey and worn like the kitchen in his and Theo's house, a combination kitchen and family room. Now that Gus had remodeled it, Martha's kitchen was also a very efficient place for her to cook and entertain guests. Her house had a living room, but he doubted he'd ever sat on one of her chairs or the plush sofa.

Martha poured coffee into mugs for him and Wade and set them on the table along with some brownies and cookies Tony was sure she'd bought at the festival. "Eat first, then talk."

"Have you talked to Mr. Espinoza since he left the Ramp Festival?" Tony spoke around the chunk of walnut in his mouth.

"No." Martha sighed heavily and pulled the corner off of her cookie and nibbled it. "I don't understand why he left so early. I thought he was having fun."

Next to him, Wade choked on a crumb. Tony glared at his deputy. "Drink your coffee."

"What's going on?" Martha didn't believe in beating around the bush. "You two are acting like some of my freshman English students."

Tony sighed. "How would you describe your relationship with Harrison Ragsdale?"

"Hairy Rags? We didn't have a 'relationship.' I detested the man. He was like some creepy movie villain who crawled out of caves and turned into a werewolf." She took a deep breath and released it slowly, obviously trying to calm herself. "I did receive a few anonymous letters that I'm pretty sure he wrote. They were all, 'I've worshipped you from afar for too long.' Or 'When I think of you, I'm transported to heaven.' "

"Hmm, lovely." Tony scribbled more notes. "So were you impressed?"

"Do you still have the letters?" said Wade.

"No, to both of you. I'm telling you, having an admirer like him did not make me happy. I can't count the number of times I would see his truck and take evasive action to get home or wherever I was going."

"And contacting your favorite nephew, the sheriff of this fair county, didn't fit into your plans?" Tony tried a stern look.

Instead of acting contrite, Martha handed him a cookie. "Honestly, Tony? I did think of it but I had no proof that it was him sending the letters, and I certainly didn't think he was doing anything illegal." She crumbled her own cookie into tiny bits. "At first, it was kind of fun to have a secret admirer. Only as time went along it didn't seem like so much fun, and then it felt creepy and I had no proof it was him, and then I just hoped it would stop and he would magically go 'poof' and vanish."

"I'd say having someone stab him with a wooden stake was something less than magical but certainly efficient." Tony picked another cookie from the plate.

"Is that what happened to him? He was stabbed?" Martha looked horrified. "What an awful way to die. I thought it was the potato."

Wade cleared his throat, looked at Tony for permission, and set his brownie on the napkin. "That's not exactly what happened." He paused to gather his thoughts for a minute and started again. "The actual cause of his death has not been established."

"Maybe you'll find that there was a whole gang of people who wanted to do away with him." Martha tried a smile but failed. "A potato and a wooden stake and what? Maybe a plastic spoon?"

"Really not funny, Martha." Tony leaned forward and patted her shoulder. "I know you're shocked by all this, but I believe at least two men were vying for your heart. What's to say there aren't more?"

"Is that why I can't get a date to take me to the movies? Honestly, Tony, I'm not the hot ticket around here that Blossom is."

"On that subject," said Wade, "who was the man Blossom was dancing with? Grace was drooling on my shoulder while she watched them. Don't you think a newlywed should have a bit more self-control?"

Tony couldn't help himself. He started laughing. The idea of Wade's wife preferring to look at some other guy while dancing with the man once voted "Most Gorgeous" in the Park County charity election tickled his funny bone. It was in the same election where he himself received the most votes for "Best Bald Head." The more Tony thought about it, the funnier it struck him. Martha evidently agreed, because she was in semi-hysterics. Then she developed the hiccups. Tony howled.

Wade simply sat and stared at the two of them while he drank his coffee and finished a thick, chewy brownie. A gleam of apparent satisfaction lit his dark blue eyes. The eyes once rated, "Best of Show."

"As for the handsome one, Jane calls him Doctor Looks-so-good. He's a dentist friend of Berry's. You might suggest Grace have her teeth cleaned if she wants a close-up view." Martha managed to blurt out the whole sentence before succumbing to the giggles again.

Waiting on his desk when Tony returned to his office was a photograph of the crumpled cars and a note from Sheila: "Although Mr. Brown continues to claim that he was on the property and no accident occurred, I have learned from sources who wish to remain anonymous (and I don't blame them) they saw Angus Farquhar ram into the damaged vehicles with his truck. According to these sources, he appeared to rev the engine up and charge toward the vehicle in front of him and make a

132

slight steering adjustment before doing the same in reverse."

Tony could have happily lived the rest of his life without seeing, talking to, or smelling Angus again. He could order Sheila to confront the man, but wouldn't. Sheila could handle Angus if she needed to, but why force the issue. At the very least, he'd send two male deputies with her. In truth, Angus was mean, ugly, and potentially very dangerous. Tony himself preferred having a partner when they visited.

Wade came into his office while he was considering the Angus problem, and Tony showed him Sheila's note. Wade's eyes narrowed and the muscles in his cheeks grew noticeably tighter. "I've seen her handle big and angry men, drunk or sober, with ease—but Angus is different—whether from hate or fear, she gives him a wide berth."

Tony silently agreed. "Can you imagine growing up in the Farquhar family?"

"I'd rather not." Wade leaned against the door frame. "You'd have to either become just like them or turn your back on them like his sister did. By the time she died, I'd guess there were few people who knew of their family relationship."

"Is his brother still at the penitentiary in Nashville?" Tony dreaded the day the vicious man was released.

"Yes, thank the Lord." Wade straightened. "He made Angus seem quite polite and refined."

Tony didn't disagree. "Those nephews ought to be sent to join their father. I know of many people, including my aunt, who tried and failed, to change the path they followed. They are going to kill someone eventually." Tony hoped he was wrong. "I want to pay Angus a visit, and you get to come too. Get your heavy vest; he's always surrounded with an arsenal."

Mumbling under his breath as he left Tony's office, Wade looked and sounded less than enthusiastic about the planned trip up the mountain to Angus's home. Tony thought he heard the deputy threaten to resign, but shrugged it off as an echo of his own desires.

A half hour later Tony and Wade arrived in Tony's Blazer, careful to park it where Angus would have trouble hitting it with either his truck or a bullet. Wade stuck the bullhorn out the window. "Angus Farquhar. This is Deputy Wade Claybough. Sheriff Abernathy and I are here to talk." He glanced at Tony. "I feel dumb."

Tony couldn't disagree. He also knew it was a bad idea to sneak up on Angus. Angus definitely preferred to shoot first and check to see who his visitor might have been later. Tony took the bullhorn and stepped out, staying behind the vehicle. "Angus?"

"Come on up, Sheriff." The voice was slurred. "I hope you brought the pretty deputy."

Tony didn't answer but trudged up the path with Wade on his heels. In the clearing in front of Angus's cabin sat the most miserable looking pickup in the history of vehicles. After the ceremonial greeting with Angus, they walked about the truck, giving it a cursory examination. The peeling paint was accentuated by a series of bullet holes. There didn't appear to be any extra damage to the front end, but it was protected by a dented steel grid, like the surface of an old barbeque grill. The rear bumper didn't have a square inch of undented surface.

As seemed to be his habit, Angus sat on the porch steps in his undershorts. An arsenal of guns rested on the warped wood next to a bottle of whiskey. He scratched his big pink belly and watched them, his piggy eyes not blinking. He lifted the bottle. "Drink?"

Wade shook his head.

Tony said, "No, thank you."

"Suit yourself." Angus took a deep swig from the bottle.

"There was an accident in the parking lot near the museum." Tony watched. No reaction. "Someone thought they saw your truck involved in it."

"Do tell." Angus spat into the dirt, barely missing Tony's feet. "Boys?" He pounded on the warped wooden frame surrounding the door behind him. "Get out here."

It took a few minutes, but finally the Farquhars' three "darlin" boys joined their uncle. Jocko, Geordie, and Shawn were Angus's brother's boys. Each was dumber and meaner than the other. Lined up behind Angus, they created a truly menacing appearance.

Tony didn't take his eyes off them, but he heard Wade quietly giving a running commentary through his radio to the dispatch desk. If they were gunned down, someone would know what had happened.

Angus said, "Any of you boys know about an accident with my truck? At the mus-ee-um?"

With the precision of long practice, the three spoke in almost perfect unison. "No accident."

Tony realized they were not denying the actions, just the intent. Without an impartial witness, his knowledge was useless. He could arrest them, but they'd get away with it. A glance in Wade's direction verified his thoughts.

"I haven't seen you boys around town lately." Tony knew he was fishing without bait, but he guessed they were behind the recent outbreak of burglaries. "Been off visiting the city?"

"What's it to you?" said the one in the middle of the line. Tony studied a little patch of whiskers on his chin, or rather on his neck about where his chin would be if it merged with his Adam's apple.

Tony tried a shrug and hoped he could maintain a casual attitude. What he really wanted to do was grab the little snot and put him in a dark hole. "Just curious." He didn't expect an answer but asked anyway. "Which one are you? Jocko, Shawn, or Geordie?"

"Geordie."

Surprised he'd answered, Tony asked the one on the left the same question.

"I'm Shawn."

Tony nodded and started to turn away.

"Don't you want to know my name?" The third brother's eyes flashed with anger.

"Nope," Tony said. "You're Jocko."

"How'd you know?" Jocko's nasal voice came through the trees.

Tony kept walking, climbed into the Blazer and sat staring at the Farquhar estate. He let out a big sigh and turned the ignition key. Next to him, Wade couldn't seem to stop laughing.

As they drove back down to Silersville, Wade finally managed to control himself. "Do you think Jocko's figured out yet how you knew his name?"

"Sheriff?" Doc Nash's voice poured into his ear. "I'm calling about the scratch marks on your victim's neck."

Tony leaned back in his chair. "Let me guess, you think he was clawed by a bear? Everyone is still looking for Baby."

"I hope you find Baby for Roscoe's sake. The man has become quite enamored with her and frankly, I'd like to examine her claws just for fun, but you're wrong." The doctor sounded positively genial. "I love being the one bearing—no pun intended—the news."

"So what are they from?" Tony reached for the pen and note-pad on his desk.

"If I'm right they're definitely human. This is just a guess, but the idea came to me over lunch. You'll need confirmation from the pathologist doing the autopsy."

Tony remembered the narrow furrows dug deeply into the flesh of Ragsdale's neck. Tony studied his own fingernails, pretending to scratch himself. If he dug hard enough to draw blood, they would leave wider and shallower marks. Maybe Ragsdale had encountered a woman with smaller hands and longer nails. "Are you thinking they'll find nail polish?"

"Nope. Not a woman." The doctor's attitude had gone past "genial" and he suddenly began laughing out loud. A real gut buster. "Give up?"

"Yes." Tony's imagination failed him, and it made him a little surly. "If you can quit laughing long enough to tell me, I'd love to know."

"A male musician who files the fingernails on his pickin' hand to a point. It's not everyone's manicure of choice, but I've seen some like it." Doc Nash cleared his throat. "Nor is it the most savory looking manicure."

Now that the doctor described it, Tony remembered seeing someone at the festival with fingernails matching his description. A male musician whose partner was a woman. Tony would be able to get the name from his aunt or mother. His initial elation over having a clue shattered with the reality of talking to those two women. "Thanks, Doc, I'll follow up on your clue as soon as possible."

Predictably, Tony found Jane and Martha together in the museum office. When Celeste met him at the door she had whispered, "See if you can cheer them up."

"Ladies?" He thought he'd try for a pleasant beginning.

Two unhappy faces turned in his direction. Silence. Okay, he'd better change tactics. "I hope you two are not trying to take personal responsibility for the death of Harrison Ragsdale." He frowned. "Unless you either finished him off or hired a hit man."

Martha responded. "I'm not sorry Hairy Rags is dead, but honestly, Tony, couldn't he have waited until he got home to die?" Her disgusted attitude seemed to awaken his mom from a coma.

Jane opened her hand and pulled out a wadded up tissue. She smoothed it more or less flat and then folded it very neatly into fourths. "I simply do not understand what happened." Looking up at him, she sighed. "Everyone was having a wonderful time. The food was good. The music was good. Roscoe and Quentin and Professor Veronica and her friend were the hits of the day."

Tony noticed her flinch when she said "hits." "In case you're concerned, the potato hitting him did not injure Ragsdale. The exact cause of death has not been established, but all the early reports say he was not harmed by the spud."

"Oh, thank goodness. I know poor Quentin has been frantic, thinking his cannon might have actually killed someone. Even if it was Hairy." Jane had to pause and wipe more tears away. "I'm so relieved."

Martha handed her sister a fresh tissue. "Did you come to tell us this?"

Tony shook his head. "I actually came to ask about one of your musical acts." Both women stared at him. "Specifically, I need the names and contact information for male string musicians."

"What do you want with them?"

"I think one of them might have left some scratches on Ragsdale's neck."

"Like these?" Martha extended her arm, displaying a strip of narrow gouges in her arm. "Someone grabbed my arm for a fleeting moment and left a mark."

Tony nodded. "I don't suppose you remember which musician did that?"

Martha thought about it. Then shook her head. "Sorry."

Silently, Jane's mouth opened and closed, making her look like a goldfish that had leaped from its bowl onto a table. Leaving her sister gasping, Martha walked to a nearby file cabinet and retrieved a folder. Inside, each musical act had a separate form, including contact information and releases from liability.

"Thank you." Tony pulled out several forms and handed them to his mother. "I don't suppose you can make copies."

Jane managed to get to her feet, took the papers and headed for a small copy machine.

Tony spoke softly to his aunt. "Is she going to be all right?"

Martha's shoulders rose and fell before she answered in her school-teacher voice, the one she used to get attention in the back row. "My sister has always delighted in taking responsibility for issues she didn't create." In a softer voice, she spoke only to him. "I don't know. This seems to have hit her harder than I would have guessed. After all, she detested the man."

"I don't—didn't detest him." Jane returned and handed Tony the papers he needed. "He wasn't all bad."

As lies went, this one was fairly obvious. Tony knew his mother rarely had anything openly harsh to say about anyone. "Coarse." Was as close to total condemnation as she could usually manage. He'd once heard her describe a serial killer as "not a very nice person."

"Okay, what wasn't bad about him?" Martha managed to blurt out her question before Tony got his mouth open.

"Give me a minute to think." Jane went quiet, holding her hand up, palm forward to insure they didn't interrupt. "Well, he did yard work for his elderly parents, but that was before they died, of course." She flashed Tony a motherly smile, one clearly taking note of his not ever even mowing her yard for her.

As a distraction, Tony considered it masterful. "You always say you don't want me to touch anything in your yard."

"True. And I haven't changed my mind." Jane was magnanimous in her victory. "Oh, and I've seen him working with a group helping do repairs on homes belonging to our needy, mostly elderly citizens. The ones without pets."

Tony realized she was right and admitted it. "I have seen him at work on a few projects. It just isn't how I usually think of him."

Jane's smile was brilliant, and she shrugged just a bit, taking the edge off her victory. "Frankly, I don't either."

CHAPTER TEN

Monday, Tony began working through the list of musicians who had performed at the festival. Thankfully they lived either in Park County itself, or one of the neighboring counties. He and Wade decided to tackle them in alphabetical order, just to have some kind of plan. The "may we see your fingernails" or "may we scrape under your nails" did not seem like a request particularly designed to make friends or gain much cooperation. If the scratcher was smart, he'd have clipped his nails off the second he left the grounds, if not before. Unless, of course, the scratches were on his neck before Ragsdale arrived at the festival and Tony was just running in circles.

Randal Byers was first name on the list. Tony wasn't familiar with the man or the name. He assumed Mr. Byers was either new, or law abiding, or both. When they knocked on his front door, a little girl opened it, just a crack. She stared at his uniform.

Tony smiled at her. "Is Randal here?"

The little girl glanced over her shoulder and back at him. She chewed her lower lip for a moment before saying, "My daddy's at work."

When faced with the question of where dad worked, she was clearly out of her area of expertise. She vanished and returned with an elderly woman.

The woman listened to their question politely enough then said, "Randy works at the fertilizer plant. He's my grandson.

They moved in here with me, and I stay with the girl." Having delivered her statement, she closed the door in their faces.

Wade made a note on their paper. "Okay, do we go to the next name or to the fertilizer plant first?"

Tony supposed being sheriff gave him the responsibility of making these incredibly difficult decisions on the fly. "Geographically, what or who is closest to our current location?"

Wade studied the list. "A who. Pops Ogle."

"No way." Tony stopped just short of the Blazer's door. "I never noticed his fingernails looking like that, and I've known the man for years."

"Me either." Wade checked his list. "But we have a witness who saw the nails on somebody."

Tony climbed in and turned the key. "Well, let's go find out. At this time of day, Pops should be in his office."

Owan Ogle, known around the county as "Pops," was the county clerk. His musical claim to fame was his amazing skill playing the mandolin. It wasn't uncommon for him to use his vacation time to go to Nashville and have his work recorded, usually accompanying gospel singers. His name was in small print on hundreds of recordings. He did it for love, barely making enough to cover his hotel expenses.

"Hey, Pops." Tony greeted the man.

Pops half rose from his position at the computer. His hands rested on the desk. Sure enough, the nails on his right hand were neatly filed to points. The ones on his left were clipped so short Tony saw no fingernail growing past the nail bed.

"Hey there, Sheriff. Wade." Pops made a half bow and sat down again. "How can I serve law enforcement today?"

Now that they were standing face to face, so to speak, although sitting put Pops at a definite height disadvantage, Tony wasn't sure what he wanted to ask.

Wade took over. "There's been some question about your

fingernails."

Pops looked down at his hands and back up. "They're mine all right." He suddenly got a case of the giggles and his belly bounced up and down. With his thin chest and round belly, he looked like he had stuffed a water balloon under his shirt. "Is someone missing theirs?" The more he talked, and the funnier he found the topic, the faster the belly moved.

Tony cleared his throat hoping he wouldn't laugh too. "I'm afraid it's a bit more serious. We're trying to piece together the events about the time Harrison Ragsdale died."

Pops blinked and went quiet. "Am I a suspect or something?"

"We're just collecting information." Wade held his notebook. "I don't remember seeing your current manicure style before. You haven't always had the right-hand fingernails filed to a point like this?"

Pops glanced down at his fingers and shook his head. "A musician friend of mine suggested I try it for the guitar. Claims he gets superior sound and control. He says it's much better than a pick."

"What's your opinion?" Tony ran his own fingernails across his palm, wondering what having claws would feel like.

"So far, I like the sound better, but my fingers get real sore." Pops gave a little shrug. "I'm guessing I'll go back to using my pick pretty soon. Like the one I use on the mandolin. My wife claims I look some wild animal at the dinner table and wants me to cut them. She won't fry a chicken 'cause she says she don't want to see me holding it with my claws."

"On that note"—Tony cleared his throat—"could we have a tiny sample of your fingernails, a clipping, even some filing dust?"

"Sure." Pops opened his desk drawer, pulled out a sheet of paper and an emery board and sawed some of the already-short nails, even shorter, leaving the pointed nails alone. "That good?"

Tony nodded and made a note on the label of an evidence envelope, folded the paper and sealed it inside.

Pops had cooperated but he wasn't without curiosity. "Don't suppose you'll tell me why you want them shavings?"

"Someone clawed Mr. Ragsdale not long before his death." Tony sighed. "We're only trying not to overlook anything or anyone, just in case."

"Then you be sure to check with that foreign-looking guy your aunt hangs out with." Pops didn't look angry, just concerned they might not have all the information needed. "He's got a real set on him."

Tony and Wade eventually caught up with Randal Byers in the parking lot of the fertilizer plant. "Can we talk a minute?"

Randal, a pleasant-looking young man, smiled and nodded. "Much longer than a minute, and my grandmother will have a fit. She's a sweetheart, but she's no spring chicken and my daughter's a busy little girl. I'm lucky she baby-sits as it is."

"Fair enough." Tony bypassed all the chitchat. "Could we see your hands?"

Randal's forehead wrinkled in apparent confusion. "Someone find an extra?"

"If you lost one, I expect you'd have reported it missing by now." Wade shook his head. "We're checking the musicians from Saturday. You do play the guitar?"

"Sure thing." Randal extended his hands palm up then turned them palm down. "Want me to make a fist or anything?"

Tony looked at the fingernails. They weren't chewed off and they weren't longer on one hand than the other. In fact, they looked about as ordinary, and as slightly dirty, as any fingernails Tony had ever seen. Not surprisingly, there were small calluses on his fingers.

Wade made a note and Tony stepped back. "Thank you, that's

all we need."

Randal climbed into his pickup and started the engine. Then he rolled down his window and looked Tony in the eye. "If you ever see your way clear to explaining what we just did and why we did it, I'd love to know the reason. Right now, I'm headed home."

Tony nodded.

"Okay, who else is on the list?" Tony slid his key into the ignition. "I'd love to get this done and go home for my own dinner and play with my own kids."

"Mr. and Mrs. Edward Hall, who live in the Oak Lawn Trailer Court." Wade read his notes. "Number four."

"Eddie and Ginger." Tony sighed. He had more than a passing familiarity with the Halls. "Mr. and Mrs. Edward Hall sound like a quite dignified couple, don't you think? Maybe pillars of the community and the first to volunteer to collect roadside garbage?"

"And they're chairing the fund-raiser to build a new library building," Wade added. He wasn't able to keep the grin from his face. "When they return from their world cruise."

Tony ignored Wade's smirk and nodded. "Maybe they'll even learn to read, if they ever sober up."

As expected, Eddie and Ginger were not involved in a discussion about the omens and portents found in *Moby Dick*. Eddie appeared to have passed out in his lawn chair and fallen backwards. In a clearly desperate and loving attempt to rouse him, Ginger was pelting him with burnt bits of hot dogs. The family pets, a pair of mangy looking curs, were crazed by the meat flying through the air, barking, howling, and yapping, they dove across Eddie's prostrate body. Just to add to the entertainment, there were episodes of fighting between the canines when one snagged a piece the other expected to eat. Fangs bared and spittle flying, they growled and lunged at each other.

Tony and Wade climbed out of the Blazer and were met with a few boos. The crux of the situation was that the audience, consisting of the other residents of the Oak Lawn, looked concerned Tony and Wade were there to break up the evening's entertainment. To relieve their anxiety, Wade waved and grinned while Tony walked over and stood near Eddie's body draped over his chair. Sure enough, his right hand had fingernails like claws and the ones on the left were chewed to the cuticles.

"I don't want to keep you from your dog training." Tony smiled at Ginger, doing his best to ignore the barking and yapping behind him. "I need to talk to Eddie about his fingernails."

"What about 'em?" Ginger's breath bore strong overtones of gin. "I hope there's a law against 'em. Ugly things. And while we're on the subject, I can't say they make his guitar picking any better."

"Well, I need his permission to take a little scraping off a fingernail." Tony hoped breathing shallowly would prevent his own alcohol level from rising.

Ginger pounced on his suggestion. "Permission, hell, take what you want. Wait! She ran into the trailer and was back in seconds with a pair of kitchen shears. "I hate those things." And with that, she clipped two of the fingernails off almost to the quick and handed them to Tony. "That enough?"

Tony agreed it was, put the clippings in an envelope, and climbed into the Blazer. As he and Wade drove away, a glance in his rearview mirror showed Ginger toss another hot dog bit. The dog show recommenced. Eddie remained oblivious.

The neighbors cheered.

CHAPTER ELEVEN

"I sure wish we'd hear something definitive about the cause of death." Tony paced in his office, cell phone gripped in one hand, willing it to ring. It did, but the caller was dispatcher Flavio Weems.

"Sir, I've got a male caller on the line who claims to be Mr. Ragsdale's attorney. Says he needs to talk to you about the dead man's will. He read about his death in the newspaper."

"I'd love to talk to him. Put him through to my office phone." Tony settled onto his chair when the desk phone rang. After brief introductions, the attorney launched into his reason for calling.

"I have the will of Harrison Ragsdale."

"Who inherits?" Tony thought if there was any decent amount of money in the estate, it could supply a motive if indeed the death was ruled suspicious. He found it hard to imagine the cause of death was anything but natural causes or an accident.

"It's quite a large estate, Sheriff, and the will is fairly complex. The main beneficiaries are his wife and nephew." He cleared his throat. "I don't suppose you can tell me anything about the cause of my client's death."

"It has not been determined as yet." Tony choked back a sneeze. "Do you have contact information for these people? Wait a minute, did you say *wife?*" Tony had never heard anything about Ragsdale and a wife.

"Yes. The wife goes by the name Jessica Baxter, and the

nephew is Randal Byers. I have Silersville addresses for both of them."

"And the rest?" Tony thought it was an interesting co-incidence Randal Byers was on this list too. He'd gone from never hearing of the man to hearing his name twice in two days.

The attorney talked on. "A couple of charities stand to get a share of it, unless one or both of these heirs is disqualified, in which case they'd get a much larger share. The remaining heir would not receive a larger portion."

Tony thought "disqualified" was the attorney's way to describe "murderer." "What *can* you tell me about your client? He wasn't our most popular citizen."

"Very little." The attorney paused. "I can't say I found him very likeable, but that hardly constitutes proof of anything. His check didn't bounce."

Tony was silent for a moment. "When did he make this will?"

"Two weeks ago." The lawyer continued. "I had the impression he expected his death to be imminent, but he certainly looked healthy enough when he came in to sign it. Even I know you can't always tell by looking."

"Imminent?" Tony pounced on the word. "Did he give you the name of his doctor by any chance?"

"No. I handled the will, that's all."

Tony thanked the attorney, disconnected, and stared at his new notes and the ones from the previous day, trying to decide his next move when the cacophony of fire trucks headed out on a call interrupted him, the sound loud even in his office. The sheriff's department and volunteer firefighters and search and rescue all used the same dispatch line, and although the fire department had their own way of doing things, a 911 call was heard by all.

The most frequent calls for the fire department involved automobile accidents and chimney fires. The first information on this call was a single family home burning. He recognized the address as one of the new houses out of town near Nina's home. It would have to be on the opposite side of the natural park named for her father, its creator. In the middle of the afternoon, with good weather, he doubted the fire was caused by lightning.

Tony assumed his office needed to provide crowd control if not more assistance. Nothing brought the citizens of Park County out in force like a disaster or misfortune. A fire of any size had potential to provide both. He headed for the Blazer. He'd drive up and see what else might be needed.

He pulled onto the highway right behind the ambulance. Not a good sign. The radio chattered with voices issuing instructions and calling for assistance. If their firefighters couldn't deal with the problem, the call would go out to neighboring counties for help. Given the location of the home, a fire might even create a forest fire. All it needed was a slight wind to fan the flames into some of the aged trees or brush.

The early spring had been abnormally dry, and it wouldn't take much to start a disaster. Before he even reached the fork in the road leading to the blazing house, Tony could see smoke and flames above the trees. As he made the final turn, he pulled onto the shoulder to let another fire engine fly past. The house, a two-story beauty built of stone with large beams and wooden shutters, had a European castle feel. It looked like everything but the stones were completely ablaze.

Huge flames rose above the roof. Tony heard the whoosh and roar of it, sounding like a tornado. The firefighters were spraying the nearby trees. Nothing could help the house. He walked closer, careful to stay out of the way, trying not to breathe in too much smoke.

Wendell Cox, the fire chief, talked into a radio as Tony approached. He included Tony in his statement. "Residents and family animals, all accounted for, all fine." He pointed to a cluster of people wrapped in blankets, huddled by the ambulance. "One of the children, the little boy, suffered some smoke inhalation, but it doesn't seem too bad."

"Any idea what caused this?" Tony flinched when the beams of the house finally collapsed and the roof fell into the flames, sending a volcano of sparks and ash into the sky. His eyes watered.

"Haven't had much time to think about it." Cox shook his head. "The place was fully engaged by the time we arrived. If it was a chimney fire, what happened to the smoke alarms?"

"I know these people, sort of." Tony focused on the family. The woman, standing with two children, was one of Theo's quilting friends, and her husband had something to do with the fertilizer plant on the edge of town. One of the few new businesses in the area. "Nice people. Where's the husband?"

"I talked to him. He's on his way. You might want to find out if they have any enemies." Cox stared past him at the burning house. He frowned. "I'm calling in an arson investigator. This is well out of my league, but even I can tell this was deliberate."

"You and your team are doing a great job." Tony didn't relish the idea of charging into a fire. He'd done some initial training with fire and knew it wasn't for him. He'd rather be shot again than enter a burning building—hot, dark, and airless.

"Hey, Sheriff." Cox waved to attract Tony's attention again and continued listening to his radio. "It's a good thing you're here. We've got a big problem, and I'm going to give it to you."

Tony didn't like the way this sounded. He stared at the almost skeletal remains of the house. How had it burned so fast? "Definitely arson?"

"Well, that too. I'm pretty sure we'll find lots of evidence pointing to an accelerant." Cox shook his head. "But what you get is the body in the garage, or what's left of the body and the remnants of the garage. Since I'm the fire chief only when called from my job as an electrician, I'm handing him over to you. You've got arson and maybe a murder."

"You're sure it's human remains?"

"Oh, yeah." Cox stared at his boots. "It's none of my crew. I'd call the doctor if I was you. I don't know what killed him, but he's certainly dead in suspicious circumstances."

Tony recognized good advice when he heard it. He called for Doc Nash and Wade. The last thing Tony wanted to deal with was a burnt body. He'd heard it would smell like roast pork. If that was the case, Tony doubted he'd be enjoying any barbeques for a long time.

As he made his way over to the homeowners, he thought wretched and miserable didn't quite cover the way Susan Smith and her children looked. The three of them were wrapped in blankets and sat with the dog, next to the ambulance. Smudged with smoke and grime, the children clung to the piece of nylon cord someone had given them to use as a makeshift leash. He guessed it was more for the children's benefit than a necessity. The dog, a big beautiful collie, shivered and whined at their feet, occasionally giving one of them a doggy kiss, and gave no appearance of wanting to leave.

"You've spoken to your husband?" Tony said.

Susan nodded. "He's on his way."

"Can you tell us what happened?" Tony and Wade and the fire chief formed a small semicircle shielding her from the sight of her destroyed house. The air reeked of smoke and ash. "Did the smoke alarms go off?"

"Yes, that's when we ran outside." Susan pulled the children closer. "It was just an ordinary school day. We dropped Zach at school and Lotti and I ran some errands while Nicholas was at story time in the library. When story time ended, the kids and I stopped for a few groceries and came home. Nothing exotic." She shivered. "We pulled into the garage and closed the door."

The little girl began to wheeze. Susan patted her gently.

"And then?" Wade said.

"We carried the groceries into the kitchen and I started putting them away. Lotti and Nicholas ran off to the family room to play." Susan paused and closed her eyes. "I heard a loud thump. And then a pop, like a balloon or small firecracker going off. Then the smoke alarms all over the house starting shrieking, so I grabbed the kids and Jeff and my cell phone. Even as we ran outside, I was calling nine-one-one." She opened her eyes. They were bloodshot and teary. "All the sudden there was another, louder boom, and everything was on fire."

"Jeff?" the fire chief looked confused.

"Jeff's the dog," said Susan. For emphasis the big dog thumped his plumed tail on the ground.

"There's no one else supposed to be here?" Tony wrote the names and her description in his notebook. "A neighbor, a cleaning woman, relatives who would have access to the house?"

"No. Why?" Susan's eyes went glassy. "Was someone found or something?"

Tony was saved from having to answer her question in front of the children by the husband making his way toward them. Medium tall, with average features tightened by fear, the man didn't seem to notice the house at first because he was clearly searching for his wife and kids. They all hugged together in a knot, the dog whining in the center of the huddle.

When Mr. Smith finally turned to look toward the house, all color leached from his face. "W-what happened?"

The chief answered. "I'm afraid at first glance, it looks like arson."

"Who-oo?"

"Ah, now's there is an interesting question." Tony and the

fire chief led Mr. Smith a slight distance from his family. "Anyone angry at you?"

"That's ridiculous." He shook his head. "I'm just an ordinary guy."

"Make any enemies at work? Get along with the neighbors? No one thinks your dog barks too much?" Tony knew all too well a motive didn't have to make sense to anyone but the perpetrator.

"We, the company, had to let a couple of people go last week. And besides, why burn my house when I'm not home? Wouldn't they come after me or some other executive?"

"What would be worse?" Tony said. "Losing your life or losing your family?"

"Oh, my God." Ashen and shaking, the man collapsed as if his bones had dissolved, sitting heavily onto the ground. "I didn't imagine."

"So what were the names of the people you had to let go? If they had nothing to do with the fire, it should be easy enough to eliminate them as suspects." What Tony didn't say was if the body in the garage was one of the unhappy former employees, it wouldn't exactly clear up all the questions.

Tony stared at the building, thinking, and watched the fire fighters putting their equipment back in order. The chief stood near the open garage, staring in. He beckoned for Tony to join him.

"What do you see, Chief?"

"It don't make sense." The chief pointed to the burned wreck of a car, the doorway into the house, and the spot between them where the body was discovered. "She had to see it there, and the kids would have seen it too."

"Maybe someone was hidden in the garage and just got caught when the fire started."

"Maybe, but I don't think so. Even a crazy person would dive for the door into the house but I've got an idea." The chief rubbed his chin, smudging it further. "There was an accelerant used on him."

At the idea of being torched, Tony's stomach protested. "Are you sure?"

"Yep." The chief's eyes were badly bloodshot and his face spotted with grime and ash, but there was no doubt he was serious. "He was burnt much worse than the stuff around him. Look at that." He motioned upwards.

Tony glanced up through the hole that had once been the garage roof. "You think he could have been on fire when he fell through the roof?"

"Yep." The chief nodded. "I'm thinking that's the way it happened."

"He was on fire and stayed on the roof until it collapsed?" Tony shook his head, trying to dispel the nausea conjured by the horrific image. "I hope he was already dead when he started to burn."

They walked farther out on the yard and stared up. Too much of the house was gone for them to gauge the circumstances. The chief slapped Tony on the back. "Don't worry. We'll get you a report that will help tell you what you need to know, but you're the one who has to figure out why our body was on the roof."

Tony sincerely thanked the chief, but found himself hoping the report would arrive in the next ten minutes and would explain every detail, especially why there was a dead man or woman, and who or what caused him to be dead. In the meantime, he wanted to talk to the family and to the recently fired factory employees.

Tony radioed for someone to pick up the two men who were the recent fertilizer company layoffs and bring them to his office, and he wanted them there by the time he drove back to town and let everyone in his department know it. If one of those men turned out to be the body in the garage, he wasn't sure if that would make things better or worse. The charred body in the garage disturbed him on several levels. Why didn't Susan and the kids see the body when they returned home?

When he studied it, it looked to him like her minivan stopped just short of the body. If it wasn't there when they got home, how much time had elapsed between their arrival and the start of the fire. Where did the body come from? Was it a man or woman? How did it catch fire?

Anger flooded through him when he thought about Susan being home alone with small children when the fire began. Until they identified the body, Tony suspected everyone, including Susan. What if Zach's birth mother came to the house, and Susan killed her and set the fires to cover it up? Stupid, but people did stupid things even more often than they committed crimes.

Tony climbed into his Blazer, opened the console, and pulled out his jar of antacids. Munching a few, he stared at the burnt-out house. The extent of the damage was shocking. The roof was gone. The upstairs, floor and all, had collapsed into the lower level. Half-burned carpet hung suspended where the staircase had been. Every pane of glass was shattered. Shrubbery was burned to a crisp. If the fire wasn't caused deliberately, he'd turn in his badge. He didn't have to be an arson specialist to see the house had burned from the top down.

But who, and why? Could it have been caused by the owners? Person or persons unknown? With what motivation? Why would someone come to a house with the intent to burn it down? Was it a spur-of-the-moment action? "I'm here and not doing anything else, so I'll burn down the house?" That didn't feel right. Did the owners expect to be paid enough in insurance to cover rebuilding and extra to pay for something else? Arson for profit?

"That is so awful." Theo was at the shop when she answered a phone call from Nina giving her the news. Nina had seen the smoke from her house and gone over to the house and taken the family into her home. "Why weren't you at school? Are they staying with you?" Theo knew she wasn't giving Nina a chance to answer one question before asking the next. She held her breath to stop talking.

Nina began. "I started feeling really ill, and since I don't have a class during the last school period, I came home early." Nina's voice lowered. "I think Susan and her family will move into the Riverview Motel later today, but Theo, they've lost everything. They're just sitting together hugging each other. I've left them alone to give them a bit of privacy. Not to mention, I doubt catching my flu bug would make them feel any better."

"It's lucky you were able to help them. Can you imagine losing everything? All the baby pictures?" Theo didn't have the flu, but she felt sick and light-headed just thinking about having all her family treasures destroyed.

"Susan doesn't even have her purse. There was not enough time to grab it." Nina snuffled quietly. "She and the kids were lucky they got out of the house before it exploded."

"Exploded?" Theo felt the shock of the word as if it hit her. "It wasn't a fire?"

"I don't think anyone knows how it started." Nina's voice quavered. "Your husband and the fire chief and Wade and Sheila were out there stringing crime scene tape when I arrived. And not just around the house. They were going partway into the woods. They looked very serious. As I was leaving, I had to show my ID to Darlin' Darren, and he's known me since I was his baby-sitter. He wrote down my license plate number and took my picture too."

Theo sensed there was more. "And?"

"And at first I didn't think Tony was going to let me bring the family here. I swear it looked like he wanted to lock them up somewhere, but I'm not sure why." Nina whispered, "He had this tight jaw and squinty look. I've never seen him look so intimidating."

Theo knew the look Nina described. When Tony wore it, something very serious was happening.

"We ought to be able to gather some clothes and toiletries from the other quilters." Theo stood by the cash register, relaying the information to Gretchen and her customer. "Can you imagine having everything go poof? Your pictures, favorite toys, your clothes, even your underwear."

Theo watched as Gretchen carefully folded the yardage she'd just cut. Her hands trembled.

"It makes me want to cry," said Gretchen.

Theo blinked back her own tears. Crying would not help. "While you keep an eye on the shop, I'm going to run up to Nina's house and see if I can get a list of sizes and their most immediate needs."

By the time she had the twins loaded in the SUV, Theo had begun a mental list of the most pressing things she could supply. She was certain Susan and her family were in shock and probably in denial.

Theo's eyes overflowed, just thinking about them losing their home. At least the whole family was fine.

As Theo approached the turn into Nina's driveway, she saw Tony's Blazer blocking it so she parked on the edge of the road. Wade had parked his vehicle behind Tony's. Tony climbed out of the Blazer and walked toward her. "Go home, Theo, or at least back to the shop."

Theo blinked, surprised. He never talked to her like that. Tony didn't give her a chance to speak; just turned his back to her and walked up the sidewalk. As she watched, Tony went inside and seconds later Nina came out of her own house, wearing a raincoat over her pajamas.

Nina climbed into Theo's vehicle and covered her face with a tissue. "I'll try not to breathe on you or the girls. I'm really sick and hope I'm not contagious. There's a fire in the area, and your husband just told me to get out of my own house."

Theo thought Nina looked as bad as she sounded. "Is the family okay?"

"As okay as they can be with their house burned down around them. No one had much to say while I was around. They were clearly in shock, so I gave them blankets to wrap up in and some hot coffee, but I think they're too stunned to cry." Nina wiped her own eyes. "I did hear John call the insurance company to ask what they needed to do first."

Theo stared at the front door. No sign of Tony or Wade returning. "I came because Gretchen and I felt so bad and wanted to see how we could help. I'm in charge of getting sizes so we can at least supply a change of clothes and some toiletries."

Nina snuffled. "Oh, look."

Theo saw Tony walking toward his car, carrying the little girl. Walking behind him was Susan. The big collie had his muzzle pressed against her thigh. Susan's husband and son looked like refugees, wrapped in blankets and moving slowly behind the rest. Theo guessed they felt like refugees too. Tony put the little girl in a car seat he moved to the backseat of the Blazer while the couple settled the boy and climbed in, their movements stiff and awkward.

Tony opened the rear hatch and the collie jumped inside. Closing it carefully, Tony turned toward Theo. She thought he must have realized he couldn't ignore her because he came to her SUV, rested his arm on the roof, and leaned in.

"Sorry I was so brusque. You can help." Tony rolled his

shoulders. "And thank you, Nina, for having the sense to bring them here. I was shocked when they vanished, but staying near the rubble of the house wasn't going to do them any good, and they would only be in the way of the fire investigation."

Theo thought he looked almost as bad as the family had. "Some of us want to help supply the basic necessities for tonight. Where are they going?"

"The Riverview Motel." Tony attempted a smile. "I'm sure the family would all appreciate some clean clothes, toothpaste, and stuff to get them through the next twenty-four hours or so. They'll have lots of talks with the insurance company and with me, and with any number of other branches of the law. We'll stop by the school and pick up Zach, the older boy, on our way, so give us a head start."

Theo sensed there was something more, something deeper, going on here than a house fire. "What happened?"

Tony stared at Theo then at Nina. "I know the pair of you are more likely to talk less if I tell you than if I make you dig the information from someone else. A person died in the fire, or shortly before the fire. We don't know who, and we don't know when, how, or why. Lips sealed?"

Shocked by the unexpected news, Theo could only nod. No wonder everyone was acting like there was some giant secret. There was.

Nina croaked. "I promise, Tony." After he turned to walk away, Nina climbed out of Theo's car. "I'm going back to bed. When I wake up, this had better be a nightmare."

Tony would be thrilled if it all turned out to be a nightmare. As he watched the family huddled in his vehicle, he doubted any dream would have such strong details. The pervasive smell of the smoke was too sharp to be imaginary. Susan's face had tear tracks etched through soot. Even the little girl had smudges of ash on her cheeks. The husband was making a valiant effort to be upbeat and to distract everyone from their thoughts, but his thoughts were all too clearly focused on what they had almost lost, what they had lost, and what else they still might lose.

"I can't imagine what happened." John Smith's voice matched his dazed expression. "How did the fire start and why did it burn so quickly? And now you say there was someone in the garage? Who?"

Susan's voice was barely more than a whisper. "There was no one in the garage when I parked in there. I would have noticed. It's not like the place is, or was, filled with lots of clutter, and it wasn't dark. The overhead lights came on as usual and sunlight came through the windows in the big door." Susan kept going over the events as if looking for something she'd missed. "We closed the garage door before going into the house, and the opener is so sensitive that once the door starts down, it will go back up automatically if even a mouse runs through the gap so I know no one came in behind us."

Tony wanted them to stop talking. He wanted to say, "It's okay. Everything will be resolved and you'll be good as new." But he knew they'd never be the same. They might be just as fine or even better, but not the same. The smell of smoke would not be a pleasant aroma for many years, if ever. Depending on what caused the fire in the first place, they might become insomniacs, or sleep in shifts just to be sure they were safe or it wouldn't happen again.

Tony stopped at the school. The dad ran inside. A few minutes later, he and the boy, Zach, a miniature of his father, climbed in and they all talked at once and tried to explain why they weren't going home.

Tony wondered if it could be the boy's birth mother in the garage. Had she come to reclaim the boy and gotten in a fight with Susan? Could the apparently broken-hearted woman in his backseat have burnt her own house in an attempt to cover another crime?

At the Riverview, John Smith used his credit card to rent a room while the rest of them stood clustered in the lobby. Behind him, Tony could hear Susan. He was sure she was talking to herself. "My credit cards are destroyed. I have no driver's license. But that's okay, because I have no car."

Tony guessed if anyone knew much personal information about the two men who lost their jobs, it would be someone at Caroline Proffitt's Okay Bar and Bait Shop. It was the unofficial clubhouse for most of the county's single men without families.

Caroline, known by her customers as Mom, smiled and waved at Tony and Wade from behind the bar. The platform she stood on added enough height for her to be able to reach the glasses behind her and across the full width of the bar. After her husband died and she took over running the bar, the platform made her work possible, and the office was converted to accommodate her children's needs. Some of her ideas had been borrowed by the equally short Theo when she was designing her own workroom.

The barroom had the ambiance of a clubhouse more than a drinking or party facility. This wasn't the place men came looking for a date. Except for the lack of beds, it was as close to a home as some of them had. They watched television together, played cards, played pool. Talked about women. Smoking was only allowed outside. Rumor said a couple of single women moved to town and went there one evening looking to meet men and ended up leaving alone and told their friends all the men were more interested in watching television and talking to each other rather than to girls.

At this time of day, after lunch and before dinner, the only customers were a couple of guys playing a competitive video game, and a lone man with bright orange hair who sat in the corner drinking ice water and reading a comic book.

"We need to ask you about a couple of men, maybe they're your customers, maybe not." Tony sat on a stool near Mom. Wade sat next to him and placed enlarged copies of two driver's licenses on the bar and turned them so Mom could see them clearly. "Do you know these fellows?"

"They've been in here from time to time. They weren't regulars, so not every week, much less every day." Mom pointed to the picture on her left. "This one I didn't much care for."

"Why?" Tony considered Mom as good a judge of character as anyone he'd ever met. She could size a man up with a glance. "He spit on your floor?"

Mom laughed. "No, he wasn't that bad, or I'd have thrown him out and never let him in again. He just struck me as kinda skeezy."

"Skeezy?" Wade held up his notepad. "You want me to write skeezy in my report?"

"Want a better word?" Mom shrugged. "I don't know. He just seemed not quite nice."

Tony pointed to the second photo. "And this one was better?"

"Yes. I did kinda feel sorry for him. I don't think he liked the other man, but didn't seem to know any of the other men who come in here. You know, like he'd moved to town and worked with the skeezy one and made the mistake of being polite to him and then couldn't get rid of him."

"He never came alone?"

"Nope. Neither of them ever came alone." Mom wiped the spotless bar with a sparkling white towel. "They came in last week, maybe Thursday, and they had lost their jobs at the fertilizer plant. They both had too much to drink, and I had Daniel drive them to their homes and give them their keys back. By noon the next day their vehicles were gone. If you need their addresses, I'm sure Daniel can help."

"Thanks, Mom." Tony glanced around. No one was paying any attention to their conversation. "What about other employees from the plant? They have much to say about the layoffs?"

"I heard a fair amount of grousing about the workers getting dumped on and management not taking a hit." Mom stood motionless. "A couple of guys said something about being relieved they still had work. You know, better thee than me kind of stuff, but sympathetic." She sighed. "There was something I heard that struck me as odd at the time, but I swear I'm losing my memory."

"If it comes back to you, give me a call. Day or night." Tony handed her a card with his cell phone number.

"That sounds serious, Tony. What's going on?"

"You'll hear about it soon enough from someone." Tony kept his voice low. "There's been a fire at the home of one of the fertilizer executives. Maybe it was just an accident, or maybe it was arson. Maybe it's a case of arson mixed with murder, but someone died up there."

"Oh, no. I hope it's not the family with the three little kids." Mom looked horrified. "I've seen them around at different events and they seem so nice—all of them. I don't know any of the others."

"No. The family escaped, but it was a close thing." Tony didn't want to go into any details. "They lost everything."

"Then who's dead?"

"An excellent question, Mom. I don't know." Tony pulled some antacids out of his pocket, dusted them off, and chewed slowly. "It might be one of these two men or neither. So far we haven't been able to locate either one of them. I'd appreciate it if you'd keep your ears open. I know you don't spy on your adult boys here, but men, beer, and bragging are a powerful trio. You might learn something I should know by a comment made in passing."

Mom nodded and put his card in the cash drawer. "I hope you find out what happened."

CHAPTER TWELVE

Rising early the next morning, Theo hurried because she expected it would be an exceptionally busy day at the shop. Between the events at the festival and the fire at Susan's home, the classroom would most likely be packed with quilters working and gossiping. As she showered, she thought she'd better pick up some extra coffee and cream on her way.

Concentrating on what needed to be done first, Theo looked at her hair in the mirror. Even without her glasses on, she could tell it was an overgrown mass of fuzzy blond curls. This was her hair's normal condition, but it looked monstrous this morning. She couldn't remember the last time she'd had it cut and decided a couple of the bigger curls threatening to completely obscure her vision needed a bit of a trim, so she pulled a pair of tiny curved manicure scissors from a drawer. Why not fix it herself? How hard could it be to shorten her hair a bit? She gently pulled on one of the corkscrew curls and clipped part of it off. Moving sort of clockwise around her head, she nicked bits off here and there and tossed them into the trash. Satisfied she'd done enough, but not too much, she fluffed her hair with her fingers, put her glasses on and headed downstairs.

She met Chris at the kitchen doorway. Behind the lenses of his glasses, his beautiful hazel eyes flickered over her face and then focused on the floor. Her mom alarm began clanging. Chris was hiding something. She leaned forward and so did he.

He gave her a little hug and whispered. "I love you anyway, Mom."

"Anyway?" Theo stood up straight. "What an odd thing to say."

Jamie charged through the doorway and stopped so suddenly that Daisy ran into the back of him and the dog and Jamie went down in a flurry of golden fur, arms and legs, and laughter.

Tony looked up from the newspaper and his lips missed the edge of the coffee cup, but the coffee continued its forward progress. "What the . . . ?" He grabbed a dishtowel and began dabbing at the spilled coffee.

Three males and the dog just stared at her. Theo felt her temper rise. "Out with it."

"Um . . ." Tony began and stopped.

"Is it supposed to do that mom?" Jamie's expression was a clear mix of curiosity, confusion, and concern.

"What?"

"Your hair." Jamie sidled toward his father as if he thought he might need protection and could dive behind the big man if necessary.

Suddenly it wasn't Theo's mom alarm ringing; it was her personal alarm. Maybe she hadn't done as good a job of trimming as she thought. Leaving the family open-mouthed, she went to find a mirror. One glance and she screamed. Tony was by her side in a heartbeat.

"What happened?" Tony peered at her coiffure.

"I thought I was fixing it." Theo stared into the mirror. The first thing she decided was either she should have worn her glasses during the trimming or not put them on at all. Instead of the neatly shortened curls she envisioned, she had ragged chunks of hair missing, almost to the scalp, next to patches of overgrown curls frothing like foam pouring over the top of a glass. She poked at a dilapidated curl with one finger. "Oh, my."

"Hmm." Tony examined the top of her head from his much taller vantage point. His expression of combined sympathy and the beginnings of laughter told her everything she needed to know. Her attempt to subdue her hair was a disaster from top to bottom.

"I wonder if Prudence takes emergency calls." Theo pressed her lips tighter together. They still quivered.

Tony tried not to smile, but the grin still happened. "You certainly qualify for an emergency haircut. I could call nine-one-one for you."

Theo tried a saucy smile and flicked the hair on the back of her head with her fingertips, only to realize there was very little hair there. Nothing to flick. The grin faded into tears.

Tony dialed Deputy Holt's phone.

"Sheriff, sir?" Darren answered after the first ring.

Caller ID had its benefits. Tony grimaced. "Good morning, Darren. Can I talk to your wife, or is she down at her beauty parlor?"

"It's a salon," Darren corrected. "She's right here."

A moment later, amid much static and rattling, Prudence was on the line. Tony explained the situation as well as he could while handing tissues to his sobbing wife. "Can you help?"

"I'll meet her at the *salon* in ten minutes." Prudence didn't wait for his thanks, but simply disconnected the call.

Theo almost ran to the car, hoping their neighbor hadn't seen the mess she'd made of her hair, and drove as quickly as she dared to the pink and purple house converted into Prudence's salon.

To her credit, Prudence didn't laugh. She checked Theo's entire head and then smiled reassuringly. "I can't put it back, but I can make it look like we planned the change."

"Th-thank you." Theo blew her nose. "I've been meaning to come in and get it trimmed, but my days are beyond full and my nights are mere phantoms."

The much taller woman gave her a little hug. "You've seen my brood of kids. I know what you're going through. It's a wonder any of us survive the early months. So far, I haven't cut my arm off when they wear me down, but I've had some near misses." She fastened a protective drape around Theo's neck and led her to the sink. Prudence kept up a steady stream of chatter as she washed Theo's hair.

Theo had to leave her glasses off while Prudence combed and clipped and filled her in on some of the events in town she hadn't heard about.

"Maybe you can tell me if you think I should tell Tony about it." Prudence clipped the hair over Theo's left eye.

"I'm sorry, what?" Theo hadn't quite understood what Prudence had been saying, and she really didn't want to distract Prudence while she was waving the scissors around.

"You know I do some part time, and very informal, fortune consulting."

Theo did know. Had Prudence seen something disturbing in Theo's life? "Is everything okay?" She couldn't control the tiny tremor in her voice.

Prudence shook her head. "Not you, honey. Harrison Ragsdale."

Theo exhaled in relief. "Did you consult with him?"

"I did." Prudence sighed. "I don't feel right talking about what I saw, but on the other hand, I'm not exactly a doctor or a priest." She clipped some more. "He had a very short lifeline. When he left, he said something about making a will right away."

"So you weren't surprised when he died?" Theo wasn't sure if she was a believer in Prudence's predictions or not.

"On the contrary, I was absolutely shocked. I've never had someone go like that and it totally unnerved me." Prudence squirted some foam on the palm of one hand, rubbed it against the other one and then worked the foam into Theo's hair with both hands. For the next couple of minutes, she was totally silent, concentrating on what she was doing to Theo's hair with her fingers. At last she handed Theo her glasses and turned the chair so she faced the mirror. "Ta-da."

Theo stared at her reflection. Instead of her customary curls, she had very short—short enough it looked almost straight—hair clipped and combed into a shining golden cap. It gave her an elfin look and drew flattering attention to her eyes.

Prudence interpreted her silence as disapproval. "You don't like it."

"Are you kidding?" Theo gave a little gasp, jumped out of the chair, and hugged Prudence. "I love it! I can't wait to show everyone my new do!"

"I won't tell anyone why it's so short if you don't." Prudence laughed. "But I'd advise you to get some sleep before you slice off your nose."

Theo nodded vigorously. "I need to buy some of that foam."

Tony felt certain only a relative of Angus Farquhar could come this close to inciting him to premeditated murder. The nephews made Angus seem like a gentleman farmer who lived to do good deeds and might eventually be nominated for some great humanitarian award.

Jocko, the nephew in the chair opposite him, had the refined features of a water rodent. The grease in his hair slicked it back from his forehead and held it firm. Small, dirt-brown eyes, set slightly too close together, gleamed under shaggy eyebrows. His nose was huge. Tony had seen a lot of noses, but because Jocko had no chin to speak of, this one appeared even larger.

"Where are your brothers?" Tony had requested the pack of them come in at the same time. That way he'd not have to spend the entire day with the Farquhar brood.

The rodent shrugged. "Busy."

"Too busy to help you out?" Tony couldn't believe it. The trio operated as one. He couldn't recall ever seeing one of the Farquhar boys by himself. Cutting him out of the herd eliminated some of Jocko's bravado.

Surprise flashed in the beady eyes. "How are they going to help me? I'm golden."

"Really? Golden?" Tony knew he was missing some detail he needed to connect the dots between what he knew and what he suspected. Could Jocko's attitude be related to the death of Harrison Ragsdale? "I'd say you were more like dirt brown."

Jocko glowered. "You think you're special. Your little wife likes me." He tried for a suggestive look, but it failed.

Tony had been treated to enough disparaging comments by Theo in the past about the Farquhar men so that he was pretty sure none of them would invite even a humanitarian interest from her, much less something more personal. In fact, he remembered one time when she'd made him promise to be her alibi if one of them turned up dead. He carefully laced his fingers together to keep them away from the man's scrawny neck. "Wade?"

His deputy stepped forward, holding a sheaf of papers. "I have a warrant for your arrest on several counts of burglary, selling stolen goods, and a search warrant for your home, all vehicles and property. You left your fingerprints all over the cash register at the Thomas Brothers Garage."

Jocko spat at Wade.

Wade had him up on his feet in a heartbeat, slipped handcuffs on him, and placed him back on his chair. Seconds later, an empty steel trash can covered his head and face.

"I'll sue you all." Although somewhat muffled, Jocko's whine was easy to hear.

"Try." Tony tapped gently on the can with his pen. "I can't

have you spreading your germs around. Someone could catch something."

A steady stream of expletives came from under the trash can.

Carl Lee Cashdollar, Jocko's court-appointed and clearly reluctant attorney, arrived at the doorway and paused. He listened briefly to Jocko's tirade, then he pounded on the top of the trashcan with one of his large, boney hands. "I'm your lawyer. Shut up."

Tony knew the squalling of twin infants couldn't come close to the annoying and loud caterwauling coming from Jocko's trashcan. Tony made a mental note to apologize to his baby girls. They were delightful and quiet and demure, even when hungry. "Would you like to be alone with your client?"

Carl Lee began with a shake of the head, then paused. "I suppose I must."

Tony left the two men in the greenhouse, their version of an interview room, together and wandered back to his office, leaving Wade to watch the door. Tony was curious about whether or not Carl Lee would remove the trash can, and seriously doubted Jocko was likely to be a cooperative client.

Maybe twenty minutes passed before Carl Lee pounded on the greenhouse door and Wade released the attorney into the fresher air beyond the door. Seconds later, he sat in Tony's office, leaving his client guarded by the deputy. "I've got a problem."

Tony hadn't seen Carl Lee like this before. He was shaking and kept knitting his fingers together one way and then switching them, compulsively. Tony doubted he was even aware he was doing it. The man had talked to some seriously bad guys in the past and let what he'd learned slide off. Carl Lee gulped, sucking in a great draft of air.

"Take your time." Tony leaned back in his chair. "Tell me when you're ready."

"But that's the problem. I can't." Carl Lee surged to his feet and began pacing, his long legs covering the floor space in two strides. "He even reminded me of attorney-client privilege, can you imagine? By now he's out on bail, and I've got a scum bucket weasel reminding *me* about ethics?"

Tony rubbed his chin. "I'm assuming that what he told you was not only incriminating, but I'm guessing it involved a crime I'm unaware of. Are you allowed to nod?"

Carl Lee nodded, agreeing with at least part of Tony's statement.

"All right." Tony thought hard. "Did it have anything to do with the recent burglaries?" There hadn't been many fingerprints left behind during the crime spree, and they were Jocko's. He assumed the other brothers wore gloves.

Carl Lee's expression was noncommittal.

Tony grinned. The lawyer hadn't shaken his head. "Okay. I'll try another question. By any chance was he near the Smith house when it burned?"

Carl Lee examined his fingernails.

Tony did notice the hands still shaking. "Were his brothers with him?"

Carl Lee froze.

Tony felt acid pour into his stomach, making him queasy. "The body in the garage? Is it one of the brothers?"

Carl Lee didn't blink.

"So I'm guessing Jocko and maybe the third brother hit whoever and knocked him out or killed one of his own brothers. I don't suppose you can tell me which one." Tony was just thinking out loud now. "It still doesn't make sense. Why was one of them on the roof of a burning garage? Where is the remaining brother?"

Carl Lee shrugged.

★ ★ ★ ★ ★

Tony received a call from the arson investigator, Scorch Single-tarry. "Why don't y'all drop by this burnt-out house and I'll give you a preliminary report."

Tony knew the lackadaisical attitude of the Alabama native was a cover. Scorch had another first name; he just kept it secret, just like he pretended to be laid back. He was a detail-driven type A personality. The casual "drop by" meant Tony should get to the house as quickly as he could. So Tony and Wade dropped the report on Harrison Ragsdale and headed out.

Scorch led them on a tour of the exterior, pointing out various burn patterns and discolorations. In the light of day with all the smoke dissipated, the house looked even worse than it had. No roof. Shards of shattered glass everywhere. Huge areas of the stone walls were stained black. "I'm thinking your fire began on the garage roof, just below this little balcony." He tapped a finger on a photograph he carried, of the unburned house. "We found some shattered glass on the garage floor beneath the body and there was an empty gasoline can and some jars near the lawnmower."

"Someone poured gas on the body?"

"Maybe poured, maybe tossed flaming jars." Scorch shook his head, the sunlight reflecting from his gunmetal gray hair. "This is a new house and until we have all the information from the builder, I'm guessing some of the burning gasoline ran under the shingles and burnt the barrier fabric and then the chemicals in the particle board took off."

"It burned awful fast," said Wade. "Is that normal?"

"Yep." Scorch pointed at the burn pattern. "Old houses burn slower than these new ones because they don't have all the glue and chemicals."

Tony wasn't sorry his wife's house was the oldest brick one in town. He hated fire.

★　★　★　★　★

Theo wondered how long it would take before one of her customers noticed her new hair style. She also considered the likelihood of her being able to pretend to have planned to change it. The odds were against her.

The first question was answered in less than a minute after she arrived at the shop somewhat later than usual. Elderly Caro stood in the classroom doorway and shrieked. "Theo what have you done to yourself?"

Theo thought the tone of the exclamation might have been better suited to, "Eek, a mouse!" Every head swiveled in her direction. Shoppers bending low to examine the fabric on the lower shelves straightened quickly. Heads, like those belonging to meerkats, popped up over the racks filled with bolts of fabric, all eyes focused on her. Theo wasn't sure whether to stick her head in a paper bag or take a bow. Trying to act casual, she patted the back of her newly cropped hair, still surprised by the smooth texture. "What do you think?"

Gretchen recovered first. "On you, it's charming. It fits your tininess." She poked at one of the braids wrapped around the top of her own head, forming a blond coronet. "Not good for us Wagnerian types."

Theo thought Gretchen was right. Her operatic assistant had glorious long, thick hair to go with her robust stature.

After the initial impact, Theo's customers examined her new do. Theo was gratified by the compliments of Prudence's skill with the scissors and continued to pretend to have been planning the change.

She was happy to see a small crowd of regulars in her shop and several unfamiliar faces. Business hadn't been good for a couple of months but now the tourists were starting to return. Thank goodness, because she had lots of bills to pay.

She struggled up the stairs carrying the twins. It was almost nap time.

Theo crept downstairs and paused in the classroom doorway checking on the group gathered there.

"The insurance claim is almost the worst part of this whole thing." Susan Smith wiped her eyes. She sat in the classroom of Theo's shop surrounded by her quilting friends. Her preschool children played on the floor next to her. "I have to list everything in the house. From the beds to the brand of refrigerator. They want a list of the kids' toys. It's impossible."

"What about in your sewing room? How does that work?" Gretchen handed her a cup of hot tea. "Will you get anything for your stuff?"

"They want to know how many spools of what kind of thread I lost. Like I keep an inventory of my thread." Susan made a choking sound. "I'm supposed to list each ruler by brand and size. The patterns, the books, the fabrics. I just don't know."

Theo joined them at the table. "Why don't you just start with the easy stuff? Your sewing machine is probably the most expensive item. What brand was it? What model? Write it down then mentally walk around your space. What else was in there?"

"I had a computer and television." Susan tried a smile before writing them on the notepad in front of her. "I was very lucky to have such a beautiful sewing area and so many nice things. And I know it's just stuff, and I can deal with those things being gone—but the baby's quilts, and the grandmother's flower garden quilt my own grandmother made for me. Those things can't be replaced."

"I can't imagine how awful this is for you." Theo meant every word. Poor Susan's life had suffered a disaster. Not knowing how or why their house was burnt to the foundation couldn't be an easy thing to deal with.

By noon there had been so many telephone calls from the

Thursday Night Bowlers asking how they could help, Theo suggested an impromptu gathering in the late afternoon. It would
start after those members with day jobs could arrive. This bit of
socialization might give Susan some distraction and some
comfort. Nothing would bring her life back to normal as fast as
having handwork to help pass the hours in their motel home.

Each bowler brought an anonymous gift—a pattern or tool or
white elephant for her, wrapped in fabric. Among the donated
items were an appliqué pattern of a basket of flowers, paper
hexagons to help her create her own grandmother's flower
garden quilt, and someone donated a half pieced double wedding ring quilt with its scrappy arcs. When Susan unwrapped
the arcs, she began to laugh. A real laugh and said, "Nina, I
remember seeing you work on this at our last retreat and, as I
recall, you spent as much time unsewing it and swearing as you
did sewing." She tossed the bag across the table. "Take it back."

"Okay, okay, don't get your knickers in a knot. I just wanted
to see how desperate you are for something to do." Nina
smoothed one of the unfinished arcs. "At least things aren't so
bad that you might consider fixing this project as a good use of
your time."

"Never." Susan dug into the next bag. "Now this I can use."
She held up a T-shirt printed with decorative quilt blocks and a
stack of neatly folded fabrics in her favorite colors. "Thank you
all. I don't know what I would do without your support."

Theo watched Tony cleaning up the dinner dishes as she stood,
swaying slightly while patting little Lizzie. The poor exhausted
baby was fighting sleep. "We had a gathering for Susan today."

Tony turned to face her. "Did you learn something?"

"You mean besides how awful her life is this week?" Theo
considered his question. "She's working on the inventory for
the insurance company and trying not to upset the children

more than she can help. And, as far as children go, I still can't believe her husband's ex-wife gave away her son like she did." She snuggled Lizzie closer. "Can you?"

"No." He poured soap into the dishwasher and turned it on. "But every day I'm flabbergasted by the things people do—to others, to themselves. Maybe she thought having a baby would be less work or more fun or, most likely, didn't think at all."

"Could she have come back to get the boy? If she changed her mind about giving him away and thought no one was home, she might throw a match or two."

"I see where you're going with the idea, but it hardly fits the situation." He gently extricated Kara from the little swing where she'd fallen asleep, curled up like a snail. "I'm pretty certain I know what happened. I'm waiting for confirmation and we're still looking for proof."

Theo glanced around. The boys were outside arguing over something trivial. "Speak to me."

"I think maybe the Farquhar brothers went to burglarize the house and got into an argument or something and fought and one of the brothers either died on the garage roof or was knocked unconscious."

Theo nodded. That sort of behavior certainly would be in character. "And the fire?"

"Why burn the house with your brother's body on it? To cover up the burglary, I guess. If the fight was upstairs, and the body was shoved from the little balcony, it would land on the roof of the garage."

"So, when the garage burned down, the body fell with the roof."

"Smart girl." Kara blinked and smiled at her father. Tony grinned back. "I was talking about your mom, but I think you're pretty sharp too."

"So, the remaining brothers are thieves and murderers."

"And arsonists. Don't forget one or both of them stuck around and filled some bottles from the recycling bin with gasoline from the lawn mower can and fire bombed the house. The way they must have gone at it, it's surprising Susan and her kids were able to get out at all."

"Susan said she heard something pop." Theo shivered, thinking about the dangerous situation.

"Most likely the pop was one of the bottles breaking or exploding and sending a wave of fire behind it." Tony's expression hardened. "I haven't argued with Gus or Berry lately. Not like I did when we were younger and they were bossing me around—but killing your brother? I can't imagine." His voice trailed off.

CHAPTER THIRTEEN

Theo answered a morning phone call from mayor and funeral director, Calvin Cashdollar. He provided sad news, shocking, but not really unexpected. Ada Walker was dead. Ada had, Calvin told Theo, according to the doctor, gone to bed and never awakened. As a way to die, it was the best. "She had you listed as her next of kin."

"I'm not really related, but I agreed to oversee her estate." Theo had to push the words past a huge lump in her throat.

What made the news so shocking was having only seen Ada the day before. Ada had been her usual salty mouthed self. The "how long, oh Lord, must I go on" followed by "Theo, honey, I'll haunt you forever if you don't find a good home for my quilting stuff." All interspersed with the steady flow of cheerful profanity.

So it fell on Theo's shoulders to arrange the yard sale. Ada herself had already set up the catered luncheon. All Theo had to do was notify the caterer of the chosen date. Theo decided to designate Susan as her official assistant, if for no other reason than to let her have first choice of the items to go on sale. Theo also arranged for Melissa, Susan's usual companion and best friend, to apply pressure from the other side by encouraging Susan to help Theo. The two of them all but dragged Susan into Ada's house.

All Susan's protestations fell on deaf cars. She soon had set aside a rocking chair, some basic quilting supplies, a good floor

179

lamp and two boxes of miscellaneous fabrics and a couple of UFOs—unfinished hand piecing and appliqué projects. Theo would not accept any money.

"Go ahead and take the lamp and this." Theo handed her an old metal fruitcake box filled with scraps of fabric. "I doubt the rooms at the Riverview Motel have good task lighting."

Susan's smile was strained, but Theo considered it a victory when Susan surrendered. Susan said, "I'll add these to the gifts the bowlers gave me. I'll have even more to occupy me after the kids are asleep." Her fingers smoothed the small bits of fabric. "Without them I would have been just staring at the motel television. Filling out more insurance forms. Or crying."

"You'll earn these things by helping me." Theo reached up to hug the much taller woman. "If you don't, I might have to employ some of the juicy swear words Ada taught me."

Ruth Ann appeared to be trying to make sense of the notes Tony left on her desk when yet another distraction hit. Orvan Lundy needed to confess.

"Not again." Tony rubbed his forehead with the heel of his hand hoping to smooth out his thoughts and wipe away the headache forming. "Could he pick a worse time?"

Ruth Ann managed to look sympathetic, but Tony wasn't fooled. He knew she lived for Orvan's confessions. He sighed. "Okay, bring him in."

Predictably, Orvan had dressed formally for the event. Clean overalls and a blue and gray plaid long-sleeved shirt with buttons on the cuffs. Tony was sure it was the same ensemble he'd worn the day of the Ramp Festival and doubted it had been washed since then. The pervasive smell of ramps still clung to Orvan. Before the old guy could finish his traditional salute and fidget, Ruth Ann and Wade arrived, notebooks and water bottles in hand.

Tony led the little parade to the greenhouse.

"I know you're busy, Sheriff, what with the little problems at the gathering." Orvan accepted a bottle of water from Ruth Ann, with a heartfelt sigh and liquid eyes. His lips moved soundlessly to form the words, "my angel."

Tony considered a possible murder a bit larger event than Orvan might describe it. To be fair, he and his department had done a good job of skirting the issue of their not knowing just what had killed Harrison Ragsdale. He pretended to himself that the moment the actual cause of death became official, it would point to the killer, if there was one, like the X on a treasure map. "Go on."

Orvan futzed a bit with his overalls and then with his water bottle. "I didn't have nothin' to do with it."

"Now, Orvan," Tony tapped his fingertips on the table. "I don't believe you're following the rules of confession. You are supposed to tell me what you *did* and leave out everything you *didn't* do."

The rheumy, cloudy eyes filled with tears. "I cannot go to my grave with you believing I could kill all them."

"Them?" Tony, Wade, and Ruth Ann managed the question in perfect unison.

"I know I'm an old sinner, but I'm not so bad as all that." Orvan twisted the lid on his water bottle. "I'll swear on the Bible. Like I said afore, I had nothin' to do with it."

"Let's back up just a bit, Orvan." Tony felt as though he'd been blindsided. He didn't usually have to do much detective work during one of Orvan's confessions; translation maybe, but not detection. "What are you talking about?"

Orvan almost had the bottle to his lips. Surprised by Tony's question, he poured a fair quantity of water down the opening between the bib of the overalls and his shirt. He squalled like a baby when the cold water soaked through to his skin. "Don't you know?"

Tony waited for the inevitable tirade. It didn't take long.

"Our taxes pay your salary. I think we're gettin' robbed. Maybe you ought to be a-payin' us."

In the time since Tony became the Park County sheriff, he doubted Orvan had made much money, and he'd swear the little menace wouldn't pay taxes to save his scrawny neck. "Talk or leave, Orvan."

Ignoring Tony, Orvan gazed at Ruth Ann. "Does he treat you right, my angel?"

Considering he'd never once, at least not recently, told her to do her manicures at home instead of at her desk, Tony thought he'd get a decent, if not glowing, review. He certainly hoped so, or neither Wade nor Orvan would ever let him live it down. And Ruth Ann would own him.

Tony watched Ruth Ann do a fair imitation of Blossom Flowers "thinking," her index finger pressed against her chin just below her lower lip. Feeling somewhat sour, Tony wondered if she and Gus practiced together.

"He's a good man, and fair." Ruth Ann finally made her pronouncement. "I think you should tell him what he needs to know. Otherwise . . ." Ruth Ann let the word hang between them, the promise or threat too much for Orvan to stand.

"It were Nem." Orvan grasped the edge of the table with both hands. "Not me, never me."

Tony's fingers itched. "And what foul deed are you laying at Nem's door?"

"Oh, it were a good deed." Orvan released the table and clasped his twisted hands together. "He buried 'em all right and proper. Even built 'em coffins."

"Coffins, plural?" Wade's voice went slightly higher than his normal baritone. "How many coffins are we talking about?"

Orvan bobbed his head and began a silent count on his

fingers. He got to four, stopped, backed one off, added one. The suspense building in the greenhouse was palpable. Tony leaned forward, watching Orvan's lips as the old guy worked his way through his list. He recognized one name.

"Roscoe?" Since Tony had seen the man just minutes earlier, he was certain Nem hadn't built his coffin, or at least he hadn't used it. "Why does Roscoe need a coffin?"

Orvan threw his hands into the air and gave Tony a look clearly calling him dumber than dirt. "For that bear."

"Has Baby been located?" Ruth Ann looked at each man in turn before what Orvan was saying sank in. Her voice trailed off to a whisper. "Is she dead?" Tears glistened in her dark eyes.

"Not that we know of." Tony reminded her of Roscoe's frequent visits asking about the bear. "He would have been crying all over the place. You know how tenderhearted he is." He turned back to Orvan. "Have you got anything else to tell us? No Martians landing on the highway and poking holes in the road signs with their magic fingers? No birds flying backwards?"

Orvan blinked hard as if puzzled by Tony's questions and his cranky attitude. "Guess not."

"Okay, let's all get back to work. Ruth Ann, if you'll show our guest the door. And Wade, follow me." Ignoring Orvan's whine as he was ushered away, Tony returned to his office and moved behind his desk, sorting the stacks and files. "Have you noticed a pattern here?"

"You mean the missing or dead pets?" Anger flashed in Wade's eyes. "Those pets are all the family some of our citizens have."

"I agree." Tony dropped into his chair. "So, assuming Ragsdale killed the pets, does that tell us who killed him?"

"No. Do we even have a definitive cause of death?" Wade studied his notes. "Last I knew, he was stabbed, and yet Doc Nash didn't think he could do the autopsy."

"The stake didn't kill him." Tony lifted the file from the top of the stack. "I just received this and haven't made my way through it all. It looks like the wooden stake was not the ultimate cause of death but it might have prevented Ragsdale from seeking help that could have saved him."

"What does that mean?" Wade looked up.

"In a word, Ragsdale was poisoned." Tony reached for his antacids. "The type of poison is unknown, and we don't know how or when it was administered."

"So, why stab him?"

"Good question." Tony chewed slowly, mulling over the facts. "Did it seem like he wasn't being affected by the poison? Did someone not know about the poison and wanted to kill him, or was someone trying to cover up for the poisoner?"

"What a mess." Wade glanced up. "Killing someone in broad daylight in a crowd takes nerves of steel."

"Or someone who has nothing to lose."

Tony turned to another page of the report. "This notation is odd. The stake used in the attack was chestnut wood."

Wade didn't look impressed. "Quite a few of the older homes still have pieces of chestnut in them. Especially some of the older cabins. There's some young trees in the area as well."

"True." Tony leaned forward. "But which of those people at the festival would come carrying a stake to shove into Ragsdale?"

"Maybe there's someone who routinely carries a stake around." Wade half-laughed at his own suggestion. "As a form of self-defense."

"You might actually have a good idea. We've got a large impoverished population. So many poor people with a grudge. Why not carry a sharp stick? It's effective and not as hard to conceal or use as a knife."

★ ★ ★ ★ ★

Theo left the girls with Jane and Martha so she could run a few errands and the ladies would stop begging for baby time. She stopped at the grocery store and spent as much time explaining why she didn't have the twins with her as she would have spent tending them. Sigh. Still she managed to fill the cart with some of the desperately needed necessities. Fruit, especially bananas, vanished the moment she unloaded her bags. Peanut butter, the biggest jar possible, cream for her coffee and an extra carton for the shop. She swept through the store, realizing her list was only the tip of the iceberg. They were out of everything. Now her family would have bread and milk, and she could do the laundry. Mountains of it. She wondered if there was a detergent delivery service that could bring it to the house each week, like milk used to be delivered.

She went from the store to the vet's office to get Daisy some of her pills.

Her last stop before heading home to put away the groceries was Doreen's gift shop. She had to admit she'd hadn't been running around town much recently, but she was shocked to find the gift store undergoing a major remodel. Nobody had told her it was happening. It looked like a new wall was under construction about twenty feet away from the existing wall.

If the shop was going out that far, its floor space might be doubled. Easing into the shop, because there was so much merchandise and the aisles were very narrow, Theo hoped Doreen would not feel compelled to buy more, but intended to spread out her current inventory.

Queen Doreen herself stood behind the counter, giving instructions to Bernice Osborne. From what Theo had gathered, Doreen had recovered from a recent embarrassment, followed by a long period of rest and restoration, including a bit of plastic surgery, in Hawaii. It was too early to know if her attitude had received a bit of adjusting along with her jaw line.

Theo liked to shop locally when she could, and Doreen's prices were fair and the quality was usually good. Referring to her employees as "peasants" was unnecessary, but she always had consistent employees, not a big turnover—including the loyal Bernice and Rex's niece Chandra. Maybe it was just the public Doreen didn't care for.

Theo chatted briefly with a couple of women she knew, both of whom were disappointed she didn't have the twins with her. "Even if I wanted to bring them . . ." Theo waved at the narrow aisles and fragile merchandise. "I'm not sure we could squeeze through safely. Our stroller is *huge*."

Waiting for Doreen to become available, Theo studied the bath salts and skin scrubs, looking for a present for a "secret sister" gift, when she overheard snatches of a conversation. At the sound of Hairy Rags's name being mentioned, she paid more attention.

"Who do you think will inherit?" said one woman.

"I understand he has a brother and a sister, plus there's always charities." The second voice was more nasal than the first. "I didn't like the man, but I wouldn't turn down some of his money."

Voice number one mumbled something Theo couldn't understand, then clearly: "What about the wife he had at the barbeque we went to. You know, the one a long time ago up at the Lodge, you know when we went to hear the world's most boring politician speak?"

"Goodness, that was so many years ago, I still had all my teeth. I do remember there wasn't enough free food to make the trip up there worth our time."

"Do you need help, Theo?" Doreen's voice came from behind her, drowning out the conversation upon which she'd been eavesdropping.

Theo turned to face Doreen, hoping she'd remember to ask Tony about Hairy Rags having a wife. Theo smiled at Doreen, more from habit than friendship. "Ada Walker's memorial lunch and yard sale are going to be in front of the funeral home, in the parking lot, day after tomorrow. I'll try to keep people from blocking your parking area, but I'll bet there will be some overflow." She saw Doreen's lips press together. "For the luncheon, I will need ten small buckets of flowers to decorate the tables, maybe something in blues and whites? I don't have an unlimited budget." Theo pointed to a steel bucket about the size of a large coffee mug. "About this size."

Doreen's expression softened. First and foremost, she was a business woman. "Something like daisies and cornflowers?" Doreen scribbled a price on a scrap of paper.

"Exactly." Theo mentally calculated the cost against the money Ada had designated for her farewell party. She still had some left to spend. "She loved the combination of blue, white, and yellow. Is there an inexpensive yellow flower we could add, or yellow bows?"

"I think we can find something." Doreen led Theo to the back of the store where the large glass doored coolers filled with flowers hummed quietly. She pointed to some bright yellow flowers Theo didn't know by name. "Those would fit in your budget or," Doreen reached to the side and pulled a length of wide yellow ribbon with tiny white polka dots. "Would you rather have this tied around your buckets?"

"Let's do the flowers." Theo knew Ada had loved flowers and hadn't been the ribbon and bow type.

"We'll bring them over when the tables are set up. Just let me know." Doreen wrote out the order. "Anything else?"

Theo checked her list. "The caterer is bringing the tables, chairs, and food. Food? Oh-oh, my groceries are in the car. I'd better hustle."

Doreen smiled at her then, a real smile. "What do you do in your spare time, Theo?"

Theo rolled her eyes. "If I ever get some, I'll let you know."

CHAPTER FOURTEEN

The lab report comparing the fingernail samples to the minute specks found in the gouges on Ragsdale's neck proved negative. There was no proof the scratches had been made by any of the people they'd checked. The technician was careful to explain the results didn't mean much. The gouges had contained almost no evidence, and he wouldn't rule any of the possibilities out.

"Very helpful, indeed." Tony frowned. "We chase all over the county looking at hands and have zero facts."

"Well, if nothing else, we almost eliminated a few people' from the scratches." Wade flipped through his notepad. He looked up. "I'm really interested in the wooden stake."

"Is there a size minimum on stakes?" Tony didn't know. "The thing didn't look much different than the handle on a wooden spoon, except sharper."

"A lot sharper." Wade handed Tony his notepad. "I made this sketch of the thing. It's got a point on it as sharp as if it was done with one of those old pencil sharpeners with a crank handle."

Tony studied the drawing. Sure enough, with the diameter of the shaft and the neat point, it resembled an arrow stripped of its feathers more than his idea of a stake. "Maybe that's how it was done—with a pencil sharpener. Do you know anyone who makes their own arrows, by any chance? This thing almost looks like it could be launched."

Wade took back his notebook. "Maybe one of the weapons

enthusiasts uses an antique crossbow."

"Now you're getting a bit far from our facts." Tony leaned back in his chair and studied the ceiling. "It had no feathers and no notch. It is made from the wood of an extinct, or more precisely, an almost-extinct tree. I understand some chestnuts still sprout, but don't make it to huge. We think it might have been sharpened with a pencil sharpener, but how was the shaft made? Was it made so smooth by man or machine?"

"Before the old chestnuts died"—Wade's eyes sparkled like he'd won a prize—"were they used for arrows? Maybe this is an antique."

The idea of another link with his family's museum made Tony sit forward with a jerk. "Please don't let this have been one of Mom's museum displays. There's already been too much death associated with the place."

Wade mimicked him. "It has no feathers and no notch."

Somewhat appeased, Tony took a deep breath. "We need more information." He dialed the museum office number. Thankfully, it was his aunt and not his mother who answered. "Are you missing anything from one of your displays?"

"Does this have anything to do with your harassment of Orlando?"

"I did not harass Mr. Espinoza." Tony sighed and rested his forehead on his fist. "The item in question might resemble the shaft of an arrow." Silence followed his question. Tony wondered if Martha was still on the line.

"No, Tony." Martha finally spoke. "I just checked the computer inventory our slave Celeste created. We never had anything like that in our museum."

Tony thanked her and disconnected. He stared at the mess on his desk. The investigation just hit another dead end.

Tony and Wade were headed to Ruby's Café when they

encountered Orvan Lundy again. Orvan was smiling and beckoning them to his side of the street. Tony considered the old guy's good mood an omen of bad things to come. Although Tony had come to almost enjoy the little man's confessions, they only occurred when Orvan was feeling a bit guilty or, more likely, lonely. A happy Orvan spelled disaster in the making.

"Howdy, Sheriff." Orvan laughed at his own imitation of a cowboy in a bad western movie.

Tony watched as Orvan tried to hook his thumbs into his imaginary gun belt but ended up catching them in the sides of his overall bib. His shoe-polished hair gleamed in the sunlight. Oxblood instead of black. Very becoming. "You seem to be enjoying the day, Orvan." Tony was not about to ask the old sinner why he was so happy.

"Yep." Orvan cackled and slapped his hands against his thighs. "Betcha wonder why, don't ya?"

"I am intrigued." And he was. To date, Orvan had avoided confessing to any of his own crimes.

"I kin solve your mystery." Orvan's faded blue eyes sparkled through the haze of cataracts. "I seed who done it."

Unwilling to be the only victim of Orvan's good humor, Tony waved Wade closer. "Orvan says he saw the killer do the deed."

Wade appeared properly impressed. "Let me get my notebook." He pulled it from his pocket and opened it with a flourish.

Orvan scampered around in a small circle, almost like he was pretending to be a clock. "Done?"

"Just tell us what you saw." Tony smelled fumes as Orvan danced past. "I hope no one waves a match around you. You'd go up in smoke like—" He broke off, suddenly reminded of the fire. Moonshine and gasoline could both be used as fire accelerants. "Let's start with where this happened."

Lower lip sticking out in a pout worthy of a three-year-old,

191

Orvan sulked. "It were at the ramp party. Us'n older folk know a thing from Hades when we see it. Have to kill 'em with a wood stake just like them vampires. Only difference is they is happy in sunshine."

Tony crossed his arms over his chest. It kept him from wrapping his hands around Orvan's scrawny neck.

"I ought not tell you 'cause he was doin' us all a kindness." Hearing Tony sigh, he talked faster. "It were old Nem. I seed it with my own two eyes. They was walkin' past each other, and Nem pulled out his special stick and jabbed it in."

"What did Ragsdale do then?" Tony felt like he was sinking in quicksand. Maybe the old guy needed an apology.

"Who's Ragsdale?" Orvan's cloudy eyes blinked, confusion furrowed his brow.

Tony wondered which one of them didn't understand the story. "Who did Nem stab?"

"Why that furriner. The count. You know, the one flying around an' suckin' blood with fangs an' wearing a black suit?"

Wade whispered. "Sounds like Espinoza."

Orlando Espinoza's name kept popping up and Tony didn't believe in coincidence. Some, yes. But time after time? "Let's go have another little chit-chat with him. Maybe he didn't tell us everything the last time."

"Like being stabbed?" Wade said, "I'll drive."

"I can't imagine why Nem would want to stab Espinoza, can you?" Tony rummaged in a pocket for antacids. "Actually, I can't imagine their paths would ever cross except at the festival."

"Maybe he's hot for your aunt too. I'll bet there is chestnut wood as part of Nem's house though. That building was put up when God was a boy and has been added on to several times, but nothing's ever been torn down." Wade gestured to the radio. "You want to tell Rex where we're going?"

Trying to push aside the charming image of romance between his aunt and the elderly Nem, Tony no more than began talking when Rex cut in.

"I think you and Wade better postpone your trip. Sheila and Darren are both involved with other calls, and there's a situation." Rex's calm voice briskly relayed a report of a man with a rifle driving a motorized grocery cart headed toward town. "The sign bandit rides again. This time he's on a stolen vehicle."

Wade turned his car and headed the other direction. He glanced at Tony. "It would be nice to clear up at least one mystery."

Tony agreed. For months someone had been destroying signs, all kinds of signs, everything from speed limits to stop signs and road markers. Their shooter preferred a twenty-two. He knew, because he and his staff had measured hundreds of holes.

When they approached the four-way stop at the bottom of the hill and looked to the right, Tony saw a motorized grocery cart. A sign on it clearly identified it as property of their local grocery store. The valuable cart was for customers unable to walk and shop, not for some idiot joyriding and destroying public property. Tony squinted but couldn't recognize the thief from this angle. "Do you suppose he knows stealing the cart is a felony?"

The driver eased to a stop, reached into the front basket, picked up a rifle, and fired. Six shots. All pinged loudly as they smacked into the metal stop sign and punched holes in the red octagon. With a satisfied grin, the driver placed the rifle back into the basket and grabbed the handlebar. He glanced over, still smiling, and waved to Tony, who sat on the passenger seat with the window down, before driving into the intersection.

Sid Lundy, Orvan's cousin, had been described as having a turnip for a brain. Tony thought it seemed wrong to malign an innocent and comparatively intelligent vegetable.

Wade made a sharp turn onto the dirt road. He flipped the light bar on and followed the cart, even as he talked to dispatch. "I'm not making this up, Rex. It's Sid Lundy. He actually waved at the sheriff right after he shot the sign." Wade honked his horn and grinned. The driver flinched but didn't pull over.

Tony reached for the vehicle's microphone. "Sid Lundy, this is Sheriff Abernathy. Stop the cart."

The cart stopped in the center of the road. Tony was gratified, if a little surprised, when the driver followed his instructions.

Wade swerved to avoid hitting the cart as he drove past it and stopped, his lights flashing a warning. "You think he'll shoot at us?"

"I doubt it, but I'm not dumb enough to risk it." Sid was Orvan's equal in cantankerous nature, but not as bright. Tony used the microphone again. "Sid, lay the rifle on the ground and put your hands up."

There was a long pause while the cart thief sat motionless as if considering his options.

Wade took the microphone. "Sid Lundy, this is Wade Claybough, I'm getting my rifle and I'll fire a round right up the barrel of that twenty-two of yours if you don't place it very gently on the ground. You know me and you know my rifle's not a twenty-two. Do it now."

Glancing around, as if just noticing he was not alone, Sid hurried to follow Wade's instructions.

Tony grinned. "Your gun's bigger than his."

Wade parked on the shoulder of the road and they both climbed out, walking toward man and machine.

"It's dead." Tears welled in the old man's eyes. He patted the cart's handlebars.

"That's not your worst problem." Tony felt more acid drip into his heartburn. "Stealing this cart is a felony, and using a rifle to destroy those road signs is going to create another very expensive problem for you. What are you using for brains?" Knowing the question was purely rhetorical didn't stop him from asking.

The man's lower lip quivered just like Jamie's had when he was two and anyone told him no. His head moved slowly from side to side. "It were fun."

"Sheriff, I'm not sure how much help this is going to be for you." The pathologist doing the autopsy on Harrison Ragsdale sounded sympathetic even through the tiny cell phone.

Tony hated any phone call beginning with such encouraging words. "Why don't you just lay it out for me anyway? Why is our Mr. Ragsdale deceased?"

"Walnuts." One word followed by silence.

For a moment Tony thought his hearing wasn't what it used to be. "Walnuts?"

"Yep. Your Mr. Ragsdale had a serious allergic reaction to something he ate. In this case, he had a fierce, and most likely, escalating, allergy to walnuts. All tree nuts were bad for him, but walnuts were the worst. He should have been carrying injectable medicine to combat the allergic reaction until medical personnel could get to him."

"I didn't see anything like that, Doctor. We shipped him to you with everything still on him." Tony searched his notebook for the inventory list. "Let's see, there was the expected watch, billfold, badge, loose change, car keys, house keys, and one implement shaped a bit like a screwdriver or a special key, a pocket knife. A revolver." Tony flipped through more pages. "I don't see anything resembling medicine."

"Then he's a stupid corpse." The doctor sounded disgusted. "I swear, if you're allergic to a common food ingredient and you stuff your face at a festival, I'm tempted to call it suicide."

He cleared his throat. "I'm not going to sign any papers until you have a chance to do a little legwork and find out if there's a reason besides poor brains that he was not prepared for an allergic reaction."

Tony groaned. "So, if someone stole it from him?"

"Yep. I might have to call it deliberate homicide."

"And if he lost it?"

"Maybe not homicide." The doctor cleared his throat. "You also might want to take a little survey of your food vendors and see how many of them were serving walnuts."

"I'm sure I ate some cookies with walnuts." Tony closed his eyes; there had been quite a few food vendors when they were all listed together—ramp recipe contest samples, the hamburger and barbeque stands, popcorn, snacks, desserts, a whole booth of desserts. "There was food everywhere. People cooking it, eating it, walking with it, spilling it."

"Don't overlook the smaller bits," the pathologist said. "Food morsels, samples, crumbs on everything including hands and lips. Maybe some woman kissed him right after she ate walnuts."

Tony thought maybe if he took all the files out of his bottom desk drawer, he might be able to slam his head in it and have it close and shut out the doctor's words. "It's hopeless."

"Well, I'm sure you'll do your best." The doctor disconnected the call.

Tony thought the doctor's pious voice sounded like his mom had when he was a boy and had produced a disappointing report card. It had spurred him to work harder back then. He wondered if the doctor's marked lack of enthusiasm would have the same effect. He pushed his intercom button. "Ruth Ann, I need your help." Maybe she could come shoot him. He really didn't approve of suicide.

Ruth Ann was reasonably sympathetic. She waved her freshly painted fingernails under his nose. "The color is citron."

Tony studied it. He might have renamed it something more like "bile." The dog had eaten something once that had re-appeared wrapped in stomach juices. It was the same color. However, he swallowed his impulse to tell her about it, because he was going to try and enlist Ruth Ann's assistance with their new research project.

"You don't look too good." Ruth Ann's comment was master-ful. "Something you ate?"

"Funny you should bring up food." Tony tried a smile. It felt a little forced, awkward.

"Something wrong with your teeth?" Ruth Ann smirked. "Maybe you should go see Tiberius. Take your mom along and let her salivate over Doctor Looks-so-good."

"Actually, I'd like you to do a little survey for me." Tony quit smiling. "Please contact each food vendor from the Ramp Festival and find out every ingredient of every food served, I especially want to know who used walnuts in any foods served in their booths, and which foods they were in and in what quantity. Mom or Martha should at least know who was selling food."

Obviously intrigued, Ruth Ann headed back to her desk.

"I meant to ask you about this before." Theo's voice came through Tony's cell phone. "I overheard a conversation, and someone mentioned Ragsdale's wife, and I didn't know he was ever married."

Shocked, he'd forgotten Ragsdale's lawyer's call because of the fire, Tony sat up straight. "That's right. She lives in Silers-ville." He began searching the top stack of papers, looking for the note he'd written himself. He found it.

"I don't know her name," Theo continued. "And it didn't seem like a good plan to say I was eavesdropping and would like to know who would marry Ragsdale and why it was such a secret."

Theo sounded as confused as he felt. "I know her name, and I know who to ask for preliminary information. I'll fill you in later." He kissed the telephone. "Thank you, sweetheart."

He charged from his office and headed to the museum. Sure enough, his mother was in the office, sorting papers. She glanced up and gave him a dirty look when he walked in. Not exactly the welcome he might have predicted. "What's wrong, Mom?"

Jane stared at him, still not smiling. "I'm sure you don't mean to create a scene every time you come out here."

"What do you mean by a scene?" Tony found his mother's snarky attitude absolutely unfair.

"I'm sure it's nothing intentional, which doesn't mean it's not your fault." She sighed, a long melodramatic exhalation. "It seems as though trouble follows you out here. As I recall, Martha and I had barely bought the land when you started this unsavory habit."

"Unsavory habit?" Tony scowled. "You make it sound like I'm the one killing off people who come onto your property. Maybe you're the one responsible." His mother had always had the gift of pushing his buttons. He almost lost sight of his reason for the visit when she frowned and squinted her eyes at him. Forestalling her next comment, he decided to test her memory. "You claim to know everyone in the county, so who married Harrison Ragsdale?"

Her mouth opened and closed without a sound. She blinked. "Why, Jessica Baxter, of course. Everyone knows it. She married him when she was still in school. High school. She was several years ahead of you."

"Thank you." Tony turned and left before his mom could get back onto the subject clearly gnawing on her nerves. Him.

Driving back to town, he called Wade. "Find out where Jessica Baxter is and let me know. I'll meet you there."

Moments later, Wade contacted him with the address. As Tony drove, he considered the little information he knew about Ragsdale's will and estate. So far, he'd learned Jessica stood to inherit part of a house including the furnishings, a sizeable savings account, and two rental houses. What he didn't know was why she was still legally married to a man she no longer lived with and it was not a recent separation. A man whom Tony had considered single his whole life.

Jessica Baxter came out of the house and greeted Wade and Tony. Tony recognized her by sight, if not name. She attended their church and shopped in the same stores. It occurred to him from time to time that he knew lots of residents by name and reputation. The ones, like Jessica, he didn't know were the ones not spending time in his jail on a regular basis. Just as he was thinking he might want to meet more law-abiding citizens, she said, "I expected you to come by."

Eyebrows high, Tony covered his ignorance with a mumbled series of words about not realizing she and Ragsdale were still married.

"Yes. Come inside." Jessica turned and went back into the house.

He and Wade followed. Once inside her house, he and Wade both retrieved their notebooks and sat. At Jessica's offer of coffee, they nodded and relaxed. Tony thought the interior of the house was well kept, although he personally didn't much care for the blond wood against the pine paneling of walls. They didn't have long to wait before she returned carrying a tray.

"I'm sure you're here because of Harrison." She handed Tony a heavy mug of coffee.

He nodded. "When was the last time you saw him?"

"I'm not sure." Jessica settled onto the sofa opposite him. "As long as you mean spending any time with him, it's been years. Of course, in a town this size, I *saw* him often."

"You really *are* still married?" Tony said.

"Oh, yes. For now." Jessica immediately realized her statement sounded peculiar. "That's wrong. Let me explain. Thirty years ago, he was a good-looking guy. I was sixteen and thought he hung the moon, as they say. He was eighteen. I think you can connect the dots." She stared at the floor. "I ended up pregnant, married, miscarried, and separated all within a year."

"Why not have the marriage annulled or get a divorce?" Wade asked.

"It didn't matter to either of us. He wasn't planning to marry and I wasn't either. Until now." Jessica blushed and extended her left hand. A miniscule diamond twinkled on her third finger.

"You don't use his name," Tony stated. "Did you ever?"

"No. We never really thought of ourselves as husband and wife, and I'd guess only a few residents would remember our quickie wedding." She studied Tony. "How did you find out?"

"A resident remembered." He wrote himself a note. He didn't mention Ragsdale's attorney knew her name as well. "So you said you didn't spend time with him. Did you talk on the telephone, e-mail, snail mail?"

"I called to tell him I would like to divorce so I could remarry, and that I'd like a dowry, as it were. After all, if he's my husband, what's his is mine, right?"

"Who's the lucky man?" Tony didn't explore the terms of her probable inheritance.

"Vic Anderson."

When she smiled, Jessica's face became radiant. If she looked this good at nearly fifty, Tony imagined she must have been stunning at sixteen. He knew she was about ten years older than he was. He recognized the name of her fiancé, a local exterminator, a man with access to and experience with certain types of poison. "And Ragsdale?"

"He said no way. Can you believe it? He said divorce was an abomination and a sin. The sanctimonious pain in the neck." Jessica's voice rose and her face reddened. "Is divorce worse than knocking up a sixteen-year-old girl?"

Tony cut her off before she exploded or wandered too far from the subject. "When was this conversation?"

"Last week." Jessica met his eyes. "I did not do whatever you're thinking. What's wrong with my wanting Vic and a bit of cash? I've seen Harrison's will. It all comes to me unless I remarry."

Tony thought she'd be disappointed by the recent changes in the will. "Only part will come to you."

"What are you saying?"

"Only that he had a new will." Tony didn't want to discuss it further. "Tell me about his allergies."

"Allergies?" Jessica looked at the ceiling. "Well, he wasn't allergic to dogs, but he acted like it just so people would keep them away. I think he was afraid of them, not allergic."

"Anything else?" Tony hoped he looked like these were his standard questions.

Jessica's big brown eyes stared into his. "You don't mean the nut thing, do you?" The corners of her lips turned down. "He acted like he was being murdered if you sprinkled nuts on his ice cream sundae."

"You didn't believe him when he said he had allergies?"

Before Jessica could answer, the front door swung open and a stocky man with bright orange hair stepped inside. "Everything all right?"

"Come in, Vic." Tony recognized the exterminator as a semi-regular patron of the Okay Bar and Bait Shop. "Why don't you have a seat? I've got a few questions for you too."

Orange hair sat. His gaze bounced back and forth between Tony and Jessica.

Tony said, "Did you tell anyone how Ragsdale behaved when nuts were involved?"

"Yes." Jessica smiled and extended a hand to the orange-haired man, and he rose to kiss it. "I told my fiancé, Vic, only a few days ago."

Tony studied the couple. Given the minimum net worth of Ragsdale's estate in property and cash, there were now two people in the room with motive, especially if they didn't know about the new will. Gaining the freedom to marry, plus cash and property, tipped the scale toward Jessica. But, if her boyfriend knew about the relationship, he might dream of a wedding and money as a package deal. Who wanted it more, and did Vic know about the money prior to their courtship?

Tony watched Vic. He did remember seeing the orange hair at the festival. It was about the same improbable shade as Blossom's dye job. He also remembered how his attention had been caught by the man's furtive expression. Maybe he just had a sneaky face. But for what cause? Cheating on his girlfriend? Stealing cookies from the bake sale? Or poisoning Harrison Ragsdale?

If there was one thing he'd learned in law enforcement—first in Chicago and now as sheriff of the smallest county in Tennessee—it was to trust your gut. If Vic wasn't involved in Ragsdale's death, he was thrilled to profit from it. What Tony didn't want to do was ask more questions without knowing a few more of the answers first. And he positively did not want these two copying the answers from each other.

"I think this is all we need for now." Standing abruptly, he signaled for Wade to follow him. His deputy managed to remain silent until they reached the street and Tony asked, "What do you think?"

"I've encountered Vic a few times." Wade pushed his sunglasses down from his head to cover his eyes. "He has motive and it makes a great suspect, but dirt's smarter. I'm not sure he's got the brains to pull it off."

Tony couldn't dispute it. "Jessica's got brains. I'd love to know when and how their relationship began."

"If we can find a video of either of them giving food to Ragsdale," said Wade, "it might not matter how they met. Love, money, and murder create a classic triangle."

CHAPTER FIFTEEN

"What do you mean, Tony?" His aunt narrowed her eyes at him. "Of course people were using video cameras, scads of them. There's no way to give you all their names."

Tony narrowed his eyes right back at her. Why was his aunt being so difficult? "Don't pretend you don't know what I'm asking. Did you have someone make an official video or not? It's not a crime you know."

She cleared her throat and looked away. "It might be."

"Why?"

"Well, one of the groups did say they didn't want anyone recording them. Something about not wanting the new song broadcast on the Internet."

"Have you done that?" Tony knew the answer. Neither his aunt nor his mother was really computer savvy enough to upload a video.

"Well, no, of course not. And we don't intend to." Martha did meet his eyes then. "It's just for us to enjoy."

"Excellent. Then you can give your unofficial video to me." Tony thought examining the videos might take weeks. All those hours of recording would need minute examining to discover someone slipping a little something extra into Ragsdale's food.

It wasn't just this video he thought they might have to study. Lots of people were using cameras and fancy telephones to record portions of the afternoon.

★ ★ ★ ★ ★

Tired of watching videos of people stuffing food into their mouths, Tony went to the clinic to have a discussion with Doc Nash about the symptoms and causes of allergic reactions.

The doctor summed it up with, "Allergies are weird."

"No kidding." Tony was frustrated and cranky. He glared at the doctor. "As a professional description, your statement lacks some preciseness."

Doc Nash took a more professorial stance. "Some people seem born with several, some none, and others have reactions that escalate over the years and some lessen. My great aunt loved shrimp. Her family lived down on the Gulf Coast and ate a lot of shrimp. One day, out of the blue, she had an allergic reaction that almost killed her and then couldn't eat shrimp anymore."

"No kidding. So we're all like allergy time bombs?" The idea of suddenly becoming allergic to some of his favorite foods had nightmare implications.

"Not necessarily." The doctor paused. "I had a patient once who was allergic to milk. Over the years, it became less severe. She had developed a tolerance for small amounts. I doubt she could drink a milk shake without suffering some symptoms, but they weren't near what they had been."

"So using someone's allergies against them wouldn't have a reliable outcome?"

"Nope." Doc Nash cleaned his glasses. "Not reliable, but possible if it's an established, escalating reaction to something."

"I'm going to go blind here." Deputy Mike Ott looked up from the computer screen and waved a hand in a gesture of despair. "I've never seen so many dull people doing such mundane things. And eat. My stomach is starting to hurt after watching that much chow disappearing down the hatch."

Tony pretended he didn't sympathize. After all, he gave the job to Mike after his own eyes, and stomach, gave out. "I guess that means no one came up to Ragsdale and dumped chopped walnuts on the man's plate."

"Not that I could see. He went to several booths, picked up a variety of samples, used the salt and pepper, piled a bunch of those little crackers onto his soup. Look, here he's talking to Vic and Jessica. They have knowledge about his allergy, and money's a powerful motive, but it doesn't look like they stopped holding hands." Mike pointed to the man on the screen. "Harrison didn't have his cane with him in this shot. Did he have it with him later? He gets behind a large group about now." Mike paused the replay.

"That's an excellent question. I'd love to find the cane. I've never seen him without it." Tony absently massaged his stomach as he stared at the frozen tableau on the screen. "Right now, let's try super slow motion of the footage showing him headed for the cordoned-off vegetable splashdown area."

"Maybe someone else has footage taken from another direction," said Wade as he stepped closer to watch. "This view shows us lots of backs."

"So far as we've learned, the only walnuts used were in the dessert booth. Ragsdale never went near it as far as I can tell." Mike rubbed his eyes with the heels of his hands. "What did you see?"

Tony focused on the screen, watching Ragsdale in super slow motion move through the crowd, headed for the pasture. Several people clearly moved out of his path, avoiding him. Ragsdale seemed to hesitate for a moment while hidden from the camera by a muscular man with distinctive long graying hair, mustache, and full goatee. Tony recognized him as one of their new residents. Bart Hudson. Tony said, "How many people do you know with allergies?"

"Lots." Mike swiveled on his chair. "Most of them are allergic to dogs or cats or bees or shellfish."

"But you know about them. It's something you learn fairly early. One of the parents of a kid on my baseball team was so allergic to bee venom that he always carried a preloaded syringe in his pocket. He told us about it so we could use it on him if he got stung." Tony shook his head. "It doesn't make sense." His focus remained on the action on the screen. "Wait. Back it up."

Mike did.

Wade muttered, "You mean like someone who would go to a food festival when you have food allergies, really bad allergies, and you don't have first aid along? Or someone allergic to dogs becoming a veterinarian?" Wade leaned in to look more closely at the screen. "What did you see, sir?"

Tony wasn't sure either. "Let's watch again."

As Tony, Wade, and Mike leaned closer to the screen, Mike started the replay. It began with Mr. Espinoza waving to catch Ragsdale's attention. Focusing on Ragsdale, Tony saw him ignore Mr. Espinoza before being eclipsed by the much larger Hudson, then reappear on the screen as if he'd fallen, or been pushed, onto his left hip. Mike paused the replay and zoomed in, making the scene more grainy, but it was clear enough to show an angry Ragsdale making a rude gesture. Definitely still alive. When the motion started again, Ragsdale regained his footing and moved into the crowd. Hudson followed, his wider body blocking their view. Not until Ragsdale passed the line of warning banners was he seen clearly again. A second later, he fell facedown.

Tony said, "Play it again." This time he watched Hudson instead of Ragsdale, trying to remember everything he'd heard about the newcomer. Hudson had purchased land in Park County about two years earlier, claiming his lifelong dream was to become a "mountain man." He dressed in long-sleeved flannel shirts, even in the heat and humidity of July and August. Tony imagined he smelled like a buffalo. He'd moved to their mountains after making big money in computer technology, grew out his hair, and bought half a mountain. Rumor, usually worth little, claimed his "cabin" had six bedrooms, air-conditioning powered by his combination generator and wind turbine. Plus, the claim continued, Hudson managed to live off the land with the help of his wife, a housekeeper, and a handyman. Unverified rumors. He rarely came into town.

"Ragsdale was clearly pushed," said Mike. "But who could guess he'd be hurt even if a potato did hit him?"

Tony looked at Wade. "Let's go have a chat with Mr. Hudson."

Mike glanced around. "Speaking of going, where's my dog? He probably needs to go out."

"Dammit got hungry watching you view the tape, and Ruth Ann gave him a couple of biscuits. He's sleeping on his back next to her desk. He covers the floor like a rug."

"Alienation of affection." Mike stood and stretched. "I'll get him."

Wade laughed. "You're just afraid Ruth Ann will paint his toenails to match her fingernails."

Tony thought Mike's expression of horror as he hustled from the room meant he had not considered the possibility.

Tony and Wade had to stop at a gate near the beginning of Hudson's clearly marked private drive. Cameras and an intercom indicated the Hudsons' security system was not just for show. Tony chatted briefly with the disembodied voice at the other end of the speaker and the gate swung open. They drove for what felt like over a mile on a narrow but smooth packed earth and gravel driveway before pulling into the parking area in front of an immense log home.

Next to him, Wade whistled in appreciation, his eyes focused on the hidden home.

Tony admired the architecture and the well planned and maintained landscape. "Not exactly like Quentin's mountain home place, is it?"

"Not quite. Maybe if they don't do any upkeep for a few years and import a couple of dilapidated trailers and a portable toilet to decorate the front yard, they'll achieve some of the same ambiance."

The heavy oak paneled front door swung open and a neatly groomed young woman gestured for them to enter. "I'm Gwen, the housekeeper. I'll show you in to see Mr. Hudson." As she led them through the expansive public areas, she explained her husband was the handyman and they had their own, smaller, cabin nearby.

Mountain man Hudson waited for them in his expansive office. Tony sniffed, but all he smelled was the scent of lemon oil. Large windows overlooked the property and the neighboring mountains.

As he studied the room, Tony counted six computers arranged in a semicircle— -some tiny, one with a screen as big as a blackboard. Today Bart Hudson's long, prematurely gray hair was combed into a neat ponytail. His clothing, khakis and a blue shirt with a button-down collar, were clean and pressed. Polished cowboy boots. Clean hands. Alert gray eyes did not miss Tony's examination. Hudson looked about the same age as Tony. Late thirties. "Where's the wild, dirty man?" said Tony.

"I like to wear a costume when I go to town. Sometimes people see what they want to see." Hudson gestured to a pair of leather chairs. "Have a seat."

Tony sat, but Wade chose to stand. "I'll come right to the point. What's your relationship with Harrison Ragsdale?"

"We don't have a relationship." Anger filled the gray eyes.

"He creeps out my wife."

Not even close to what Tony expected to hear. "How?"

"He stands too close to her. Stares at her. Tries to touch her." Hudson leaned forward, his fingers tightly laced. "It's subtle, but unpleasant."

Tony could imagine the truth of his statement. It sounded a lot like his aunt's. "Did you talk to him about it?"

"Yes. At the Ramp Festival." Hudson balled his hand into a tight fist. "I told him what I thought and punched him in the stomach. Then we left."

A pair of bright-eyed pugs trotted into the room and greeted them all before settling into matching beds near the unlit fireplace. Tony said, "Any problem with him and your animals?"

Clearly thrown off guard, Hudson sat back, his eyebrows pulling low. "No. Why?"

Tony didn't answer. "May we meet your wife?"

"Sure." Hudson stood and the pugs dashed toward him, their corkscrew tails wagging with apparent delight. "Her studio is next door."

Tony's definition of "next door" was measured in feet, not in yards. The three men and two dogs eventually arrived at a separate building attached by a broad enclosed walkway dotted with windows. Hudson knocked twice then entered.

Mrs. Hudson, like her husband, was not any older than Tony. Tony had barely greeted her before he stopped to stare at the painting of the Smoky Mountains in progress on an enormous easel. "That's beautiful."

"Thank you." She smiled, but her expression spoke of distraction and her fingers tightened on the brush in her hand. He'd invaded her space.

Tony thought her expression was similar to Theo's when she was designing a quilt and said so.

"Call me Olivia," Mrs. Hudson said and all the tension in her expression disappeared as she gave him a real smile. "I've been in your wife's shop and seen some of her work. I actually own a quilt she made." She gestured to the wall behind them. "It's a compliment to be mentioned in the same sentence with her. Your wife uses fabric like I use paint."

Tony recognized the humorous quilt hanging in the alcove. Theo had made it and called it "The Girls," her name for the eight appliquéd frogs she'd decorated with costume jewelry, beads, and embroidery. Theo had not planned to sell it, but said a man—now Tony knew who—had purchased it as a gift for his wife. Theo had laughed and claimed she sold it practically at gunpoint to a desperate man and received a large check in exchange.

When Tony asked Olivia about Harrison Ragsdale, she stopped smiling. "He often stared at me, you know, not in a nice way. One time Gwen drove me into town, and I swear he followed us when we left. I wasn't sure if the gate at the road would close quickly enough to keep his truck out, so I made Gwen drive all the way to Maryville and back to make sure we lost him."

From the corner of his eye, Tony saw Bart Hudson's hands ball into fists again. Tony couldn't blame him.

Tony walked toward the wall of windows, noticing the heavy wall coverings that could be lowered like shades. He knew there was a name for them that he couldn't place, but it didn't matter. The view encompassed part of the mountain and had a full view of McMahon Park. The burnt-out rubble of the Smith house filled the center of their bright, spring-green lawn.

To the left of the glass wall were more large windows flanking a pair of French doors opening onto a balcony. He thought he'd never be able to write in this room. He'd spend every moment staring out at Mother Nature's playground. "Did you see the fire down there?"

"Yes. I called nine-one-one."

It wasn't until she walked to join him by the windows that he realized she used a cane. His expression must have shown his surprise. He glanced lower and noticed she wore paint-smeared cropped pants and walked on two prosthetic legs. "I had no idea."

"I know. Thank you." Her smile was radiant. "It's the first thing most people do notice. But not you."

"I guess I was too busy thinking how much you're like Theo, and also admiring your view, to pay attention. I didn't notice any special markings."

Olivia gestured to the wide door. "If you look, you'll find there's a button for the automatic door openers. I did not want bright blue handicapped pictures all over my home." She smiled warmly at her husband. "Bart can work anywhere in the world, and he built this palace for me after the accident. Pouring over the plans and sample books gave me something wonderful to think about. Bart's a sweetheart."

Tony thought Bart was almost embarrassed by her statement.

"I wanted to add an ivory tower, but she said no." Bart leaned against a wall, but did not look particularly relaxed.

As much as he was enjoying talking with this couple, Tony had a job to do. "What did you see?"

"Bart was in California." Her hands trembled and she looked away from the windows. "It was terrifying." She took a deep breath as she forced herself to turn back to the windows. "I saw three men on the roof of the house that burned and thought they were working on it, but when the woman's van returned and the garage door opened, they sort of hid, you know, flattening themselves out. Then the garage door closed behind the van and almost immediately a fire started right below the window opening onto the roof. I went to get my cell phone, but I'm not very fast. When I got back to the balcony again, huge flames were coming out of the upstairs windows, and a river of fire covered the garage roof below the little balcony. As I dialed nine-one-one, I saw the mom and kids run out with the dog. By the time nine-one-one answered, they were safely away from the house." She trembled. "I just remembered. I took some pictures of the men with my phone."

"Photographs of the arsonists?" Tony wondered if Bart would object to his wife being kissed by the sheriff. "Awesome. May I see?"

"I doubt they're very clear. I didn't look at them." Olivia retrieved her state-of-the-art cell phone from a drawer and handed it to Tony. Her expression was only half apologetic. "I hate it ringing when I'm working."

Bart nodded. "I can't tell you how many times I've called her and she doesn't answer."

"Did you see where the men went?" Tony could only think of three men who ran in a pack, the Farquhars.

"They ran away from the house, down to the dirt road on the edge of the park." Olivia pointed through the trees before looking at Tony. "But I only saw two leave."

Tony made no comment. He now knew for certain what he had only guessed before.

Olivia swallowed hard and began scrolling through the tiny pictures on her phone. "Here's where they start." She turned it so Tony and Wade could see, showing each one at full size, which was still the size of a playing card. "Will they help?"

Wade said, "The second one looked pretty clear. I'll bet a photo genius can make it poster size."

Theo couldn't believe how exhausted she suddenly felt; like she'd fall over if she had to stand up for another minute. She glanced into the kids' corner of her office. Chris and Jamie were battling some video game monster with yellow teeth and spots.

It reminded her of someone. She couldn't place who though. "Are you boys at a stopping spot?"

"Not now mom." Chris said, "Almost. We have to get into the castle and collect the coins first."

"Our sisters are sleeping." Jamie gave her a pitiful look. "Are you going to wake them up?"

Theo yawned. Behind the boys, the trundle bed called her name. "How about I take a nap and you can wake me up when you're ready to go home."

"Deal." The boys turned back to their game.

She moved some stuffed animals aside and curled up on the bed. Within seconds, she was sound asleep.

"Theo?" She heard Tony's voice in her dream. "Theo, honey, wake up."

She felt someone shake her shoulder and slapped at it like it was mosquito. "No."

"Mom?" Now it sounded like Jamie's voice was right inside her head. Warm breath tickled her ear. "Are you in there? It's time to go home."

She blinked a few times. All three Abernathy males were staring at her. "Tony? What are you doing here?"

"Not that I don't envy you sleeping away the afternoon, but are you ready to go home?" He had a baby in each arm. "The boys called me when they couldn't wake you up."

"I'm sorry." Theo managed to sit up. "I was just so tired and thought I'd nap for ten minutes while the boys finished up their game." She glanced toward the window. "At least it's not dark."

"Yep, but it will be soon. Let's go home and you can sleep there."

Theo got to her feet and staggered a bit before managing to get her purse and keys and all the babies' stuff together. "Would you mind if we just order pizza for dinner?" If she wasn't so wiped out, she might have cared that Tony and the boys looked relieved she wasn't planning to cook.

Curious about Harrison Ragsdale's nephew, Tony thought he'd have time to return to Randal Byers's home before the pizza could be delivered. He found the young man in the back yard helping his daughter practice shooting a basketball. The hoop was only about five feet off the ground, but she still struggled. When Randal noticed him, he smiled and walked toward him. "Sheriff?"

"Sorry to disturb you and your daughter." Tony stepped backwards, hoping the young man would follow until they were out of the girl's earshot. "I have only recently learned you are the nephew of Harrison Ragsdale."

Randal nodded. "I'm not real proud of my family tree. I think learning about it was part of the reason my wife left me. She thought the whole family, including my daughter, is tainted by bad blood." Anger vibrated in his voice and made his eyes narrow. "If you've got any similar ideas, you can stuff them."

Tony shook his head. "I'm just collecting facts. Can you tell me about your relationship with Ragsdale?"

"We've barely even met and never really spoken together. His sister is, was, my mom. She drank herself to death about two years ago. And my uncle, their brother, is in the penitentiary in Illinois. We don't visit." The young man stared into the distance, past Tony's shoulder. "Quite a family tree, isn't it?"

"I've known better and worse." Tony wasn't without sympathy. "I don't suppose you know anything about Ragsdale's will."

"If there is one, I know nothing about it. You can ask my grandmother, but she's my dad's mom."

Tony thought the young man's facial expression was half-belligerent and half-desperate at the idea of an inheritance.

"Grandma did say some man with a cane stopped by one day and wanted to meet my daughter. I thought it might be my uncle Harrison. Grandma said she took a broom and swept him off the porch; didn't like the looks of him. He never came by again."

"How are your finances?"

"Without Grandma's help, I couldn't afford to live here. The fertilizer plant pays okay, but if I had to pay a baby-sitter, I don't know how I'd do it."

"About your ex-wife." Tony felt like a louse asking him painful questions. Randal acted like a good father and a hard worker but the law was *his* job. "Do you have joint custody?"

A bitter-sounding laugh was part of Randal's answer. "Nope. I have full custody and eight kinds of paper to prove it. She didn't want any part of us. It seems I was fun for a little while, but she didn't think being a mom was worth the effort. She bitched a lot about stretch marks and stuff. I'd guess she used all the money I gave her to pay for some plastic surgery. Last I heard, she was headed to Hollywood."

"Is she an actress?"

Randal laughed long and hard. A real, deep-from-the-belly laugh. "Thank you, Sheriff. I swear that's the funniest thing I've heard in weeks. Yeah, she thought she was finest actress ever, and to be fair, she convinced me that she loved me, for a while." He tossed the ball to his daughter.

Tony watched the little girl trot after it. She watched them over her shoulder. "She looks concerned."

Randal's voice dropped to a whisper. "The first few weeks we were here, she was afraid her mom was coming to take her away."

"She didn't want her mom?" Tony didn't like the way this story was getting hinky. "Does she think she's going back to live with her?"

"No, not anymore, but it's taken a lot to convince her she's just mine." Randal kicked a rock with his toe. He squinted as he raised his eyes. "One of the reasons, besides every dime I had, my ex-wife finally signed the papers giving me full custody was because I threatened to call the cops and have her arrested."

"Abuse or neglect?" Provoked by his anger, Tony's stomach gnawed.

"A little of both, and neither obvious." Randal looked directly into Tony's eyes. "When you're working two jobs and are rarely home, it's hard to keep track of all the little details. There were just lots of things my wife said or did that didn't quite add up." He heaved a big sigh. "Then one day, I came home and she, my wife, was entertaining a man in our bedroom and my daughter was locked in her room. I went ballistic."

"I think I've heard enough." Tony extended his hand. "Good luck with your daughter. As long as all this is substantiated, I'm on your side."

"Do you think? Is it possible?" Randal couldn't quite ask the question.

"Do you mean are you in the will?"

Randal nodded.

Tony lied. "I don't know. We haven't found one yet. But if you are, you'll be contacted by the lawyers." Tony sincerely hoped Randal was as innocent as he seemed. "We're still looking into your uncle's death, so it may take a while. Don't give up hope, and remember your time is worth more to your daughter than the things money buys."

"Yes, sir." Randal picked up the ball and tossed it. The little girl ran after it, giggling and suddenly at ease, almost as if she sensed a possible threat to her happiness had been averted. Her hair flew behind her and the old lady opened the door and called them to dinner.

"Good luck." Tony whispered and went home to hug his own kids. Running around in circles was not conducive to thinking things through, and money was still one of the oldest and best motives for murder.

"I want to know what the three Farquhar boys have been up to for the past week or two." Tony addressed the day shift—Wade, Mike, Sheila, and Darren. "And I wouldn't be disappointed if one of you should learn one of them fed Ragsdale a handful of walnuts."

"They haven't been in town for a while." Sheila tapped her notebook. "Or they're being low-key. I had to drag two of them out of the Okay a couple of weeks ago. Mom Proffitt said she'd shoot one if they came back. They are definitely not welcome in her establishment."

Mike said. "The only certainty is they're drinking somewhere. They were pretty liquored up at the festival. I bumped into one of them, and he started to take a swing at me, but his brothers pulled him away."

"So they're probably doing their drinking at home or over at the Spa," said Sheila.

Tony thought about his next move. The Spa was the nickname for the Spot. No one ever seemed to think pronouncing the whole "spot" was worth the effort. Neither was spending much time in the Spa. Unlike the Okay, the only reason anyone went there was to have too much to drink and maybe chum up with someone else over-imbibing. It was a dump. A dive. A cesspool. And thankfully for the county budget, it was conveniently near a really fine place to set a trap for speeders and DUIs. "I'll go to the Spa myself. I need to have a little chat with Fast Osborne about his customers being over-served. Wade, come with me."

"I'll watch the roads while you two chat with the Farquhars," Sheila looked at Mike and Darren. When they nodded, Sheila relaxed a bit, making Tony wonder what she wasn't telling him. Sheila said, "Have you noticed the shrine near Dead Man's Curve seems to be growing?"

"Larger?"

"Flowers." Sheila used her hands to suggest the width and length. "The center is planted with crocuses and some other small bulbs, and around it is a border of something else, and so on. There's at least four borders, and each contains a different kind of plant. I've been taking Alvin out there to clear the weeds from his grandparents' memorial and we've noticed lots of changes."

"Any idea who is gardening there?" Tony leaned forward. "Or what, if anything, is buried there?"

"No." Sheila gestured again. "The center has had a handmade cross ever since the man from North Carolina drove into the stone wall and you rescued Catherine. It's pretty crudely done but identifiable. Now there's an additional wreath of artificial flowers on a stand. The way the shrine is getting larger kind of gives me the creeps."

"Here's your chance to do some detective work. See what you can learn about it. I remember seeing it not long ago, but it sounds like after several years untouched it is definitely changing. Find out why." Tony knew Sheila would handle the assignment with her usual efficiency. He looked at Mike and Darren. "You two, watch out for those Farquhar boys. I suspect they are our burglars as well as our arsonists."

"Do you think one of them was the body in the garage?" Mike absently massaged Dammit's ear. "I wouldn't put it past them to kill one of their own."

"Me neither, so be extra careful. Don't turn your back on them." Tony stood. "Wade, let's go bar hopping."

In Tony's opinion, if there was ever a case of a nickname not matching the establishment, it was the Spa. Where the Okay Bar and Bait Shop was built like a box, sort of a whitewashed wooden cube, the Spa was long and narrow and built of cinderblocks. The original owner named it "the Spot" and had painted a huge red circle on the front of the building, encompassing the door. The rest of the cinderblocks were painted the same dull gray as their natural color.

No one had painted anything around the Spa in years, and most of the red paint had flaked off long ago. No one had trimmed the weeds growing through the gravel of the parking lot. No one had filled the ruts either. Driving across the parking lot in the patrol vehicle, Tony had to wonder how the Spa's customers could afford to keep their vehicles in alignment.

"Good thing we brought your vehicle. It has higher clearance than mine." Wade gripped the window frame of the Blazer as they dropped into a vicious rut. "I doubt the Thomas Brothers could straighten the frame if I drove here in my car."

"I was thinking along the same lines." Tony parked right in front of the bar's front door, mostly because it was the flattest part of the parking lot. He looked at Wade. "You'd better suck in all the oxygen you can. Last time I went inside there wasn't any, just old tired air." He climbed out of the Blazer and headed inside, Wade followed close on his heels.

"Sheriff?" The owner/bartender, Fast Osborne, peered through the haze. "Is there a problem?"

Tony ignored the question. He'd have taken a seat on one of the stools, but guessed the back of his khaki pants would bear the stains forever. From the corner of his eye, he noticed Wade wipe one with a corner of his handkerchief. He folded it carefully and put it in his jacket pocket, but not before Tony saw the brown sludge folded into the middle of it.

"Have you seen the Farquhar boys lately?" Tony thought he'd skip the pleasantries.

Osborne just stared at him. "Huh?"

"I know they're customers of yours. Jocko and Geordie and Shawn Farquhar." Tony's skin started itching. He was no stranger to walking into unclean buildings, crime scenes, and accidents, but this room felt like a biology experiment in action.

The bartender still didn't respond, but from an even darker corner, near the back, a man's voice, raspy from years of smoke and whiskey, said, "Two of 'em was in here this morning."

"Okay, that's a start. Which two?"

"Can't tell them apart." Behind the bar, Osborne found his voice at last. "They're all dumb, dishonest, and drunk most of the time."

"So, some of your favorite customers." Tony guessed the "boys" spent all the money they stole right here.

"They do keep me in business." Osborne's breath came out in a great gust. "Is that a crime?"

Tony backed away from the fumes emanating from the bartender. He'd evidently been sampling the wares himself. "It is a crime if you over-serve them and send them out on the road." Tony wouldn't want the bartender behind the wheel either and hoped he still lived on the premises.

"They's grownups, ain't they? I don't serve no kids in here." The little man puffed up like an angry bird. "I run a class eee-stablishment."

"Yeah," Wade muttered near Tony's ear. "If A is good, this is definitely E rated."

Tony nodded. "Tell me about the two Farquhar boys who were in here this morning then. Were they talking big, flashing money, anything unusual for them?"

With the palm of his hand, the bartender smashed a black bug staggering along the bar, then wiped the remains on the side of his dirty jeans. "You know, seems like they was a bit quieter than usual. Maybe 'cause there was only two of them, but they was kinda huddled together at that table." He nodded to a corner table in almost total darkness.

"Who took them their drinks?" Wade tipped his notebook to

let the paltry light shine on it so he could make his notes.

"I did. They each had a couple of beers and left." Osborne spat on the floor behind the bar.

"Anyone talk to them?" said Tony.

"Naw, but I wouldn't say that's any different than usual. Those boys ain't real friendly 'n' most times they's generally left alone."

Feeling there was nothing to learn and anxious to be outside, Tony beat Wade to the door. As soon as they were in the fresh air, he took huge gulps of the stuff, trying to purge his lungs of stale Spa air. "Can you imagine spending more than ten minutes in there?"

Wade shook his head and wheezed. "I feel like I need a shower and a fresh uniform."

As they prepared to pull back onto the road, Jessica's boyfriend, Vic, drove past them in his work van. A giant plastic bug lay, legs up, on the roof. The logo on the door said "Vic's Victims, Exterminator." Tony glanced at Wade. "Mom Proffitt called earlier and said she remembered Vic talking about coming into big dollars—like he was marrying an heiress. What do you think?"

"I think it might be interesting to hear what he says when Jessica isn't around. She strikes me as a no-nonsense woman with a firm grip on the reins."

"My thought exactly." Tony followed the van until it stopped in front of a house and parked. Calling out and waving to Vic, Wade got out first.

The three men gathered near the oversized, fake deceased insect. After a brief meet and greet, Tony said, "Did you know about the houses Ragsdale owned?"

"Sure." Vic's expression hinted of pride. "He had me spray all of them each spring and fall. Said the riff-raff couldn't be trusted to watch for termites or creepies."

Wade made a note. "How many houses?"

"Six or seven." Vic scratched his head. "I have the addresses in my files. Guess there's no reason not to show them to you."

"So, you've been doing this for several years?" Tony leaned casually against the van thinking the number of houses was quite different from Jessica's version. "How's business?"

"There's always bugs." Vic chuckled. "They're my job security." His laughter faded. "I imagine you've heard I have been having a bit of difficulty paying my bills."

Tony hadn't, but kept his ignorance to himself. "Did you ever consider Jessica would lose all her inheritance if they divorced?"

"But she's his widow." Desperation rang in Vic's voice. "Don't she get it all?"

Tony was frustrated and busy, but he still made time to help at Chris's baseball practice. He was walking across the park from his house to the ball fields when he encountered a coach from a rival team. Andy Marks.

"My wife said I should talk to Doc Nash, and I did, and he said I should talk to you." The man said as he approached Tony in the park. "I think it's silly."

"What's that?" Tony's curiosity was certainly piqued. He shifted the baseball equipment bag on his shoulder. Andy carried a similar one.

"Well, it was something that happened at the Ramp Festival. I have allergies and ate something with nuts in it there and had to leave early." Andy gazed off in the distance, a slight smile on his lips. "I would purely have enjoyed seeing Hairy Rags go down. Missed the whole rocket potato. My tongue started swelling, and my wife got me out of there and jabbed me with my emergency anti-allergy syringe." He flexed his beefy arm and pointed to a small dark bruise. "I mean it. She jabbed that sucker in hard."

Tony wasn't sure if he was supposed to laugh or arrest the woman. "But it did the trick for you?"

"Yeah, I still had to go to the doctor and all, but there wasn't a big rush and all's well. Anyway, the doctor said for me to tell you I'm allergic to nuts, and now I have." Looking somewhat embarrassed, Andy turned to leave.

"Wait." Tony set his bag down and pulled out his notebook. "Tell me everything you can remember from before your reaction—what did you see, eat, smell, taste?"

Andy stared for a moment. "You really want to know all this, do you?"

"Absolutely."

"Well, the wife and me wandered around the crafts booths first. The food lines were really long when we got there, especially for the ramp pies." Andy paused. "This is really what you want to know?"

Jotting down a note, Tony smiled and nodded. "You're doing great. Just keep talking."

"Okay. Well, the wife bought a few cookies at the bake sale, but like I said, I couldn't eat any because of the nuts. Honestly, that woman's wonderful, she loves nuts and she takes the cookies to her office and eats them. She's really good at brushing her teeth and washing her face after she eats them, but it's not enough. When she eats stuff with nuts in it, I can't kiss my own wife because of the nut thing."

"I'd say it's a pretty severe allergy then." Tony didn't think he'd ever heard of someone having such extreme reactions to anything. "Have you always had it?"

"Yep. But, it does seem like it's been getting worse, like each time I have a reaction, the next time it's stronger. I didn't used to have to carry medication." He patted his jacket pocket. "Before you start thinkin' my wife isn't good to me, you're wrong. She does the cookies thing only about once a year when the ladies of the church have their bake sale. One of those ladies makes a walnut, chocolate, caramel cookie to die for, so to speak." Andy cracked a wide grin. "My wife indulges with my blessing."

Tony made a note to chat with the church ladies. Even if it turned out it wasn't part of the case, he thought he should investigate just how good the cookies really were. "So after visiting the crafts and bake sale, were you feeling all right?"

"Just fine. My wife had the ladies seal the cookies up in the triple plastic bags she brought along. Everyone was very careful. Then she stashed it in her purse and zipped it up." His pride about the way his wife worked to protect him was obvious. "So then we watched some of the entertainment. And by the way, if you should shoot them Elves, I'll give you an alibi. Name the day and time, and I'll say you were with me." His head bobbed emphatically. "I'll swear it on the Bible."

Tony nodded, afraid if he opened his mouth a laugh would escape.

"So, anyway we went over to the ramp stuff. I got a slice of ramp pie and the wife got a cup of the soup. Those relics—I can't believe that's what they want to be called—but they had the name printed on T-shirts. Anyhow, they were handing out napkins and plastic spoons and offering salt and pepper and hot sauce. I guess if you sprinkle enough fiery sauce on the ramps, you don't notice the taste so bad. I had two bites and my lips started to swell, and I could feel my throat closing. I handed the wife my pen, she stabbed me, and we left." He made a snuffling sound. "Didn't get to see those vegetables fly."

Tony studied the man's expression. He was clearly more disappointed about missing the vegetable weapons display than anything else. "Do you have any idea what happened?"

"Nope. I guess there were some nuts in the pie, but I can't say I saw any or tasted any." He clearly considered the interview over and shifted away. "That it, Sheriff? I need to get to practice."

"Me too." Tony picked up the equipment bag at his feet. "Thanks for the information." Glancing toward the ball fields, he saw Chris waving and hustled to practice.

Luckily, Tony was only an assistant coach to the assistant coach. His attendance was erratic because of his work, and although his body was there today, he couldn't get his mind off the story he'd just heard. Had someone poisoned everyone with nut allergies? Accident or not?

Theo took Jamie to his team's practice. Actually, she and the stroller filled with the twins accompanied Daisy as they walked behind Jamie. When they were almost at the ball field, Kenny Baines, whose daughter played on Jamie's team, signaled for Theo to join him and Blossom. His tiny little girl was not a great hitter, but she could catch the ball and had an accurate throw for a girl so young. The little girl smiled and patted Daisy before trotting next to Jamie, who had waved to everyone but kept walking.

Blossom and Kenny sat side by side on folding chairs under a shade tree with bright green spring leaves starting to unfurl. Theo noticed the couple was holding hands. As usual, Daisy carried her leash in her mouth and she abandoned Theo and trotted over to investigate the puppy by Blossom's feet. Miss Cotton was about the size of Daisy's head, but she was unfazed by the difference in their sizes and ambled to greet the huge golden.

Fighting with the double stroller as she pushed across the uneven ground, Theo followed more slowly. "It's a beautiful evening."

Blossom and Kenny agreed. A moment later, without a word, Blossom extended her left hand so Theo could see a new ring on her finger. *The* ring finger. A diamond flanked by a pair of emeralds sparkled in the late afternoon sunlight.

"You're engaged?" Theo thought she might have shrieked a bit.

Kenny kissed Blossom's cheek. "Yes, we are." His smile was tender and triumphant.

Theo was delighted. "Congratulations!" She gave each of them a hug and a cheek kiss. "How exciting! When did you decide?" What she really wanted to know, and wouldn't ask, was if they had already told Tony. Their competition to have the freshest news first was ongoing and semi-serious.

"This afternoon." Blossom beamed. "Kenny and the girls asked me when he came by to pick me up to come here."

"So just minutes ago?" At their smiling nods, Theo picked up Daisy's leash. "We'll leave you to make your plans. Should I keep it a secret?"

"No," said Kenny. "Tell everyone you want to. We haven't set the date, but it might be as early as June." He kissed Blossom's hand. "The choice is my fiancée's, but I hope it's soon."

Theo wanted to know if they'd broken the news to DuWayne, but managed not to blurt out her question. Glowing with self-pride, she managed to wait until she was out of earshot from the couple before she pulled out her cell phone, and still fighting the stroller, hit speed dial to contact Nina. "Guess what I just saw!"

Chapter Sixteen

"Okay." Tony stood in front of his small staff. "I know we've gone over part of this before, but let's do it again. I want to know everything you've learned about nuts and the festival. Sheila, you start."

"Several of the cookies and candies sold at the dessert booth contained walnuts, pecans, almonds, or almond paste." Sheila flipped through her notes. "The ladies swear they had a few people who questioned them about the ingredients. A few didn't buy, presumably because of allergies, but it could have been an excuse they gave to make it look like they were willing, not cheap." Sheila paused and looked around. "No one thinks Ragsdale came within twenty feet of the bake sale booth, and since most of the women looked like they'd spit on his grave, I believe they'd remember."

Wade stood. "I checked the ingredients in the ramp dishes as well as the foods offered by the vendors. No one used tree nuts in any dishes or walnut oil in their cooking. Not even in the salad dressing." He turned to Tony. "And I didn't just take their word for it. I took samples of the dressings and sauces and had them tested."

"Maybe someone bought a cookie from the ladies and crumbled it and dropped it on his food when he was distracted." Mike feigned pointing to the side and dropped a paper wad on the floor.

"There's a good idea," said Tony. "If we can somehow get a

list of people who knew about his allergy, who were at the festival, maybe someone will remember selling a person a cookie. Or maybe I'll find a winning lottery ticket in the morning mail."

"Sheriff, I have some video you might want to see." Rex Satterfield's voice came through the radio.

Tony had asked everyone in the department to check any photographs or videos they or a family member had taken at the festival. Rex was the only one saw far who had seen anything of interest. He hurried to the dispatch desk to view the recording. The footage showed swarms of spectators moving toward the field, apparently focused on Harrison's body, but beyond them the Farquhars, including Angus, ran the other direction. Tony saw them knock over a few people before one of the younger Farquhars dumped the money from a tip jar into his bunched up shirttail and rejoined the pack.

"I want to talk to the Farquhar 'darlin' boys.' All of them."

"Damn those Farquhar boys." Tony's outrage propelled him from his chair. None of his deputies could find a single one of them. "When I want to talk to them they vanish, and when I don't, they turn up on every corner I turn. I'd like to ship every Farquhar out of this county, the state, and the country. One-way. Let's just pack them into a big, strong crate with a few air holes and a couple of bottles of water and nail it shut. Send it away." Tony moved to pace in the hallway outside his office. "Forget the water."

Watching from her desk, Ruth Ann's dark eyes showed no sign of shock. She very precisely placed the polish brush into the bottle and twisted the top closed. "What country are you hoping to provoke into a war? Receiving a gift like a box of Farquhars couldn't be excused."

"You're starting to sound more like a lawyer every day." Just saying the words gave him a chill, cooling some of his anger. "Did you pass your bar exam?"

"I don't know yet." Ruth Ann blew gently on her brilliant blue fingernail polish. It matched the color of her blouse. "Word should come in soon though. I feel pretty good about it."

Tony settled onto the chair next to her desk. "I'm sure you'll pass." His stomach gnawed and he realized he felt close to panic, thinking about what would follow if Ruth Ann did pass the bar exam. "And then? What's your plan? Abandoning us?"

"Do you want me to leave?" Ruth Ann's dark eyes met his.

"Hell, no." He studied her expression. "Are you planning to practice law and keep up with your manicures and run this office?" Tony ticked each item on the fingers of his left hand. "Plus there's Walter. Now that his mama's moved from your house and back to her own, you get to go home to your husband at night."

"I do enjoy being at home much more now. When Walter was unable to be left home alone, she was a necessary and helpful visitor." Ruth Ann did smile then, her teeth brilliant white in her cocoa-colored face. "I don't miss her."

Tony felt a glimmer of hope. Maybe Ruth Ann wasn't going to jump ship, at least not any time soon.

"Our new trailer has arrived." Tony led the deputies and Ruth Ann through the law enforcement building and into the small parking area in the back surrounded by a ten-foot fence topped with razor wire. It looked like part of the jail facility exercise yard. A shiny new trailer painted green and white and decorated with the Park County sheriff's logo sat in solitary splendor in the enclosure.

"Wow." Several voices spoke in a ragged chorus.

"It looks bigger in the cage than it did on the parking lot." Tony had some experience hauling a trailer, but not much. He was going to have to do some serious practicing before he would feel comfortable parking it in front of witnesses. He had no desire to become the laughingstock of the county or, even worse, to back the thing off the side of a mountain. Some of their narrow, twisting roads were difficult enough to navigate with the Blazer; he wasn't looking forward to dragging the trailer, however useful it might be.

"What's going inside?" Ruth Ann stared at the paint job.

"Emergency stuff." Tony thought he'd leave it at that. Knowing he'd have to practice parking after midnight, he wasn't in the mood to discuss the projected contents.

The first night he decided to practice, he felt a little awkward backing the Blazer into just the right spot to hook the trailer onto the back of the vehicle. Actually driving and pulling it felt somewhat different, but not difficult. He learned fairly quickly about how much extra time he needed to make a smooth stop. He turned a few corners too wide and realized he needed to compensate more. Driving up and down the hills of the county after midnight gave him a different perspective of his world. When he was first elected sheriff, he had made lots of nighttime drives and soon realized the lack of sunlight was not the only difference. A completely different set of people traveled the dark roads.

His parking and backing-up practice was not immediately successful. After almost tipping the whole business on its side, he quit sightseeing and studied the various problems he encountered, hoping to solve them. A family of possums sat by the side of the road staring at him. The mom and her little ones wore the same avid expression his boys displayed when watching cartoons and video games. He suspected he looked much the same when watching baseball on television. At least the possums were quiet and well mannered. Lined up in the weeds, they simply watched, offering no advice. When Tony managed to make the turn, backing up a little, forward a little, until he could head in the other direction, he was sure he heard them cheer a bit. It felt good.

He passed J.B.'s cruiser several times. The deputy had preferred to work the night shift for as long as Tony had been sheriff. On this lovely evening, driving around in the moonlight, Tony could almost understand why. Illuminated by the full moon, the landscape was darker than the sky. Occasional yard lights or headlights on other vehicles on the road were blindingly bright after the shadows. His headlights reflected from the wide eyes of critters out for an evening stroll. A huge owl swept from the sky, picked up an unwary mouse and soared silently past his windshield. He passed so close Tony could see individual feathers. A few miles closer to town, he saw Sheila parked by the side of the road. She was supposed to be off-duty, and it looked like she was trying to break up a fight between a short, squat woman and a much larger man. Tony pulled over to help.

In the light from the headlights, the woman appeared to be winning the fight. Her waist was wider than her chest. Her stringy, dishwater blond hair flew about her face, accentuating her missing teeth, almost all of the ones on the left. She shrieked. "He's the one you ought to arrest. He's cheating on me."

The man pressed both hands over his bleeding nose. "Come on, Candy, that's not fair. She's my wife."

"Well, you ought to treat me better than her." Candy hauled back and threw a punch. The boyfriend ducked, and Candy's fist slammed upwards into Tony's left cheekbone.

"That's enough." Tony held Candy's wrists together and Sheila handed him a pair of handcuffs.

Tony thanked her. "What are you doing out here?"

Sheila tipped her head to her car where a teenage boy sat in the passenger seat. "Alvin called. He was afraid his mom was headed for trouble."

"I'd say he had good instincts." Tony led Candy to his Blazer and put her in the backseat. The cage had a shield to prevent her spitting on him. He turned to watch Sheila load the boyfriend into her car. When she drove away, Tony followed. He left the Blazer and the trailer in the back lot and led Candy through the double set of doors into the jail intake area. Candy squawked and continually whined about her no good SOB boyfriend cheating on her. With his wife, of all the women in the world.

Sheila put the boyfriend in a chair and took Candy off his hands. "She'll sober up and stay through breakfast, then we'll cut her loose. Unless the boyfriend presses charges."

"And Alvin?" Tony headed outside to retrieve the boy. "Should I leave him in the kitchen?"

"Could you make him a couple of sandwiches?" said Sheila. "This won't take me very long and then I'll take him to my folks."

Tony thought he could use a snack too. He led Alvin to the kitchen and pulled an assortment of sandwich makings and cookies from the jail kitchen's well stocked refrigerator and cupboards. The jail cook, Daffodil Flowers Smith, kept a jar on the counter for either cash payments or vouchers to cover anything eaten by staff or guests. Staying away from the subject of his mother, Tony and Alvin made small talk about Alvin's desire to study botany, his makeshift greenhouse and the possibility of doing yard work for the Abernathy family. Tony dutifully obeyed Daffodil's rules.

Once Alvin was fed and drove away with Sheila, Tony took the trailer back to its spot. Parking it in the lot was trickier than he expected. After several attempts, he managed to get it lined up right and locked it up and went home. He passed Theo at the top of the stairs as he headed to bed and she went to soothe an unhappy infant.

CHAPTER SEVENTEEN

Theo sat in the workroom with Susan. Together they continued trying to fill out the Smiths' insurance forms. It had to feel like a hopeless task. Poor Susan kept crying and saying, "I don't know. What do you think?"

Theo couldn't really offer more than sympathy. She knew she had sold a fair amount of fabric, thread, and quilt batting to the woman, but had no idea how much. Or how much Susan had used on various projects, or how much she might have purchased from other shops. Quilters—and Theo was certainly no better than her friends and customers—loved to visit every shop they come across. One of the popular books she sold in her shop was a listing of other shops. Driving down the interstate, she'd seen signs pointing to the exits and instructions on how to reach the quilt shop. A motel might not be listed, but the quilt shop was. Theo didn't think of herself as a fabulous businesswoman, but she was no dummy. She had ads in the book and her own little shop paid for a couple of signs.

Jane and Martha breezed into the shop chattering away. Theo couldn't imagine the two women could have anything left to talk about. The sisters spent about ten hours a day in each other's company and witnessed the same events.

"Oh, Susan, we're so sorry to hear about your house." Martha settled onto a chair. "How can we help?"

Overcome, Susan just shook her head, chin quivering, and patted the little girl sleeping in her arms.

Jane whispered into the silence, "We could throw a fund-raiser out at the museum."

Theo wasn't sure if she should be horrified or enthusiastic. Hairy Rags hadn't even been buried yet. "After your last big celebration?"

Martha clapped her hands. "It will be so much better this time. We won't have to invite those Elves or eat smelly vegetables."

"Everyone should bring a covered dish, and Susan will get to keep the dish," Jane babbled now, bouncing on her chair like a toddler. "And all the quilters can wrap theirs in fabric, and can't you just see it?"

Theo hated to throw cold water on their plans. The threat of another huge event strengthened her resolve. "Why don't you wait until the family is not living in a motel room? They really don't have any place to store anything."

Tears welled in Jane's eyes. "I forgot."

Tony decided he could give himself a couple of hours at the house. He might even get some writing done, but more likely he'd spend his time cleaning up the yard. Once inside, he still had his hand on the doorknob when Daisy trotted past him, plumed tail high. Something pink hung from the side of her mouth. Her tongue, was his first thought, but immediately realized it was fuzzy. He followed Daisy into the small parlor. That was normal, since she practically lived on the love seat. Instead of jumping onto it, she wriggled behind it until all he could see was haunch and tail.

"Daisy?" The tail thumped in response. "Come." He patted his leg. The tail thumped faster. "Now." She scooted backwards enough to turn her face to look at him. Sorrowful brown eyes in a big face met his.

He went to her and bent forward, looking into the corner

behind the love seat. Wedged between the furniture and the wall was a sizeable pile of tiny socks, hats, T-shirts, and a soft toy. Not one of her toys. Daisy's nest. "Good dog." He rubbed the dog's ears. "You've kept them all safe." He reached in and gathered the missing items into his hand and pulled them toward him.

Daisy watched anxiously. A soft whine came from her chest.

"It's okay, girl." He spoke softly, hoping to mitigate her distress. "Maybe you can keep this one." He pushed the toy, a fuzzy yellow duck, back into the corner and carried the tiny clothes to the laundry. At least one mystery was solved. Theo would be relieved the socks had returned and he was thrilled the washing machine didn't need repairs, or replacement.

He glanced out the window and saw Gus amble back and forth across the yard. Tony thought his expression was more intense than usual. Genial and affable were the adjectives more likely to describe this brother. He went outside, joining Gus, wondering what the problem was.

Theo headed to the dump. She was off to visit Katti. Since learning of Katti's pregnancy, Theo was determined to help as much as she could. Katti had done so much for her family when she was pregnant, more than she was paid to do. Theo felt almost guilty.

Claude came out of the house when Theo turned into the driveway. He must have seen her pull off the road. With the flashy yellow paint job on her new SUV, a blind man could see her coming.

"That's some vehicle. Would you like to trade for my truck?" He gave her a big wink. "Either one, the dump truck or the Crown Vic."

"Maybe the pink Cadillac?"

"I'm not the owner of the caddy." Claude ambled toward the

aromatic dump truck. "And since Katti loves the car and I'm sure she'd go wherever it went, I'll have to say no." His voice dropped to a whisper meant only for Theo. "She's not been feeling too good, mostly in the mornings. Maybe you can help."

Theo nodded, understanding. "It's different for everyone, but morning sickness usually passes in a few weeks." She carried the girls into the house and looked into the living room for Katti. The mail-order bride was stretched out under a pink blanket. Not surprisingly, a long array of crocheted, antebellum girls sitting over rolls of toilet paper, rescued from the post-festival garbage, had found homes on a bookcase in the cramped space next to her.

"How are you feeling?" said Theo.

Katti's complexion was slightly green. "I feel . . ." She struggled to find the word in English. "I feel like dog poop."

Theo handed her a package of saltines and a large bottle of sports drink she'd brought with her. "Only a little at a time."

Katti waved her toward the deep rose velvet sofa. "You sit. Tell Katti of joys of motherhood."

And Theo did.

Frustrated by Gus's refusal to explain what was going on, Tony drove to the museum after asking Wade to meet him there.

"Tell me about the process followed at the food booth. I have a witness who is allergic to walnuts who had an attack after eating some ramp pie." He raised his palm toward his mother to keep her quiet. "Aunt Martha, you start."

"We have a commercial, inspected, and licensed kitchen, Tony." Martha clicked her heels together and placed her right hand over her heart. "I swear, I have no idea what could have happened."

Jane shot to her feet and stood next to her sister. "Honestly, Tony, you can't think we poisoned the man. If we were going to do it, we would never have waited this many years, and we certainly wouldn't have done it at our own party."

Tony released a sigh in a gust. "I don't think you actually did it. You two couldn't have kept it a secret, at least not for more than fifteen minutes."

Jane crossed her arms over her chest and sat again. "That hurts."

"I don't mean it as a criticism. You're just too nice, too honest and . . ." He stopped, not wanting to hurt her feelings.

"And a chatterbox." Martha finished his sentence. She hugged her sister. "I don't think we want to be suspects."

"He's insulting our kitchen." Jane apparently wasn't over being miffed.

Tony rubbed the back of his neck. "Let's attack this from another angle. Who else besides you two worked in the kitchen that day?"

"Well," Jane raised her left hand in a fist. "Martha and me." Ignoring his request to leave themselves out, two fingers went up. "The church ladies." One at a time a finger went up as she went through the list. She passed ten and was starting through her hands again when Tony surrendered.

"Let's try this another way." Tony thought for a moment. "Was there anyone in the kitchen you were surprised to see there, or who shouldn't have been there?"

The two women conferred for a few minutes.

Tony felt like humming a game show tune always played before the big answer. When they shot him a dirty look, he realized he had started doing it out loud. "Sorry." He concentrated on being quiet.

"No." The women spoke. "Everyone in there had a job and was doing it."

"Wait," said Jane.

Tony and Martha leaned forward waiting.

"The man from the burger booth. He was in there when we arrived." Jane rubbed her left ear. "I was surprised to see him. He put something in the refrigerator."

It wouldn't surprise Tony to learn that the man did put something in the refrigerator, but he couldn't imagine it was nutty. Still, he'd better find out.

"Yes, I put mayonnaise and some of my meat in their refrigerator. Wasn't I supposed to use it?" Big Ed snarled at Tony. "I certainly wasn't the only one besides your mom and aunt storing food in there. There were some mighty tasty looking desserts in there too, and real cream for coffee." Big Ed looked like he was just warming to his subject, his face was turning a deep red. A large vein in his forehead throbbed and grew even larger.

Tony thought it was fine for Ed to use the refrigerator. If a bunch of people had gotten sick on spoiled food, the situation would probably be worse. One man dying of an allergic reaction was far removed from the potential disaster with hordes of aging people and small children suffering from food poisoning. Tony shuddered at the horrendous idea. "I'm sure Mom and Martha were just answering my question about who was using the refrigerator. There's no reason to be concerned. As you said, there were many hands involved in the feast." Which, as Tony saw it, made the whole issue of the nuts even more complicated.

"Well, that's good." Big Ed's high color eased a bit.

Big Ed might not be mollified, but at least he wasn't clutching his chest. Tony wanted to do CPR on the cook about as much as he wanted a heart attack of his own. "Did you see anything unusual in the refrigerator or notice anything that contained nuts?"

"Some of them little cakes had nuts on them, but they was wrapped up good and tight."

Ed looked a bit miffed about it, and Tony wondered if he had hoped to snag a treat without paying for it. "Unless there's something else you can tell me, I'll look into those. Thanks for coming by." Tony watched Big Ed waddle out the door and promised himself he'd cut back on the pie and spend more time exercising. Tony turned to Wade. "You learning anything we can use?"

Wade flipped through his notes shaking his head, then he grinned. "I'm learning I might want to eat less at Big Ed's booth. The man looked like he was about to have a heart attack."

"I agree." Tony turned back to stare at the empty doorway. "What are we missing? There were nuts on the desserts, but everyone, including the pathologist, swears Ragsdale didn't eat a dessert. Everything was wrapped up tight, so the nuts didn't fall off a cookie and land in his burger."

Theo stared at the shop telephone. She was elated, excited, and thrilled. The call she'd just ended came from a well-known quilting magazine. Her shop had just been chosen as one of the top ten in the country by a committee. The wonderful news was followed by the immediate request to set up the appointment for a photographer to come and take the pictures for the magazine. Theo glanced around. Currently the shop looked like the back of her closet—a mess comprised of some really good stuff and some trash. They needed to do some serious cleaning. And the article was supposed to remain a secret for a while. Keeping such a huge secret was *not* going to be easy.

"Gretchen!" Theo trotted down the stairs, made sure they were out of earshot, and whispered, "Guess what? We can't tell anyone yet, but we're going to be in the magazine—one of the top ten."

Gretchen presented her normal unflappable persona but Theo

saw her hands shaking. "How wonderful! What should we do first?"

Before Theo could say a word, Nellie Pearl Prigmore, whose dementia had continued to worsen daily while she still lived in Silersville, slammed the door open and stalked inside. "Where is she?" Anger vibrated in every syllable.

Behind Theo, a customer quietly approached. "You think she escaped? I thought her daughter took her to California or something." Theo thought so too. Nellie Pearl's daughter had spent a couple of months living with Nellie Pearl, trying to sort out the good possessions from the garbage she collected and make sure her mother took her medicines as scheduled. At the end of that time, she had put Nellie Pearl's house on the market and left town, taking her mother with her. Theo greeted Nellie Pearl with as much warmth as she could summon. The two women had never been friends. "Hi, Nellie Pearl."

The old woman turned toward Theo. She bared her teeth and hissed at Theo. Taking a step closer, she raised her hands, holding them like claws ready to attack.

Theo froze, thinking there were wild animals you should try to outrun, and there were others where staying absolutely still was the recommended approach. What kind was this demented old woman? Nellie Pearl looked much cleaner than she had when she and her daughter had stopped by on their way out of town. At least she wasn't wearing her former clothes: layers of dirty clothes, usually men's shirts. If it weren't for the anger and confusion in her expression, she'd actually be a very pleasant-looking older woman. She wore jeans and a clean blue and green plaid shirt, open, over a navy T-shirt. It was weather appropriate. The hands held like talons were clean and the fingernails neatly trimmed and polished.

The next moment, like an internal switch flipped, Nellie Pearl relaxed and looked around the shop, a soft smile on her face.

Curious, but nonviolent.

The bell on the door chimed softly as someone entered. "Oh, thank goodness, she's in here." The speaker addressed someone on the sidewalk.

Theo thought Nellie Pearl's daughter looked better too. She had been so exhausted and bedraggled by the time she left town with her mother that the two women looked almost the same age. There were still lines of strain in her face, but nothing like there had been.

"Mom?" The daughter walked up to the older woman but didn't touch her. "Have you come to talk to Theo?"

"Theo?" The older woman's manner changed again. "Yes, I remember her. She's a tiny little thing with big eyes and glasses. An orphan. Lives with her grandparents."

"That's right." Theo realized Nellie Pearl was living somewhere in the past as her grandparents had died almost twenty years ago.

The daughter smiled at Theo. "We've come to sign the papers. Mom's house has sold." Her shoulders lifted slightly in a gesture conveying uncertainty. "I hope it's not too upsetting for her, but I've decided not to take her out to the house. You've known her a long time, do you think I should?"

"I can't see how it would be of any benefit. Her reality is not present day but maybe twenty to thirty years ago." Theo herded them to the back room. "Some coffee? Some of her contemporaries are working on a quilt."

"That would be lovely." The daughter looked a bit anxious, but bravely guided her mother. "Mom talks about them all the time now. When we first moved her away from here, she was so frightened and angry, but now she's become quite sweet." Her grimace told Theo she hadn't forgotten her mother's behavior mere moments ago. "Usually."

Theo thought Alzheimer's, or any dementia, must be the

most awful of all diseases, robbing people of their memories, even of themselves.

Tony decided to take the trailer out on another night's foray. He wasn't quite ready to demonstrate his skills, or lack thereof, in the very public venue of the law enforcement center parking lot. The lot sat in plain sight of not only law enforcement, including the jail, but search and rescue headquarters, the fire department, and the court house. He hadn't ever been the class clown and wasn't prepared to begin now.

It was two in the morning when he silently left his sleeping family and headed for the trailer. The night dispatcher, Karen Claybough, was an efficient but decidedly uncurious person. Perfect. Tony eased the Blazer into place to hook up the trailer. The task went fairly smoothly, much better than his first night attempts. Feeling more confident, he headed out, determined to travel around most of the county's main roads. As before, he saw little traffic and lots of critters. Making his way around the treacherous Dead Man's Curve, he had to travel quite slowly to keep to the right-hand lane. He hadn't picked up any speed when his headlights illuminated a man in overalls, kneeling by the side of the road at the ever-increasingly large memorial.

Tony eased past the man and parked in the first turnout. As he climbed out of the Blazer and headed toward the shadowy figure gardening by the glow of an old-fashioned kerosene lamp, he recognized old Nem. Nem held a pair of trimmers that looked like one of the antiques in the museum, like shears for sheep. The old man did not attempt to stand, but continued kneeling even as he greeted Tony.

"Evening, Sheriff."

"Nem." Tony studied the memorial display. At the center of it was a handmade cross of two branches lashed together. Surrounding it was a colorful array of plants, a mixture of blooming spring bulbs and newly planted summer flowers. Bright yellow pansies and a blue flower he didn't recognize shared space with some thin, sad, red petunias. Next to Nem was a small arsenal of garden implements, all antiques, a plastic watering can and a small wooden box. The box looked homemade and reminded Tony of an old-fashioned coffin. It hadn't been long since someone had said something about Nem "building boxes," but at the moment he couldn't remember the context. "Why are you out here in the dark?"

"It's public land, ain't it?"

Tony wasn't sure but nodded anyway.

"Well, I'm public." Nem turned back to his gardening, ignoring Tony.

Although it irked him the way Nem dismissed him, Tony wasn't sure he could dispute the old man's logic. Tony studied the assortment of wreaths on stands and small statues in amongst the plants. A wooden cane protruded from a cluster of flowers. "There seems to be quite a display here, a mixture of real flowers and fakes." He leaned forward, shining his flashlight into the garden, and spotted a plastic fire plug. "That looks like a dog toy." The moment the words passed his lips, he suddenly understood. "It's a pet cemetery."

Nem didn't flinch. "Yessir, they needed burying."

Tony glanced at the small box again. "A casket?"

"Made it myself." Nem sounded quite pleased with himself.

Tony thought for a moment. "What kind of wood is that?"

"Dunno. I took apart an old shed on my place." He cackled. "It's even older than me."

"Could it be chestnut?"

"Ain't they all dead?"

"Pretty much, but not all." Tony considered the question. "Your shed has to be over a hundred years old."

Nem nodded and poured some water on a new planting.

Tony had hoped the old guy would volunteer some information, but it wasn't happening. "What's in the box?" He pointed with the light.

Nem dusted off his hands. "A bird."

"And the rest of these?" Tony ran the light over the various memorials.

"Cats, dogs, critters." Nem patted the box. "God's creatures."

Feeling half sick, Tony asked anyway, "A bear?"

"No, sir. No bear." Nem shook his head, emphatically. "If you're a-thinkin' I've planted Roscoe's Baby in here, you're wrong."

Tony believed him, if for no other reason than Roscoe wasn't weeping and wailing all over the county, and Nem couldn't have hidden what he was doing from Roscoe. As he glanced up and down the highway, he saw no sign of a vehicle, a meaningless situation since the old guy didn't normally drive unless he was delivering eggs or selling boiled peanuts. He must have walked a million miles over his lifetime. "How'd you get out here?"

Nem cackled. "If'n you was to walk straight through there"—he pointed at the woods across the road—"you'd come out at my place less'n a mile away."

Tony realized he was right. The road made an almost complete loop. He felt like he'd made enough small talk with the old man. "We found a slender stake with a sharp point embedded in Ragsdale's side."

Nem nodded. "I tried to kill him."

Tony saw moonlight reflect in the sheen of tears in the old man's rheumy eyes. He suspected they were from frustration, not regret. "Tell me."

"It come to me whilst I was a-workin' on this here memorial patch of ground. I could carry a sharp stick inside my suit coat and just slip it out and stab him in the heart, even as small as it was."

"But you didn't." Tony almost felt guilty about insisting Nem admit failure.

"Oh, but I tried." The old man stared at his palsied hands. "I ain't got the strength no more and couldn't keep a tight enough hold on it. It slid right through my hand and stuck in his shirt." He sighed deeply. "I'd have pulled it free and given it another try, but he walked away."

Tony thought the old man was the personification of disappointment. "I'm glad I won't have to arrest you for murder."

Nem smiled, cheered up by his words. "I reckon I wouldn't like life in jail very much, and the hens would probably stop layin' too. They don't cotton much to strangers."

"Tell me about the cane." Tony returned the flashlight's beam to the curved wood.

"I found it on the ground after the ambulance carted Ragsdale away." Nem stood straight. "I figured these poor critters would enjoy having it here amongst the flowers."

"Why?" Tony thought they'd hate it.

"Long as it's here, he'll never use it on another poor beast." Nem lifted rheumy eyes to meet Tony's. "I didn't think anyone would want it. Do you?"

"No." Tony couldn't imagine a better place for it.

Satisfied, Nem returned to his gardening.

Following Ada's specific instructions for her memorial, Theo arranged the buckets of flowers on the long tables. Other helpers had covered them with white paper and taped it in place. The caterer's truck sat at the opposite end of the dining area from the tables displaying the remaining possessions of Ada Walker. The small crowd milled about, waiting to learn whether food or shopping was first on the afternoon agenda.

Theo and Nina had worked late into the night sorting through every item in Ada's house. Thankfully, the old woman had already done a fair job of disposing of many of her possessions. She had even put price stickers on a few items herself. Theo had felt ghoulish at the beginning of the process, but pricing and loading the contents of Ada's house into her SUV cured her. Everything, even a box of toothpicks for a penny, went to the sale.

Anything not sold would either go to the dump with Claude Marmot or be donated to charity. Money earned was earmarked for the senior center.

Theo glanced at Susan. Dressed in new jeans and sweatshirt, she looked fairly rested and almost normal. The haunted expression in her eyes and the tension in her face told the real story. According to her friend Melissa, Susan had not wanted to attend the luncheon. The two younger women had enjoyed Ada's company, though, and felt obliged to pay their respects. Theo waved them over. "I set aside a few more things I'm sure Ada would have offered to you first. If you don't want them, I'll just slap them on a table."

Stashed together in a corner were some basic quilting supplies like scissors, a mat, rulers, and a rotary cutter.

Susan smiled. "I'll take all of the quilting stuff. Even if I don't have room for it and it's not my favorite fabric or pattern. I promise I'll take care of it."

"Good." Theo released a breath she hadn't realized she was holding. "Ada threatened to haunt me forever if her fabric and projects don't find a good home."

As if they'd been waiting for an invisible signal, the remaining senior citizens from Ada's group joined them. They sorted through Ada's things and bought little but sat together, enjoying the outdoor luncheon, and called encouraging instructions to those more avid shoppers.

"As payment for lunch," Theo said, rising to her full petite height. She blew a whistle to cut through the chatter. "I think it would be nice if each of us would tell an Ada story. I'll go first." Theo paused. "The first time Ada came into my shop, she was with her daughter. Ada had just moved here and the two of them were exploring downtown Silersville and stopped by. Ada said that living near her daughter was fine, but having the charity quilts to work on made life worth living."

Tony stood. He'd joined them just before Theo began to speak. Theo thought he looked tired or sad or some combination of the two. "I've never met anyone, man or woman, who had a finer repertoire of cuss words, and I'm certain I learned at least three very useful ones from Ada."

"No kidding," Theo whispered. "I'm sure Chris and Jamie have heard a wide variety of curses over the years, but it made me cringe whenever a mom was in the store and Ada started telling a story. It was blankety-blank this and blankety-blank that. Have mercy, I thought." Unchecked, fat tears rolled down her face. "I'll miss her."

Tony rested a comforting warm hand on her back, just below her neck. "I know."

RUNNING IN CIRCLES
A MYSTERY QUILT
THIRD BODY OF CLUES:

Cut the 5 1/2″ squares of fabrics (B) (C) (D) (E) (F) and (G) diagonally twice to make quarter square triangles and stack them and label them by color letter. To protect the bias edges from stretching, handle as little as necessary.

Divide fabric (B) into two stacks and place, center points touching.

Lay all 48 triangles of (C) into one of the spaces between the (B) stacks and place the 12 triangles of each remaining fabric into the remaining space. Sew together forming 12 hourglass blocks of each layout. Press and trim to 4 1/2″.

Stack the strips made in the Second Clue—D+B+A+B+E on top of each other.

Stack the squares labeled (B+F) with stripes horizontal and place above center (A).

Stack the squares labeled (B+G) with stripes horizontal and place below center (A).

In the corner spaces, stack the hourglass blocks with (F) triangles touching the left end of (B+F).

Stack hourglass blocks with (G) triangles touching the right end of (B+G).

Stack hourglass blocks with (D) triangles in space remaining with (B+D) and (E) triangles touching (B+E).

Before sewing, look at the arrangement. There should appear to be four arrows aligned counterclockwise around center block (A). Sew upper row blocks into strips and lower row blocks into strips. Press. Sew on appropriate side of center strip. Press away from "A".

Make 12 blocks. Trim to 12 1/2″.

CHAPTER EIGHTEEN

"Yes, of course I knew Harrison Ragsdale. We worked together for quite a few years." Douglas Seaborn sat at his desk, his thick fingers laced on his old-fashioned blotter. Behind him was a poster about the danger of forest fires. "What can I tell you? He did his job. I did my job. We didn't socialize."

Tony thought Ragsdale's supervisor was evasive, and no wonder. If he gave Ragsdale a glowing recommendation, he'd be lying, and if he told the truth, he'd be a suspect. Tony slipped an antacid into his mouth. He could already tell this interview wasn't going to go smoothly and exchanged glances with Wade who sat next to him. "I'm sure he followed the guidelines as written."

Seaborn nodded but offered no further information.

"Maybe you can tell me if your office received any letters or phone calls complaining about him."

"Do you need a warrant to ask these questions?" Seaborn remained still.

"I can get a warrant to arrest you for obstruction." Tony didn't believe himself to be a man who was easily angered, but within seconds of sitting down he was furious. "I can't see what the problem is. He's dead. Unless you killed him, I'd think you'd want to know how and why he died. So maybe I'll just arrest you and lock you up on the presumption of guilt." All patience exhausted, he rose from the chair.

"Okay, okay." Seaborn raised his hands. "I'll tell you the

truth, but I really don't want to have to testify. I hated the man. I hated seeing him, hearing his voice. I hated getting phone calls about him. In fact"—he paused to catch his breath—"I don't think paying you to search for whoever might have speeded his departure from this planet is a good use of taxpayer dollars. How's *that* for an opinion?"

Tony relaxed a bit. "I'd say it's honest and well-earned." Seated next to him, Wade shifted but remained silent. "Will you answer my questions now?"

Seaborn nodded as he stood up and crossed to a four-drawer file cabinet. He patted the drawer below the top one. "It's filled with letters of complaint about Ragsdale. They date back to almost his first day on the job." He opened the drawer and retrieved a thick folder. "This file contains phone messages complaining about him. I only kept the ones where the caller identified him or herself."

"Pardon my asking this, but why?" Tony searched for the right way to ask his question.

"Why didn't we fire him?" Seaborn sat and went back to his laced hands pose. "Because he followed the letter of the law. Believe me, we watched to see if he put department gasoline in his personal vehicle or violated policy in any manner. Although we investigated, most, but not all, complaints about him, he either hadn't done anything technically wrong, or there was no evidence. One whole file is filled with letters from elderly ladies of the county who were miffed because he didn't hold the door open for them at the store or carry their groceries to the car."

Tony could sympathize. His own small staff did the best they could to accommodate the county citizens, driving them to appointments or helping carry groceries, but they did have their own jobs to do. An accident or burglary had to take precedence over courtesy calls, and while most of the seniors were understanding and grateful for the assistance they did receive, there were a couple of cranky, squeaky wheels. "I've got some of those too."

Seaborn leaned back in his chair, more relaxed than he had been. "I couldn't fire a man for rumor and innuendo, and while I'm sure he committed every one of the foul deeds in that file, he never left any evidence." Seaborn suddenly leaned forward, knocking his pencil holder to the floor, scattering its contents. He ignored it. "My own mother's dog went missing, and she said that she 'knew' he did it, but didn't see it and I couldn't help her."

Tony didn't feel like they were getting anywhere. "I've never known another employee of your office or any other, federal or state, whose job entailed anything to do with animals having such a poor attitude about them, have you?"

"Once before, back when I was still living in Pennsylvania as a boy, I met a man very much like Ragsdale. He lost his job fairly quickly because he wasn't as cagey as Ragsdale." Seaborn said. "I did nothing to Ragsdale, but I often dreamed of the day the animals would get their revenge. I had rather hoped it might be something painful and prolonged, but I understand he went down fast."

Wade raised his pen from his notebook like a student interrupting a professor. "Were you aware of Ragsdale's allergy to nuts?"

Bull's-eye. Tony watched Seaborn turn an unbecoming shade of gray.

"I was." Seaborn rested his hand on Ragsdale's personnel file. "He didn't make a big deal about it, but it was part of his required information, plus his wife is my niece." He cleared his throat. "I understand that's what killed him?"

"Really?" Tony was curious. "I wasn't aware a final determination had been announced."

"I presumed. I mean, that *is* why you're asking about nuts, isn't it?"

Seaborn became so flustered he stopped making much sense.

Wade consulted his notebook. "You were one of the people in the booth serving ramp pie just before he died."

"One of many. There was a crowd back there, cutting and serving or handing out napkins and stuff, and more pies coming from the kitchen and empty pans going back there. One whole crew stayed in the kitchen cooking." He exhaled sharply. "We were shocked so many people wanted to eat ramps."

Tony clicked his pen. "Perhaps you could make a list of the names of the people you remember seeing during your shift. We can compare it with other lists."

Eagerly, after retrieving a pen from those scattered on the floor, Seaborn began writing on a sheet of stationary. "Do you only want those of us serving?"

"Not necessarily. You can list them by job if it makes it easier for you." Tony was lazy enough to let other people divide things into similar groupings for him. He really doubted Seaborn was the guilty party and thought it unlikely he'd seen anything of importance. Unlikely things happen all the time, however, so Tony sat calmly watching the man scribble, waiting for him to look up. At length, he did. "If you were going to guess who on your list did it, who would you pick?"

Seaborn scanned his list. "Carl Lee Cashdollar."

"Why?" Tony sat forward.

"I understand he thought Ragsdale ran over his wife's Siamese cat and barely missed hitting Jill when he drove away. I never saw Carl Lee so angry before. He's usually pretty laid back, but I think I heard him suggest putting ground glass on Ragsdale's slice of ramp pie so he could suffer what he called the 'miseries of hell.' "

"And?" Tony sensed there was more.

"He left before his shift was due to end." Seaborn handed him the list. "Said he needed to take Jill home."

Tony thought about it. Just because Carl Lee was an attorney, and a defense attorney at that, did not make him immune to doing wrongful acts. Like Tony himself, he saw lots of people doing bad, criminal, or just plain stupid things every day. And he loved his wife. So if his wife was crying about the senselessly run-down pet, he might consider it an act of public service to try and give the perpetrator a taste of misery. He himself might have given the man something laced with walnuts if he'd known about an allergy, never dreaming it would kill him, but hoping the man would break out in itchy welts.

They found Carl Lee sitting in the hallway outside the courtroom. "Hey, Sheriff. Hey, Wade." Carl Lee smiled broadly as he watched them approach. "How's it going?"

Tony looked into the man's pale blue eyes and saw no concern in them. "We're still looking for clues about the poisoner of Harrison Ragsdale."

"He was poisoned?" Carl Lee's focus flickered away and then back. "I suppose you've heard about me threatening to feed him a bit of ground glass."

Tony nodded. "So you did threaten him?"

"Not to his face. I was spouting off about him in the serving line."

"You didn't take a little extra something with you and slip it in his food?" said Wade.

Carl Lee shook his head, but there was anger in his eyes and expression. "I wasn't planning to be one of the food servers, or I might have. My wife cried for days. Ragsdale drove by and her cat went missing. It might not have been quite so traumatic if he hadn't done it right in front of her." He held out his skinny wrists. "You want to slap the cuffs on me, go ahead."

"Did you hear anyone else talking trash about the man?" Tony kept his hands away from the handcuffs on his belt.

"Everyone." Carl Lee lowered his hands. "I can imagine the Farquhar boys thinking it's cool to have everyone in the county either hate you or fear you, but what did Ragsdale get out of being so mean-hearted? Since I'm a stay-at-home-in-the-evening kind of guy, I guess he could have had a secret life, hanging out in the bars or going to city for fun kinds of things. For all I know, he was a karaoke fan."

"Not that I've found out so far." Tony paused to think about Carl Lee's question. What had Ragsdale done with his spare time? He thought maybe he'd explore the man's house. He might learn something useful.

He had already checked Ragsdale's cell phone records. Besides lots of calls to his office, most of his calls were to Pops Ogle. What did those two men have in common? Pops's loves were music and fundamental religion. Tony tried to imagine Harrison Ragsdale being involved with either of those things and failed miserably.

The Ragsdale house sat at the far end of the two-block long street from Blossom's house with the new, and quite lovely, white picket fence. It was not the house Ragsdale grew up in, but in a town the size of Silersville there wasn't a lot of distance between any two buildings.

Wade parked in front of the house, and he and Tony stared at it for a while.

Tony thought it looked like half the houses in the county. A single story, white house with a sloping roof that extended over the front porch. Four large posts supported it. The front door was painted dark green and neatly divided the front of the house in two sections, each one with a pair of sash windows placed side by side.

He climbed out of Wade's car, adjusted his heavy-duty belt and glanced at his deputy. "Take as many pictures as you want." Walking over to the ruts worn into the lawn, he looked to the back of the property. A detached garage sat at the end of the ruts. It was big enough to hold a single car. Ragsdale's work vehicle, a pickup with the official insignia on the doors was parked at the curb. "Wade, do you have any idea what happened to the vehicle he drove to the museum?"

"Not right offhand, but I'll find out." Wade talked into the microphone clipped to his shirt while he took the camera from its case and took a few pictures of the house and lawn. He glanced up at Tony. "No vehicle was abandoned or towed to the storage lot."

"So how'd he get out there?" Tony checked the mailbox. There were a few pieces of junk mail, nothing personal. "It's hard to imagine he went with friends and they kept it secret."

Wade shook his head. "Frankly it's hard to imagine he had friends, isn't it?"

"There's not a tree or a bush or a flower, just grass." Tony's gesture encompassed the entire site. "Considering the growing habits of plants around here, that's quite a feat. Most of us spend time chopping stuff down."

"Maybe he poisoned everything else." Wade snapped a picture of the barren patch where a former flower bed had become simply dirt with some clumps of grass.

Tony thought it looked like someone had been digging there recently.

He took the keys from the evidence envelope and unlocked the front door. He didn't know what he expected the inside of Ragsdale's house to be like—maybe one or two recliners and a giant flat-screen television or plain bare rooms—but when he stepped inside, he came to a sudden halt. What would be a living room in most houses was here set up as a workshop. Unfinished furniture pieces sat at one end, and large, well-maintained and very expensive tools filled the dining area. Two closed doors, one in the dining area and one in the living area, were the only parts of the main wall not covered with peg boards displaying small tools. "Wow."

"You got that right." Wade's voice was almost drowned out by the clicking of the camera shutter. "Who knew?"

"Let's see what else he has, and then you can come back and take more pictures." Tony guessed the door on the left would be the kitchen and on the right, maybe a pair of bedrooms. He headed into the kitchen. He was correct. It was a plain room filled with a sink, stove, refrigerator, a worn countertop, and cabinets. The flooring looked like it hadn't been replaced since the house was built, probably seventy years earlier. A rescued school desk, the kind with the seat attached to it and a wooden writing surface hinged over a storage area was the only place to sit or to eat.

"That's weird." Wade had opened the refrigerator. "He's got piles of sandwiches made up and wrapped in bread sacks."

"Ah, hell, I'm going to have to say something nice about him." Tony recognized the bags. He'd seen some like them not long ago. Rumor said an unidentified man had been handing out bags of cheese sandwiches and peanut butter sandwiches to the hungry and homeless. "Either he was the secret sandwich fellow, or he was stealing bags of sandwiches from the needy."

"So he probably planned to deliver these on Saturday afternoon or evening. That's the usual schedule." Wade started to reach for a bag. "He missed this week. I could take them if we knew the drop spot."

Tony was pretty sure he knew the spot and positive the sight of a county sheriff's department vehicle would keep the intended recipients from accepting them. "Let's call Pops Ogle and get him to do it. I'll go out on a limb and say he was involved anyway."

"How could Ragsdale make peanut butter sandwiches and not have an allergic reaction?"

"He was only allergic to tree nuts." Tony was quite proud of knowing the answer. "Peanuts do not grow on trees."

Minutes after Tony's call, Pops Ogle arrived at Ragsdale's house. He opened the back door of his car, and Tony could see a row of insulated totes. Pops trotted to the kitchen door as if he'd done the same thing many times in the past.

"I thank you, Sheriff, for calling me. It was making me ill, thinking about all this good food going to waste." He started loading the bags of sandwiches into a cardboard box he carried. "I drove him to the festival and planned to pick up the sandwiches and stuff when I dropped him off again. After he died, I took the bags I had and passed them out there and told them I'd be back with more, but between you and me, I weren't real sure if I could."

Tony and Wade helped Pops carry the food to the car. "Is this the normal amount?"

"Yessir." Pops's whole body nodded along with his words, then he stopped. "No, there's the right amount of sandwiches, but there's usually a treat and some cartons of milk for the young'uns."

The three men trooped back into the kitchen. Once the bags of sandwiches were out of the refrigerator, there was not much left except a half-bag of deli fried chicken and some orange juice. They checked the freezer. Bingo. It was filled with snack cakes. A picnic cooler sitting near the door held small cartons of milk and cooler ice.

Tony picked up one carton of milk and pressed it against his cheek. He was relieved to find it very cold, so they loaded all the stuff into Pops's car. "Why'd he ride with you? Why not drive out there in his own vehicle?"

Pops wasn't known for his ability to tell convincing lies, so when he said, "It had something to do with an undercover operation," Tony believed it was what he'd been told.

They sent Pops on his way to deliver the food.

"Undercover operation?" Wade watched the car disappear around the corner and looked back at the open kitchen door. "I never would have guessed Hairy Rags would do anything halfway decent. I just don't know what to think. All these years, all the bad feelings."

"He certainly didn't make any attempt to make people change their minds about him. Maybe he was told to do something good in the community, or else?" Tony wasn't proud of his feelings, but the cynical part of him distrusted the idea of there being such a wide gap between Ragsdale's public image and the private do-gooder. "Maybe we should see what's in the rest of the house. So far, I'm wondering if he actually lived here."

"It's a bit creepy. I'd feel more at home in Quentin's trailer." Wade grabbed his camera again.

Tony tried to stifle a laugh, but comparing this living space to Quentin's dilapidated trailer was like comparing a jet airplane hangar to the Thomas Brothers' garage. Not quite in the same league in size or cleanliness.

The single bathroom was functional. One bath towel hung from the shower curtain rod. There was no soap or shampoo in the shower. Without realizing he was doing it until Wade turned to locate the sound, Tony pressed his lips together and made a humming sound.

There were two small bedrooms. One was used as the lumber storage area. A rack made from two by fours held the boards flat and up off the floor. Tony could almost feel Wade's anticipation, mixed with his own, as he turned the knob on the second door. It was locked.

"Okay," Tony mumbled. "I'm going to get into that room if I have to take an ax to the door."

Wade jangled some lock picks in front of his face. "Won't be necessary," Tony said. "This one fits." Seconds later, the lock released and the door swung in.

Tony stared, not as surprised as he was shocked. "Look at them all."

"Do-it-yourself taxidermy?" Wade's camera clicked several times. "Or professional?"

"And why lock this door? It's his own home." Tony flipped on the light switch, and the overall effect became more of a natural history exhibit than trophy room. "Are they valuable?"

"Where did he sleep?" Wade stepped inside, taking more photographs. "There's no furniture in the house."

"Did you see a basement?" Tony backed out of the taxidermy room. "I'll check." He did find some stairs behind a door in the kitchen that had been overlooked in the excitement of the sandwich situation. Opening it, he found a pull cord to turn on a light. It lit three bulbs spaced out along the length of the basement. A dirt floor. A water heater and the furnace. The ceiling was too low to make the space useful for much else. He'd have to walk bent over at the waist just to get to the far end.

They returned to the woodshop. "Where did he live?" said Wade.

"The garage is the only place we haven't checked." Tony doubted it doubled as a bedroom.

So they trudged out to the garage. The door wasn't one of the newer "overhead" doors but two wide, hinged doors. A padlock kept it shut. Wade had it open in seconds.

Tony wasn't sure why, but he held his breath as the well-oiled doors swung open. A perfectly ordinary pickup truck sat next to a perfectly ordinary lawn mower, and perfectly ordinary yard and garden tools hung from hooks and nails. With a whoosh, the air left his lungs. He felt better when he heard the same sound from Wade.

Just for fun, they placed seals on the house and garage doors and strung yellow tape about the place to discourage visitors. "Let's go have a chat with our county clerk and see how much more property Ragsdale owned. So far his wife and her fiancé think it's two to six houses."

CHAPTER NINETEEN

"He owns *how* many houses?" Tony stared down at county clerk Marigold Flowers Proffitt's wig of the day, noting absently how much it reminded him of an apricot poodle's fur. Not his favorite of her rotating supply of wigs and turbans. She was one of Blossom's sisters, and her approach to the family tendency to carry thin hair and excessive weight was to shave her head and not eat. "Did you say eight?"

"Yes, eight." Marigold squinted at the screen. Just as she refused to eat, she also refused to wear glasses. "I can print this list of addresses out, and you can take it with you."

"Thank you." Tony understood the message. She wanted him out of her office. He probably smelled like apple pie, and she wouldn't stand for it. He felt a bit dazed as he carried the printout from the courthouse to his office in the next building over. The paper gave the addresses, legal description of houses and lots, and current values for property taxes. The late game warden owned roughly a million dollars' worth of land and buildings. Tony considered his and Theo's own financial empire, a house she'd inherited and her shop building they owned jointly with the bank. Her bright yellow SUV was a gift or they'd never be able to afford it.

As he walked past Ruth Ann's desk, she waved her nail polish brush to attract his attention. She'd purchased a headset so she could talk on the telephone and leave both her hands free for her day job, the manicures. She spoke into the headset. "If

you'll hold on just a second, I'll see if the sheriff is available."
She pushed a button with the eraser end of a pencil.

"Do I want to be available?" Tony thought he wanted to study
the real estate papers, but Ruth Ann was capable of running his
office, studying for the bar exam, and painting her fingernails.
He didn't want to admit, even to himself, how much he
depended on her. She nodded. "It's the pathologist. He's made
positive identification of your crispy critter from the fire."

Tony hurried into his office and picked up the telephone
receiver. He knew this was news he needed. He doubted it was
going to improve his life or solve his problems or cases. "Doctor?"

"I'm busy, you're busy." The doctor's staccato words punched
through Tony's haze. "Your dead body is Geordie Farquhar. He
suffered a severe blow to the back of his neck, possibly paralyz-
ing him. I talked to the arson boys. According to them and the
burn pattern, someone splashed his body with gasoline before
he fell to the garage floor."

Tony came to attention. "So this is no accident?"

"Nope." The doctor coughed as if he had just inhaled smoke
himself. "I'm calling this a homicide. Whoever hit him and left
him on a burning roof—not even his own burning roof—killed
him. There was some extra damage caused by the gasoline and
the fall. You want to hear about it?"

"No." Tony thanked the doctor and said to put everything in
the report. "I know his two brothers. I'll have to decide whether
to arrest the first one to rat out the other, or the one ratted on.
Maybe both."

It wasn't until he and Wade entered the third house belonging
to Harrison Ragsdale that they could find signs he lived there.
The first house had been the official address on his employment
records, and it was where his mail was delivered. The second, a

block to the west of the first one, was a tiny home, maybe two rooms. A family of six lived there. When interviewed, the nervous residents admitted they paid cash to Ragsdale and used a post office box for their mail.

The third house was two blocks to the east. It was larger than the others. Several rooms remained empty, but there was a normally furnished living room with a recliner, couch, and a television, a room containing a bed, dresser, and closet full of clothes. The bathroom cabinet held toiletries and a supply of medications, including allergy-symptom reducers. Normal food items filled the refrigerator and cabinets.

"Why use a fake address, park there, and walk to this house to sleep and eat?" Tony stood in the living room, glancing around.

"To hide from your enemies?" Wade scuffed a toe across the carpet. "And how much do you want to bet he's not paying taxes on the cash he's getting for rent?"

Tony couldn't disagree. By the time he and Wade located the five remaining houses on the list, and learned the tenants paid in cash and had post office box addresses, he was certain Ragsdale was not on the up and up. In his local bank account, he maintained a decent but unremarkable balance. No safe deposit box.

"So, what did he do with the cash?" Tony absently stared out the window. "With several houses yielding monthly cash infusions, I'd think his balance might fluctuate. His salary is the only deposit."

"Does he own all of the houses free and clear?" Wade sat forward on the chair. "Maybe every dime is used to make the payments."

"Nope. He paid cash each time he purchased a house, but he hasn't bought one in the past ten years."

"At least not here." Wade scribbled in his notebook. "He

could own property in other cities or states."

"Or countries." Tony groaned. "He had to keep his documents somewhere. Home ownership entails reams of paperwork. Let's search houses one and three again. He didn't seem to spend any time in the others."

By the end of the afternoon, both men were exhausted. The more they explored Harrison Ragsdale's belongings and real estate holdings, the freakier Ragsdale became. Only by constant searching did they find his cache of money and deeds, hidden behind a sliding panel built into the back of a display box in the taxidermy room.

"If you keep it behind a locked door, in a locked house, can you call this a display?" Wade was busy emptying the contents of the first case into a box, keeping a running tally of the types of documents.

Semantics aside, Tony admired the beautifully constructed display. The box appeared to be made of something like maple inlaid with cherry and possessed a space containing a safe, a fireproof box requiring a key to open it. He flipped through the keys, pulling out the one he wanted. "So that's what the peculiar key opens. That lock looks like it needs the business end of a Philips screwdriver to open it."

Wade glance up from his cataloging. "Ragsdale was a freak. Who hides money like this?"

"A paranoid one."

"A rich one." Wade stared at the stacks of cash resting on another sheaf of legal-sized documents. "Maybe too paranoid to pay taxes."

"Someone is certainly going to be a lot richer."

"Even without counting it all, I'm thinking this much money is a powerful motive. One might immediately suspect the heir."

"Probably his wife." Tony mused. "Or someone engaged to the heir."

"One who was about to become an ex-heir when the divorce was final. Grab the money and run? Or possibly a tenant who felt Ragsdale was taking advantage of him. Maybe he over-charged his tenant or threatened eviction."

"Certainly, the more we learn, the more motives show up." Tony picked up a stack of bills, hundred-dollar bills, and ran his finger across them. "There's at least five thousand dollars in this little bunch."

Wade sat back on his heels. "And there are piles of those."

"Let's get the money all counted and logged into evidence before either or both of us succumbs to temptation." Tony began working on a list of his own. "Have you seen anything like records we could check against?"

"Nope. Just cash and property deeds." Wade put the lid on the box. "I wouldn't mind inheriting the lot."

"With a million dollars in real estate and cash to be lost in a divorce, Jessica and Vic have a powerful motive. Do you suppose they knew Ragsdale was changing the will?" Tony was not expecting an answer. His cataloging was interrupted by a call notifying him the Farquhars were in custody. He sighed. "Let's lock it up and go talk to the remaining Farquhar boys. Like we haven't had enough fun yet."

It was getting claustrophobic in the greenhouse. Tony sat in his favorite chair and waved his suspects, Jocko and Shawn Farquhar, into the seats facing him. Wade pulled a chair to the corner of the table, leaving the Farquhars' attorneys with what was left of the seating. Folding chairs.

Tony considered interviewing the boys separately, but decided he might learn more if they could bicker with each other.

The whining began before the brothers reached their designated spots. Jocko waved his manacles, showing them to an uninterested audience. "You see the way he treats us? Like we're some big shot criminals or something."

Only Shawn had a response. "Yeah. Like we're really bad dudes." His smile indicated his pride and joy in the moment. Being accused of a felony, arson, and potentially the murder of his brother appeared to be the highlight of his career in crime. He swaggered to the chair and sat.

Tony started with some simple questions, like verifying their names and addresses. Ones even the Farquhar "darlin' boys" might be expected to answer honestly. They did. Preliminaries over, Tony said, "Why were you boys at the Smith home on the day of the fire?"

"We was out for a walk, it bein' a nice day and all." Shawn nodded to emphasize his ludicrous statement.

"So, to make sure I have this straight," Tony squeezed his pen. Hard. These boys had never been known to walk across the street without a beer waiting on the other side. "You, all three of you, went for a walk in the sunshine." They nodded. Tony jotted a few words in his notebook—never happened. The entire interview was being recorded on video, but taking notes was a habit, a good one so he also wrote down what they said. "Go on. Just tell us what happened next. You got to the Smith house?"

Shawn must have forgotten the script and silently began digging for something in his nose while he thought about it. Jocko took over. "It looked like someone upstairs was stuck in the window and calling for help."

"Um-hum." Tony wrote down a word—fantasy. "And then?"

"We climbed up to help." Finger out of his nose, Shawn rolled his eyes, making his opinion clear. "What didja think?"

Tony squeezed his pen more tightly. When he felt it start to bend, he forced himself to relax. Thanks to the photographs he'd recovered from Olivia Hudson's cell phone, he felt he had the upper hand in this interview. "Go on."

Jocko, marginally more perceptive than his remaining brother, said, "We shoved Geordie up on the garage roof so he could check on them. When he got to the window, it was open and he found one of them drop-down ladders and me and Shawn climbed up to help."

Tony believed two-thirds of the story. It certainly explained how they got inside the house to burglarize it. "Who was calling for help?"

The Farquhars shook their heads.

"Okay, then, let's go on." Tony watched the attorneys sit up a little straighter. To this point, their clients had confessed to nothing more sinister than attempting to rescue a family from an unknown threat. "What happened next?"

"Geordie fell through the roof of the garage." Shawn waved his shackled hands making his chains rattle. "It was the owner's fault our Geordie died. We'll sue."

Wade checked his notes and cleared his throat. "I thought Geordie went inside and dropped the ladder down?"

Shawn and Jocko looked at each other and fell silent. The lawyers stood and said their clients had said all they had to say.

Tony assumed the group hadn't quite worked out all the glitches from their confessions. He wasn't surprised. He switched off the recorder. "We'll let you confer with your lawyers for a moment. I want to hear how Geordie ended up dead." He and Wade stepped out and closed the door behind them. "What do you think? Who's the weak link?"

Wade said, "Shawn."

Tony agreed. A couple of minutes passed before one of the attorneys knocked on the door. When he and Wade were back into position, Tony turned the recorder back on. "What happened on the roof?"

Jocko nodded, giving Shawn permission to talk. "Geordie started actin' all goofy. Said he just come along to get some pills, only they wasn't any around and we should leave. He said those people didn't act snooty like some."

Tony watched Jocko. He was known to be a hard case, amoral, and a liar of the first order, the worst of the younger generation of Farquhars. He turned to Wade. "Put Jocko in the holding cell." Tony escorted Jocko's attorney from the greenhouse before turning to Carl Lee. "It might do Shawn some good to hear his options from you. When Jocko's near, Shawn's brain—what there is of it—shuts down." He left them alone.

Carl Lee wasted little time before he knocked on the door.

Tony returned and sat after turning on the recorder. "Let's try this again, shall we?" He rested his laced hands on the table. "You said Geordie liked the Smiths."

"He did." Shawn's oversized upper teeth gnawed on his lower lip.

"Did he work for them?" Tony asked. Shawn stared, open-mouthed. Tony thought employment was not a concept that meant anything to him. "Okay, so how'd he know them?"

"From the park. Geordie liked kids, an' he thought the mom was good to 'em."

"So, did Geordie know it was the Smiths' house?"

"Not until later." Shawn wiped his nose on his wrist and struggled to wipe it onto his pants. The manacles made the maneuver difficult. "He said there's no pills, let's leave, 'n' Jocko hit him to wake up his sleeping brain and said Geordie should look around 'cause even if there's no pills there's got to be tons of money in a place like that, and he shoved him and Geordie fell out the window and landed all crooked on the garage roof. He didn't move."

Tony was sure he wasn't going to like the next part but forced himself to leave his two remaining antacid tablets in his pocket. He felt acid drip into his gut and felt his stomach rumble. "And then what happened?"

"We looked around the bedroom and grabbed a pretty little

box, 'cause Jocko thought it might have jewels in it." Shawn's lower lip jutted forward. "It didn't."

"What was in it?" Wade looked up from his notepad.

"Little bitty teeth."

Tony doubted they would be able to recover the carefully saved baby teeth; not one treasure saved for the devastated family. "Where are they?"

Shawn didn't answer. He scrunched his face. He twitched. Using both hands, he picked up a bottle of water and gulped the contents. He shook his head. "Left 'em there."

"Okay, Shawn, what happened next?"

"Jocko started to use his lighter to set Geordie's shirt on fire. Said we had to. Then he looked down at the ground and saw a box full of empty jars, and the next thing, he's fillin' 'em with gasoline from the mower can and we're both tossin' them at Geordie and in the windows. Splash, splash and everything went whoosh." Shawn laughed. "Oh, man, it was an awesome fire."

Tony swallowed hard, thinking of the damage they'd created. "Then what?"

"There was only a little gas left, and the house was burning like crazy." Shawn's eyes reflected his excitement.

"What about Mrs. Smith? When did she come home?"

"Don't know." Shawn shrugged. "Got no watch."

Since Tony could see one on his wrist, he thought, as lies went, this one lacked something in cohesiveness. More likely, Shawn couldn't tell time on a non-digital watch. Tony assumed it was stolen. "Did you see her come home?"

"Yep." Shawn grew more confident when he told the truth. "She drove into the garage and closed the door when we climbed down for the gas."

Everything Shawn told them explained the photographs on Olivia Hudson's phone. Tony wondered if Geordie had been dead before the fire. He wasn't sure he wanted to know. "I don't understand why you torched Geordie's body."

Shawn shrugged. "Seemed like a good idea at the time."

Theo volunteered to drive Susan and her children to Knoxville. Susan had gotten a temporary replacement for her driver's license and needed to get to the rental car agency recommended by her insurance agent. At least they had been able to purchase a new car seat for the baby in Silersville. The downside to living in such a small community was the limited availability of certain products and services.

Twins and a toddler filled the backseat of the SUV, and the younger boy remained with his father. Thankfully, all the other children were in school. They'd have to rent a bus if they wanted to take everyone.

Theo slowed down even more than usual as they went around Dead Man's Curve. Standing off to the edge of the road was a small group of people looking at the memorial. Theo thought they looked curious rather than bereaved.

The sight of them awakened Susan from her haze of sorrow and confusion. "What happened there?"

Theo had to admit she didn't know. Suddenly she saw a man standing near the road, he lunged toward them, waving wildly. Roscoe. Theo pulled over to stop in a turnout. Before she could lower her window, Roscoe was pulling her door open.

"Baby's here. I found Baby." Roscoe all but dragged Theo with him, leaving Susan in the car with the children. "You've got to call for help."

"Is she hurt?" Theo looked around and didn't see the bear and nothing made sense. This was miles away from Quentin's mountain land. She couldn't believe the bear traveled this far on her own.

"Don't think so, but she's stuck." Roscoe danced around,

pointing to a shrub. "In there."

"Stuck?" Theo finally saw Baby under a large mountain laurel. Sure enough, it looked as though she had shoved her arm into a length of plastic pipe and couldn't work her way free. Baby lifted her head and made an odd heartrending cry. "How'd she get all the way down here?"

"She musta gone riding in the back of Quentin's pickup. She loves to nap back there in the sunshine." Roscoe's chin quivered, and he fell on his knees next to Baby. He whispered in her ear.

"We need lots of help." She used her cell phone to call Tony. "I'm with Roscoe. He's found Baby."

"Is she okay?"

"She's alive, but she's stuck. Can you bring something to cut heavy plastic pipe, without cutting her arm?" Theo stepped away far enough away so Roscoe couldn't hear her. "And the vet or a paramedic. I'm not an expert but I think she's badly dehydrated. Her eyes are pretty glassy."

"Stay on the line a minute," Tony said.

Theo heard conversations in the background between her husband and several different people before he spoke to her again. All sounded willing and happy to come help extract Baby from her predicament. Unofficially. Theo heard the girls wake up in the backseat of her car. "Help is on the way," she told Roscoe and hurried to rescue Susan from her twins.

The bear had been rescued and given fluids and a bowl of strawberries before being driven up the mountain again. That errand complete, Tony called Wade and Mike into his office. He hoped they were prepared to explain their latest search of the museum and its property.

Wade began. "We went back to the kitchen and checked every spoon, bowl, and can for evidence. We found eighteen million partial fingerprints in there." He rubbed a hand over his bleary features. "Everyone we were able to identify had a legitimate reason for being there."

Tony sensed there was more and held his silence. Wade and Mike deserved to be allowed to tell the story their way.

"But three prints were unusual, mostly because they were clear, not overlaid with others." Mike took over. As if of one accord, they leaned in, listening intently. "We found Ada's on the hot sauce, Nem's on the pepper shakers and Letty Bainbridge's on several of the clean, unused plastic forks."

"Which led you to do what?" Tony hated the idea of any of the relics turning up guilty.

"We tested the hot sauce. The chemist said there's nothing in it but red peppers and vinegar. The plastic forks are clean, but there's ground walnuts mixed in with the black pepper," said Wade. Next to him, Mike nodded his agreement.

"No kidding?" Tony leaned back in the chair. "So Nem put walnuts in the pepper and tried stabbing him with the stick?" It didn't make sense to him. "Why plan to do both?"

Wade said, "Belt and suspenders. If one failed the other should work."

"The old man's buried a lot of Ragsdale's innocent victims. Nem's a good man, but he's been pushed too far," Mike added.

Tony couldn't dispute Mike's take on the situation. Didn't want to disprove it. They finally had means, motive, and opportunity, so why couldn't he believe it? "Let's bring him in."

Tony watched Nem. The old man sat proudly at attention in the greenhouse. He took a sip of his water. He examined his fingernails, broken and dirty from his gardening. He refused the services of an attorney, but Tony called Carl Lee down anyway.

"Talk to him." Tony welcomed Carl Lee. "He's not our killer. I don't want him lying and then lying about telling me a lie."

"Why not?"

"I've known him a long time." Tony glanced away. "He's an honorable, if irritating, old guy, and telling a lie that size will eat at his soul. I don't want to be responsible for it. I want to find the real killer."

Carl Lee slapped him on the back. "You're a fair man and good sheriff. If you let it, this job will make you crazy."

Tony nodded. "I'm not too sure it hasn't already. I'm going to watch the videos again and see if I can catch Nem in the act. How subtle can you be and poison someone in a food line?"

He returned to his office and watched every video they had been able to find with coverage of the food line at the ramp booth. They were almost identical to each other. Pies in, pies out. He tried concentrating on the hands and saw people eating, getting forks, dropping napkins. Talking, waving, and laughing. Shaking hands. Hands shaking. Young hands. Old hands. Hands shaking hot sauce. Gnarled hands shaking pepper on pie.

RUNNING IN CIRCLES
A MYSTERY QUILT
PUTTING IT ALL TOGETHER:

Lay the completed blocks into four rows, three blocks wide. Play with different arrangements if you wish or simply place them all in the same direction. Sew four rows of three blocks then sew the rows together, taking care not to rotate them.

Carefully measure length and width of quilt top. Cut 2 strips to each measurement from the strips of fabric (D). Sew onto quilt top, using 2 1/2″ squares of fabric (C) as cornerstones, to form first border.

Repeat the process using 4 1/2″ wide strips of fabric (A) and 4 1/2″ squares of fabric (C) as cornerstones.

Quilt as desired, and bind with remaining 2 1/2″ wide strips of fabric (A).

CHAPTER TWENTY

The majority of phone calls to the Park County sheriff's office were from people looking for lost animals—whether pets or livestock of some nature. The second was a tie between complaints about road conditions and reporting accidents. Then there was a predictable mixture of excessive alcohol, domestic violence, items lost, and items found. Tony rubbed his head. People called to complain about their neighbors' music, barking dogs, power outages, and television glitches. Reports of UFOs came in spurts, causing some discussion about the possibility they were real.

Most challenging were those reports about issues with mentally ill individuals. The line between criminal behavior and insanity was unclear, at least out in the field.

The dispatch desk heard it all, sent officers to investigate, notified the utility departments and had to remain calm in tense situations. Maintaining contact with the officers during a call was vital. A missing deputy could need backup.

Flavio Weems had, after the first rocky months, become a solid, dependable dispatcher. "Sir, we may have good news for a pet owner." Flavio's nasal voice came through Tony's radio. "Sheila has a pregnant Siamese cat cornered. She would like some assistance. Evidently the cat has a bad attitude."

"Where is she?" Tony's first thought was Two Bit. Maybe it was Jill Cashdollar's cat. The address Flavio gave was maybe half a mile from Carl Lee and Jill's home. He asked Flavio for their telephone number and punched it into his cell phone.

Jill answered on the second ring.

"It may not be your cat, Jill," Tony began. "But Sheila is evidently dealing with a feisty, pregnant Siamese."

"Pregnant?" After a moment, she said, "We had an appointment to have Two Bit spayed, but missed it. I guess it could be her."

"If you have a favorite treat and a carrier, you might grab them and meet me at the corner of Oak and Third. There's a storage shed in the back."

Jill didn't hesitate. "I'll be there. Whether it's Two Bit or not, the cat needs help."

Within minutes of each other, Tony and Jill arrived. Sheila, covered with dirt and leaves, greeted them with a smile. "I got her herded into the shed. Good luck catching that one."

Jill held the carrier in one hand and an open can of cat food in the other as she slipped past Sheila. "Kitty?"

Tony and Sheila waited. Several minutes passed with occasional soft words from Jill and angry cat sounds in response.

Finally Jill reappeared, clearly ecstatic. "It is definitely Two Bit."

Tony could see the outline of the Siamese cat's head through the mesh on the side of the cat carrier. At least someone was having a good day.

Prosecutor Archie Campbell dropped by Tony's office. "I'm going to have to prosecute Slow Jr."

Tony nodded. "Thanks for the heads-up. I almost forgot about him. We'll find the best place to house him we can."

"You're assuming I'll win."

"Yes, I know you will." Tony didn't want a crook in the office. It was his job to catch them and Archie's job to punish them. "He might learn a valuable lesson from a stint in jail."

"What about the person who killed Harrison Ragsdale? Any progress?"

Tony nodded. "Sometimes my job, like yours, is fun, and sometimes it breaks your heart." He gathered his papers and straightened his tie. "I have an appointment."

Tony found Portia Osgood standing outside the grocery store with the aid of her walker, a cloth bag holding a few items hanging on the front of it. The walker and a can of peas added together would weigh as much as she did. He parked the Blazer near her and climbed out. "Let me take you home." It wasn't a request.

She gave him a single nod. The royal sign of acquiescence.

Tony walked up to Portia. In the years since she'd been his fourth grade teacher, they had both changed in size. He had grown a couple of feet taller while she'd shrunk. The top of her head wasn't much above his belt buckle.

As a lad he'd been absolutely intimidated by her authoritarian demeanor and talents with a twelve-inch wooden ruler. Not so much so now. With sheer size, not to mention weapons, on his side—if she attacked, it would be like a flea going after a junkyard dog.

He opened the passenger door and pulled out the folding step stool Theo and the boys used to get inside. She allowed him to assist her. He put her groceries and the walker on the backseat. They drove the six blocks to her home, an older house shaded by ancient walnut trees. She had lived there as long as he could remember. The house next door had gone through a succession of owners, one of them the Ragsdale family.

"The trees look healthy." Tony said as he helped her to the ground. "They produce a good crop of walnuts last fall?"

She nodded.

"You knew he was allergic." It was not a question.

"They moved away from this neighborhood because of it."

Her head turned in the direction of the former Ragsdale home. She spoke softly. "I was not sorry. He was a nasty little boy and grew into a nasty man."

"Did you have help?"

Portia stared straight ahead. "No."

"How did you manage it?"

"Habits rarely change. He was a piggy little boy and put pepper on everything I ever saw him eat. I was sure he'd come to the festival, and if he didn't, he didn't." Her attempt at a casual shrug failed. "I have bags of walnuts in the house and there was no hurry. I broke some open with a hammer and put the nut meats in my electric coffee grinder."

"And then?"

A winsome smile made her appear younger. "We relics were put in charge of condiments. I brought a box of black pepper mixed with ground walnuts."

He gave her points for dignity. She stood before him, her twisted fingers almost useless, faded eyes clouded with cataracts. He found it unthinkable and impossible to imagine her having the speed and dexterity needed to put ground walnuts in anything. She didn't look capable of unscrewing the lid on a pepper shaker. She didn't look capable of unscrewing a light bulb. The lids on the pepper shakers were not tiny, but not large either.

"You had to ask someone to unscrew the lids for you?" Tony guessed that's how Nem's fingerprints got on the shakers.

"I did. And I added the walnut and pepper mix to each of them. My shaker assistant had no knowledge of my transgression."

Tony said, "Why now?"

Her voice was soft, but her words were clear. "There are no more pets waiting at home for me. He killed the last one." The frail hands shook, and tears blurred her faded eyes. "I never guessed he would die."

"What did you envision?"

"Hives, welts, horrible itching." She looked up at Tony. "Maybe some wheezing. In short, more misery, not a release from it."

Rage, hot and unexpectedly intense, surged through him. Not at Portia, but at Harrison Ragsdale, who had deliberately caused so many people much sorrow and loneliness. "I'll carry your groceries inside."

"I don't have to go to the jail?" Portia's voice was barely audible.

Tony couldn't imagine locking this woman in his jail. "Are you planning to run away?"

"No." She lifted her chin and met his eyes. "I'll be here when you want me."

"I trust you." Tony massaged the back of his neck. "Get a lawyer. It's up to Archie Campbell and his crew to decide what to do. My job is done. The case is solved." A thought occurred to him. There was probably better food at the jail than she ate at home. "Unless you'd prefer . . ."

"Here, please." She patted his arm. "You were always a good boy."

That made him laugh out loud. "I always thought you hated me."

"Having favorites is unavoidable. Hiding it is preferable." She winked. "I knew you'd be a good man and hoped you would stay in Silersville. I missed you when you moved away."

Tony's mouth opened and closed. It must be his week for being rendered speechless.

"Do you write anymore?" Portia said. "You used to make up the most wonderful stories. A bit far-fetched, but very imaginative."

Still stunned, Tony managed to nod.

"I'll confess," she gave him a wide smile, and continued. Clearly her language abilities weren't disabled, and she knew it. "I never would have guessed you would marry tiny, reclusive Theodore Siler."

"You don't approve?"

"I think it's wonderful." A delighted smile shifted all the wrinkles on her worn face. "She was another favorite of mine."

Gus knocked on the front door. "I want to see your kitchen." Confused but agreeable, Tony ushered him down the hallway and into the kitchen Gus had visited hundreds of times before. As if never having never seen it before, Tony glanced around the room, wondering what Gus was looking for. The kitchen and its living area were warm and inviting. Tony loved coming home to it. Normally.

Today the space felt more crowded than usual, and Tony realized they had gradually been increasing the amount of items in the room. The kitchen end, with its old wood-burning stove and the modern one, was somewhat cluttered with baby bottles, but the living end was packed with extra stuff. In addition to the normal chairs, television, video games and Theo's quilt-in-progress and slippers and books, there were his books, magazines, and the whittling project he'd found intriguing. Plus a trash can. Added into the mixture was a playpen, bouncy seats, a high chair, and swing. Balls, cars, trucks, stuffed animals, and a couple of empty cardboard boxes littered the boys' area. Currently the family couldn't build a fire in the raised hearth because of the overflow. Heaven help them, they were drowning, and there was no lifeboat was in sight. Tony couldn't even see room for an oar.

Gus cleared his throat, almost like he was nervous. Not Gus's style. Tony felt a vague sense of alarm. His brother was acting peculiar.

"Can I ask you something?" Gus fidgeted and didn't make eye contact.

"Sure, anything." Tony couldn't imagine what was going on. His older brother was supremely self-confident, sometimes to the point of arrogance.

"Well, Catherine and I have been talking, and here's the deal." Gus paused. "We want to put an addition onto your house. This place is a claustrophobe's nightmare."

Tony could only stare. He certainly couldn't dispute Gus's assessment about feeling smothered.

Gus waved a hand. "We could build off the back of the house." He pointed out the window. "We wouldn't lose the light from this window. You've got a huge lot. If we angle out between those trees, you'd still have plenty of yard even though it would eliminate the historical purity of the exterior. I was thinking maybe a large bedroom, a small office, and three-quarter bath." He paused to breathe.

"You're serious." Tony couldn't quite take it all in. "You've been designing an addition?"

Gus nodded.

"Wouldn't that require serious money?" Tony didn't want to guess how much they'd have to pay for supplies, plus the cost of labor. Certainly more than they could afford.

Gus didn't deny it. "Not your money."

Still trying to understand, Tony shook his head. An addition to the house was far more than he and Theo could accept. Wasn't it? "Why?" Tony couldn't seem to think coherently.

Gus didn't answer. He just grinned and stood with his arms crossed over his chest and his legs spread. Tony understood why both his own wife and Catherine often accused the two brothers of resembling pirates. All Gus needed to complete the picture was a cutlass and a ship. Maybe a parrot. Gus shook his head.

Tony considered shooting his brother out of pure aggravation, wondering if the courts would rule the homicide justifiable. Maybe he should just choke the information out of him. Gus might have a slight edge in the muscle department, but Tony wasn't exactly a lightweight himself. Plus, he had advanced hand-to-hand fight training. He flexed his fingers. "I can kill someone with my bare hands."

Capitulating, Gus grinned and answered. "It's from Catherine. She's paying for all of it, and she said to remind you of the day she promised to find a way to pay you back." Gus became very serious. "She's got the money and wants to do this, but we both owe you." Gus breathed hard, as if he'd been running.

Tony remembered the incident Gus referred to, but disagreed about them owing him. It had happened the second night after he took the office of sheriff. He was driving the roads of the county he'd sworn to serve when he saw Catherine rising from a soggy ditch, covered with mud. She was almost blue from the cold, slimy and wet, with sticks and grass clinging to her skin and hair. Her blouse was missing. Her eyes were swollen shut. A date gone terribly wrong had brought her from a wealthy North Carolina suburb over the mountains to the back roads of Park County. She'd sprayed her date with pepper spray, getting some of the stuff in her own eyes, and jumped from the car when he slowed down. She'd hidden in the ditch until Tony found her, shivering and half dead. What they didn't know at the time was that her date did die. He'd been driving much faster than the speed limit, when he crashed into the wall of stone at Dead Man's Curve. He wasn't wearing a seat belt, and he still clutched Catherine's ripped blouse in his hand when he was thrown through the windshield.

Gus spoke as if answering a question. "You know Catherine runs a *very* successful Internet business. She considers my income to be somewhere in her petty cash range." He chuckled.

"It works for me. I don't mind being her boy toy."

Tony shrugged away the idea of his big brother being a gigolo. No one worked harder than Gus. "Not to trivialize the incident, but I didn't exactly do anything but wrap Catherine in a blanket and take her to the doctor. She defended herself quite handily. If some of the spray hadn't gotten in her eyes, she wouldn't have needed any help from me or anyone."

"True." Gus appeared to be breathing normally again. "Still, she wants to do this, and it's *not* charity."

Tony felt his eyebrows rise. "What would you call it?"

Gus thought for a moment, possibly stymied, then he grinned. "It's a gift. A baby gift."

"A baby gift?" Theo knew she was whispering, but it felt like a shriek. "A hat or a blanket is a gift. An addition to the house is . . . is a miracle."

"Can we accept it?" Tony squeezed into the cramped nursery. "He's waiting in the yard for our permission to get started."

Trapped in a space the size of a milk carton, Theo shook her head. At the same time, she said, "How can we not?"

Tony reached for a blanket. "Gus said something about our giving him the greater gift."

"What's that?" Theo felt a beat off, like she had stepped into someone else's life.

"Catherine."

"Nonsense. We didn't give her to anyone." Theo slipped behind Tony. "Let's go down and talk to him."

Sure enough, Gus stood in the back yard, almost hidden by the trees. He turned at their approach and didn't give them a chance to say anything. He poked a stick into the ground. "Out to here." He turned and took a few long steps, perpendicular to the stick. "To here." He strode back toward Tony and Theo, but turned and studied the layout. Silent, he squinted for a while before turning to Theo. "Would you like a garage for your pretty little SUV?"

"A garage?" Theo could barely breathe. "You mean attached to the house?"

Gus nodded.

"I wouldn't have to carry the children outside in the rain?" Theo hadn't realized she was crying until tears dripped onto her hands.

"It is all for them, you know." Gus ignored the tears. "They are the two sweetest little girls. Ever."

Theo waited for Tony to say something, but he couldn't seem to speak.

Gus said, "It's easy. We'll put the extra rooms over the garage and build a hallway where the girls sleep now, connecting the whole thing." He pulled a notebook from his pocket and, ignoring his brother and sister-in-law, began measuring.

Theo whispered, "Do you realize that in the past year someone has gifted us with a new car and now an addition to the house? What are the odds?"

Tony shook his head but remained silent.

ABOUT THE AUTHOR

Barbara Graham began making up stories in the third grade. Learning to multiply and divide paled in comparison. Born and mostly raised in the Texas Panhandle, she later lived in Denver, New Orleans, and East Tennessee. Inspiration for Silersville comes from her Tennessee period. An unrepentant quilting addict, she has been a travel agent, ballet teacher, and stay-at-home mom. She lives in Wyoming with her long-suffering husband and two dogs. She is a long distance member of various writing groups including Mystery Writers of America, Rocky Mountain Fiction Writers, Sisters in Crime, and International Thriller Writers.